THE SECOND BOOK OF SWORDS

Also from Orbit by Fred Saberhagen:

THE FIRST BOOK OF SWORDS

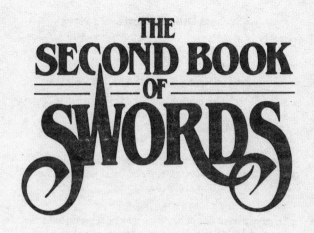

THE SECOND BOOK OF SWORDS

FRED SABERHAGEN

Futura

An Orbit Book

Copyright © 1983 by Fred Saberhagen

First published in the USA by Tor Books

This edition published in 1986
by Futura Publications, a Division of
Macdonald & Co (Publishers) Ltd
London & Sydney

ISBN 0 7088 8150 5

Printed and bound in Great Britain by
Collins, Glasgow

Futura Publications
A Division of
Macdonald & Co (Publishers) Ltd
Greater London House
Hampstead Road
London NW1 7QX

A BPCC plc Company

CHAPTER 1

Fire from the sky came thrusting down, a dazzling crooked spear of white light that lived for an instant only, long enough to splinter a lone tree at the jutting edge of the seaside cliff. The impact beneath the howling darkness of the sky stunned eyes and ears alike. Ben winced away from the blinding flash—too late, of course, to do his shocked eyes any good—and turned his gaze downward, trying to see the path again, to find secure places to put down his sandaled feet. In night and wind and rain it was hard to judge how far away the stroke had fallen, but he could hope that the next one would be farther off.

Ben's thick and powerful right arm was stretched forward across the rump of one heavily burdened loadbeast, his hand grasping the rope that bound the panniers on the animal's back. Meanwhile his left hand, extended backward, tugged hard on the reins of the loadbeast reluctantly following.

The little packtrain was composed of six loadbeasts, along with the six men who drove and led and cursed the animals forward. A seventh animal, considerably more sleek and graceful than the six that carried cargo, came a few meters behind the train. It bore a seventh man, a cloaked and hooded figure who rode with a cold, flameless Old World torch raised in his right hand. The torch shed an unflickering light through wind and rain, projecting some of its rays far enough ahead to give the train's drivers some hope of seeing where they were going.

Like some odd crawling compound creature possessing three dozen unsynchronized feet, the packtrain groped and struggled its way forward, following a mere sketch of a path across the wild landscape. Ben was pushing the first animal forward, more or less dragging the second after him, and trying to soothe them both. Hours ago, at the beginning of the trip, the drivers had been warned that tonight the usually phlegmatic animals were likely to become skittish.

There would be dragon-scent about, the officer had said.

Another flash of lightning now, fortunately not quite as close as the last one. For just an instant the rocky and forsaken wilderness surrounding the small train was plain to see, including the next few meters of the path ahead. Then darkness closed in deeper than ever, bringing with it harder rain. Its parts linked by the push and pull of human arms, the beast with three dozen feet advanced, making slow progress over the treacherous footing of rain-slicked rocks and yielding

sand. Meanwhile the wind howled continuously and
the rain assaulted everything.

Ahead of Ben, the soldier leading the first loadbeast
was wrapped and plastered like Ben himself in a soggy
blue-gold uniform cloak, with a useless helmet drizzling
rain into his eyes. Now Ben could hear him loudly
calling down the doom of demons and the wrath of
gods upon this whole situation—including the high
functionaries whose idea it must have been, and who
were no doubt somewhere warm and dry themselves
this moment. The man was almost shouting, having no
fear that the priest-officer, Radulescu, who rode behind
the train, might be able to hear him above the wind.

The cold torchlight from behind suggested, and the
next flash of lightning proved, that the scanty path the
train was following was now about to veer sharply to
the left. At the same time, a large indentation in the
line of the nearby cliffs brought their potentially fatal
edge sweeping in sharply toward the path from that
direction. Ben, not liking this sudden proximity of the
brink, leaned harder against the animal whose rump
his right arm was embracing. Using his great strength
and his considerable weight, he forced the beast a
little farther to the right. Now the packtrain was moving so close to the cliff's edge that when the lightning
flashed again it was possible to look down and glimpse
the pounding sea. Ben thought those rock-torn waves
might be a hundred meters below.

He supposed that a common soldier's life in any
army was not a happy one. More than one old proverb,
repeated mostly among soldiers themselves, testified
to that, and Ben had been given plenty of chance to
learn the truth of the proverbs for himself. But what

worried him tonight was not the usual soldier's concerns of dull abuse and passing danger. Not the storm. Not really the danger of falling off this cliff—that risk was obvious and could be avoided. Nor was it even fear of the guardian dragon up ahead, whose presence the drivers had been warned of because it might make the loadbeasts nervous.

What bothered Ben was a certain realization that had been growing upon him. If it was correct, then he had more than dragons to worry about. So, for that matter, did the other drivers who were here tonight; but Ben had no reason to think that any of them had yet realized the fact.

He wondered if he was going to have a chance to talk to them about it without the officer overhearing. He decided that he probably was not. . . .

By Ardneh, how could any man, even one afraid for his life, manage to think straight about anything in the middle of a storm like this? Ben couldn't even spare a hand to try to wipe the rain out of his eyes, or hold his cloak together. Now, sodden as the garment was, it had blown loose from its lower clasp, and streamed out uselessly in the wind. Even in the brilliance of the lightning the cloak no longer looked gold and blue. It was so wet and matted that it might have been woven out of the gray of the night itself.

More lightning, more wind, more rain. Through it all the twelve linked bodies of angry men and burdened animals kept struggling forward. Under ordinary conditions, one or two men could have managed six loadbeasts easily. But Ben had to admit that whoever had assigned six drivers to this job tonight had known what he was doing. Certainly two or three men would not have been enough to manage it tonight, when lightning and the scent of dragon rode the air together.

Radulescu had earlier reassured the drivers, telling them that he had at his command powerful spells, sure to keep the dragon at a distance. Ben believed that. Blue Temple officers, he had observed in his year's stint as an enlisted man, were generally competent in matters that they considered to be important. And this trip tonight had to be important . . . and that led Ben back to his new private worry. He wanted to be able to argue himself out of that dreadful idea, but instead the more he thought of it the more real it became.

And the less time was left to try to deal with it.

They had been told nothing about the nature of the cargo, so well-wrapped, so compact and heavy, that they were transporting through the night. Other hands than theirs had wrapped it, and loaded it into the animals' panniers. From the way it weighed, and felt, it could hardly be anything but heavy stone or metal.

Ben couldn't really believe that it was stone. He could tell from the way the animals moved that it must weigh like lead. But of course Blue Temple, the proverbial worshippers and hoarders of wealth, were unlikely to be trafficking in lead.

That narrowed the possibilities down considerably. But there was more.

When the packtrain had left the local Temple, some hours before dark, it had been accompanied by an escort of some three dozen heavily armed cavalry. These were mercenary troops, speaking only some bizarre dialect of their own; Ben thought that they must have been recruited from halfway around the world.

Progress had at first been easy; the sky was threatening but the storm had not yet broken. The armed escort had surrounded the packtrain most of the slow way, the loadbeasts had been docile, and the six drivers had been able to take it easy, riding themselves on six spare mounts. Their journey, along back roads and then increasingly slender trails leading into the back country, had been entirely on Temple lands—or so Ben thought; he could not be completely sure. Such a heavy escort, on Temple lands, seemed to be overdoing it a bit—unless of course the cargo was very, very valuable.

And to think that didn't help the new worry at all. . . .

Just before nightfall, the train had halted in a small clearing amid the scrubby growth and boulders of the wasteland. In a smooth and evidently prearranged fashion, the laden animals with their six drivers had been detached at this point from their escort, and under the command of Radulescu had continued forward over this rugged thread of trail.

According to the announced plan, their escort was to wait in the clearing for their return. As the separation was taking place, and almost as an afterthought, the six drivers had been ordered to leave their own weapons behind in the escort's care. Swords and daggers, Ben and the five others had been told, would not be needed up ahead, and would just get in their way when they went to work on the unloading.

Radulescu had been the officer who told them that, raising his crisp professional voice above the rising wind, while behind him the cavalry sat their own mounts, waiting silently. And when the weapons of the six drivers had been collected under a waterproof, and the spare cavalry mounts returned, Radulescu had ordered the train forward along this unknown thread of a trail. Then he had followed it on his own steed.

Ben had never set eyes on the priest-officer before today, and as far as he could tell the man was un-known to the other drivers as well—even as they were to each other. Certainly Radulescu was not one of the regular cavalry or infantry officers assigned to the local Temple's garrison. Ben suspected that he came from somewhere very high up in the loftier strata of Blue Temple power—perhaps he even had some con-nection with the Inner Council that ruled the Temple in all its branches. All of the regular officers had deferred to him, even though his uniform of plain gold and blue was devoid of any of the usual insignia of rank. That, thought Ben, had to mean he was a priest. Still, Radulescu seemed perfectly at home astride his cavalry mount, and also quite at home with giving orders in the field.

And now through the night the men and animals continued to struggle on, to move their heavy cargo forward. Ben thought it might not be all gold that they were carrying. He could imagine, inside the heavily padded, shapeless bundles that filled the wicker baskets, a certain proportion of jewelry, for example. Precious stones, and maybe some things of art . . .

With every minute the worry that had fastened upon him grew and grew. And the wind continued to blast the little procession, as did the rain, until even the four-footed creatures were slipping and sliding on the wet and rounded rocks that made up so much of this poor excuse for a path.

Again Ben shoved against the beast whose hind-quarters were under his right arm. He shifted the animal bodily a small distance to the right, farther away from that dreadful brink that now again came curving in from the left to run close beside the path.

And now, to Ben's mild surprise, the officer came cantering forward on the right side of the small train. Radulescu was urging his mount to a greater fraction of its speed, so that it quickly got ahead of the slow loadbeasts. Lights and shadows shifted with the change in position of the cold torch still held in the officer's hand. That torch was a thick rod whose rounded, glassy tip glowed steadily and brightly white, impervious to wind and rain. Ben had seen similar lights in use a time or two before, though certainly they were not common. In that steady light, Radulescu's officer's cloak shone, glistened as if it might be waterproof, and his head was neatly dry under a hood instead of wet in a damned dripping helmet. From under his cloak on the left side a sheathed sword protruded like some kind of stiffened tail.

As soon as Radulescu had gotten ahead of the train, he turned back into its path and reined in his swifter mount. And now, with a motion of his light, he signaled to the drivers that here they were going to leave the precarious path. He was waving them inland, across utterly trackless country.

The driver just ahead of Ben cursed again.

With the officer now riding slowly on ahead of the train, his cold light held high for guidance, the first driver got the first animal turned off the trail and headed inland, to the west. Ben followed, leaning on the first animal's hindquarters as before. The animal behind had to agree, with Ben's grip still on its reins. The others followed.

Now, moving across country on footing even worse than before, they were traveling even more slowly. From what Ben could see of the surrounding land, it was absolutely trackless and abandoned. All six of the drivers were cursing now; Ben was sure of it, though he could hear no maledictions other than his own.

The edge of the cliff was now safely distant. But now men and animals had to pick their way over uneven slopes of sand, push through prickly growth, negotiate more rocks whose surfaces were slicked by rain. This land, thought Ben, was in fact good for nothing but raising demons, as the old folksaying had it of the deserts. If indeed a large dragon was nearby—and he did not doubt that it was—then it was hard to imagine what it found to eat.

He thought that the dragon was making its presence known. The farther west and south the loadbeasts were made to struggle, the more restive they became. And now Ben, who had more experience than most in locating dragons, thought that he could detect the unique tang directly in the wet air, coming and going with variations in the wind. In that scent there was something swinish, and something metallic too, and something else that Ben could not relate to anything outside itself.

And now, unexpectedly, the packtrain was jouncing and stumbling to a halt. A few meters ahead, the priest-officer Radulescu had already reined in his animal and was dismounting. Reins held firmly in one hand, Radulescu lifted his torch high in the other, and began to chant a spell. Ben could not hear him chanting, but could see in profile a regular movement of the officer's short beard, chewing words boldly out into the wind.

And now something else came into view, above and beyond the cowled head of Radulescu, who now turned fully away from Ben to face the apparition. First the two eyes of the dragon were born in the midst of darkness, greenly reflecting the Old World light. The height of those eyes above the ground, and the distance between them, were enough to impress even an experienced dragon hunter. In the next moment, as the monster drew in a slow breath, there appeared below and between the eyes a red suggestion, glowing through flesh and scale, of the inner fires of nose and mouth, an almost subliminal red that would have been invisible by day. The purring snort that followed was a nearly musical sound, the rolling of hollow metal spheres in some vast brazen bowl.

Ben's sense of magic in operation was not particularly strong, but now even he could feel the flow, the working of the chant. The spell had already held the dragon back, and now was turning it away. With blinking eyes the great landwalker snorted again, and then melted back out of the train's path, disappearing into storm and darkness.

With the going of the dragon, Ben's real worry only sharpened. He had no trouble now in concentrating on it. In fact, as he waited for Radulescu to conclude his spell, demonstrating how firmly the powers of the Blue Temple were in control, it was impossible for him to think of anything else.

The worry that deviled Ben was not rooted in any

single warning, any one thing that he had seen or heard. Rather it had sprung into existence like some kind of elemental power, out of a great number of details.

One detail was that all six of the drivers here tonight, including Ben himself, were newcomers to this particular Temple garrison. That meant, Ben supposed, that none of them were likely to have friends around. All six had been transferred in from local Temples elsewhere, within the past few days. Ben had managed to discover that much from a few words casually exchanged while they were waiting for the train to start. He had not been given any particular reason for his own transfer, and he wondered if the others had, for theirs. So far he had had no chance to ask them.

At the time, the transfer orders had seemed to Ben only one more incomprehensible military quirk; in a year's service with Blue Temple he had gotten used to such unexplained twitches of the organism. But now . . .

In Ben's memory, repository of a thousand old songs, one in particular had now come alive and was dancing an accompaniment to his thoughts. He couldn't remember where or when he had heard it first. He probably hadn't heard it at all for years. But it had popped up now, as an ironic background for his fear.

If only, he thought, he was able to talk to the other drivers. They might be able to shout a few words back and forth now through the wind, but Ben needed more than that, he needed time to ask them things and make them think . . . he suspected he wasn't going to get the chance.

He had only a very little time in which to decide whether to act, or not to act, alone. And if he decided wrong, either way, then very soon he would be dead. . . .

The priest-officer, in the act of concluding his spell, used his wand of light to make one long, slow gesture after the departing dragon. Then Radulescu held the wand upright again, looking after the retreating beast and perhaps trying to listen after it through the storm. Then he remounted, turned to the waiting drivers, and once more motioned the train forward.

The drivers moved reluctantly. The loadbeasts were more easily convinced than their masters that the dragon had in fact departed. With dragon-scent now vanishing quickly in the wind, the animals moved forward again with more willingness than they had shown for several hours. And now, as if to suit the improvement in the atmosphere, the rain began to lessen too.

There followed a hundred meters more of stumbling along their trackless way, now and then tearing clothes and skin on thorns. Then the officer reined in again, and again motioned the packtrain to a halt. Another dragon? Ben wondered. He could perceive no other reason for stopping at this point. Radulescu was indicating with his light the exact place where he wanted them to halt the animals, close beside a rocky hillock that looked no different than a hundred other rocky hillocks that surrounded it. There's nothing here, thought Ben . . . and then he understood that that was just what he was supposed to think.

Radulescu had dismounted again. With torch still in hand he moved to stand beside the lower end of a great slab of stone that in itself made up a large portion of the hillock's flank. Putting one hand on this huge stone, he raised his voice above the wind: "You men, secure the animals. Then gather here and lift this rock. Yes, here, lift, I say."

The boulder he was indicating looked too heavy for a score of men to budge. But orders were orders. The drivers hobbled their beasts, and crowded round. Some of them were brawny men and some were not—but anyway, the priest was proven not to be mad. As soon as they lifted, the enormous stone went tilting and tipping up with surprising ease, to come to rest balanced in a new position. Now where its lower end had been, the dark triangle of a cave opening was revealed. The black hole in the hillside looked to Ben a little too regular in shape to be entirely natural, and was about big enough for a single man to be able to pass through it readily.

First in was the officer, moving confidently, holding his cold torch before him to light the way. The utter interior darkness melted before that light, to reveal a single-chambered cave, with its flat floor sunken three or four meters below the land outside. There was room on that floor for perhaps a dozen people to stand without crowding. From where Ben stood at the triangular entrance, a narrow stairway crudely carved from rock twisted down to the floor, and now in the center of that floor Ben noticed, between two lips of stone, another man-sized aperture, this one leading into deeper blackness.

When he reached that lower opening, Radulescu stopped. He leaned his torch against a wall, and from some inner pocket, evidently waterproof, brought out two stubby candles. He produced a flame—so quickly that Ben did not see just how it was done—and in a moment had placed a lighted candle on either side of the hole in the floor.

And now he looked up to where the drivers' faces were crowding the small entrance. "Begin unloading," Radulescu ordered briskly. "You are to carry the sacks of cargo down here, carefully—carefully! And drop them here, into this aperture." With a light stamp of his foot he indicated the opening in the floor. He had given the last order with special clarity and emphasis, as if wishing to avoid having to repeat it for those who thought they had not heard it properly the first time. On either side of Radulescu the candles burned, blue wax and golden flames; and on the flat rocks where they stood, Ben could see drippings, encrustations of old wax. It was evidently not the first time, nor the second or third, that a cargo had been delivered here.

The six drivers, as they drew back from the upper entrance, getting ready to obey orders, all looked at one another for a moment. But there was really no time for Ben to talk to them. He could see surprise in some of their faces, but nothing like his own fear mirrored.

Will it be here, he thought to himself, as soon as the unloading's finished? And if so, how? Or do I have a little more time, until we get back to where the cavalry's waiting . . .

"Move! Quick! Unload!" Radulescu was climbing the stair with his bright torch in hand. He was not going to give them time to think about anything except getting the job done.

The men had been trained, in a hard school, to obedience. They sprang into action. Ben moved with them, as automatically as any of the others. Only now, as he lifted his first bundle from a pannier on a loadbeast's back, did he realize how effective the Blue Temple training had been.

The bundle he had taken was small but very heavy, like all the others. It was wrapped against weather in some kind of waterproof oilskin that had been sewn shut. Inside the outer covering Ben could feel thick padding, that made it hard to tell what the true shape of the contents might be. To Ben the loading felt like several metal objects, all of them heavy, hard, and comparatively small.

Despite the weight, Ben could have carried two of the bundles at once easily enough. He did not do so, wanting to prolong the unloading. He might have only the time it took to do that job in which to try to think, to nerve himself, to act. . . .

As he passed through the upper doorway of the cave for the first time, bearing his first load down, he looked carefully at the great stone as it rested in its raised position. Ben was struck by how close it must be to its point of balance. What six men had heaved to open, it appeared, could be easily tilted shut again by one.

Going down the crooked stairs for the first time, watching carefully by candlelight where he put down his feet, he noticed that the stairs were beginning to be worn. As if many processions of laborers had borne their burdens here. . . .

Think, he ordered himself. Think! But, to his silent, inward horror, his mind seemed paralyzed.

Down in the cave, putting his first bundle obediently down into the dark hole in the floor, Ben noticed something else. The heavy bundle made no noise of fall or landing when he released it into darkness.

Either it was still falling—or it had somehow been caught.

Moving in slow procession with the other drivers, now emerging from the cave to get his second load, Ben saw that Radulescu had again set his Old World torch leaning against a rock, this time just outside the entrance. The officer had gone back to his tethered riding beast and was taking something from the saddle, untying a light, long bundle that Ben had not really noticed until now. The bundle was just about the same size and shape as the sword that Radulescu wore, and heavily wrapped like all the other cargo.

Ben kept moving as he watched. He shouldered his second load, lightening another animal's burden. Again the weight of the package he picked up was startling for its size. No, it wouldn't be lead that the Blue Temple was putting down into the earth so secretly.

The location of their main hoard had been a subject of stories and speculation for generations. At least one song had that hoard as its subject—the same tune that was still running, very unhelpfully, in Ben's mind.

The other five men in the line of treasure-bearers gave no indication that they had guessed what they were about. The implications of their situation, as far as Ben could tell, had simply not dawned on them at all. Their faces were dull, and set against the rain; set against knowledge, too, as it now seemed to Ben. He saw no possibility that he would be able to talk to them meaningfully before he had to act.

Both the stairway and the upper entrance to the cave were so narrow that the process of carrying in the cargo was necessarily slow and inefficient; men moving down always had to stop and wait for men moving up to pass them, and vice versa. Even so, with six steadily at work, the unloading wasn't really going to take very long.

Six men, Ben kept thinking, who now know where Benambra's Gold is really buried. Were there six other workmen still living in the world who had managed to learn so much?

The unloading proceeded, and it seemed to Ben that the process was going very fast. Outside the cave there was the light of the Old World torch to work by, and inside the warm smoky flicker of the two blue candles.

"Move along there!"

Ben had just dropped another bundle into the dark hole in the cave floor. He was in the act of straightening up and backing away when he brushed lightly against the officer who came moving forward just behind him. As the two men grazed past each other, the tip of the bundle that Radulescu carried brushed Ben's arm. Even through his sleeve and the object's wrappings, Ben could feel the passing presence of some power of magic. It tugged at his memory as some old perfume might have done, some fragrance lost since childhood and suddenly known again. And the incident made his fear suddenly more powerful than ever.

Ben had climbed the stair and was outside again, getting yet another bundle to carry down, when Radulescu also emerged from the cave. When the officer looked sharply at Ben, Ben looked dully back.

In his twenty-three years of life, Ben had learned that there were only two things about his own appearance that were at all likely to impress others. One, that never failed, was his squat bulk; he was really not shorter than average, but so heavily built that he appeared that way. The second thing was his apparent dullness. Something about his round slab of a face tended to make people think he was slow-witted, at least until they knew him. For some reason this effect was intensified by the fact that his body was so broad and strong. It was as if no one wanted intelligence and unhandsome strength to coexist in the same man. Ben had convinced himself that he was not particularly slow of mind, but he had learned also that there were times when it was helpful to be thought that way. He let his jaw sag just a little now, and returned the impatient officer's gaze blankly.

Radulescu stepped closer to him. "Move along, I say. Are you taking root there? Do you want to stand out in this storm all night?"

Ben, who would have been delighted to settle for just that, shook his head slightly and let himself be spurred again into obedient motion. Mechanically he rejoined the slowly shuffling line of the other drivers.

Burdened again with what he thought must certainly be gold, heading down once more into the cave, he observed again how precariously the great sealing rock was poised near its point of balance. One man standing outside the cave ought to be able to close that doorway quickly, with one hand. Whereas six men caught inside would never be able to crowd themselves into position to reach the rock and lift it open. Of course, if given time, they ought to be able to manage some way of getting out. If given time.

The rock was not going to come crashing shut behind him this trip. Not all of the treasure had been unloaded yet.

As he let this weighty bundle slide down into the hole in the cave floor, Ben started back reflexively. Half a meter or so below the level of the floor, a pair of hands, inhumanly large and white, had come momentarily into view to catch the package. As quickly as they had appeared, the hands were gone again, all in utter silence.

Ben turned away again, saying nothing. As he moved past a line of burdened men all waiting to drop more cargo into the pit, he realized with a pang of fear that the unloading must now be almost finished. He took quick strides toward the stair, wanting to make sure that he got out of the cave again before the job was done.

At the upper entrance, the officer had just delayed the last driver, who was just about to start down with what must be the last bundle on his shoulder. "Wait for me below, out of the rain," Radulescu was telling him. "I want to speak to all of you."

And the last man, burdened, entered the cave. Just inside the entrance Ben shouldered past him. Ben got out, leaving behind him a voice that muttered obscene protests at almost being forced off the stairs.

The officer, with his Old World light once more in hand, greeted Ben's emergence with another look of disgust; this time there was perhaps something more dangerous in the glance as well. And Radulescu cursed Ben wearily. No real curse fortunately, but one of the hollow forms used automatically to relieve feelings and abuse subordinates: something about an Emperor's child, lacking in both wit and luck.

"Sir?" Ben responded numbly. Now, he was thinking to himself, I must move now, before it is too late, before . . .

"The unloading is finished," the officer informed him, speaking slowly and plainly now, as to the company dullard. "I want all of you to assemble in the cave. Go down there and wait for me."

Behind Radulescu the six unburdened loadbeasts were waiting patiently. And down in the cave the five other drivers waited, displaying the same kind of patience. Ben felt unable to move. He had the sensation that he was about to be forced to jump from a high tower into unknown darkness.

Something must have altered in his face, for the officer's own expression suddenly grew dangerous. "Inside!" Radulescu shouted, and in the same instant cast down his torch and began to draw his sword.

Ben could feel the dead weight of training on him, and also the weight of fear. Terrified at his own obedience, he took a step toward the cave. But when he looked down through the entrance at the burning candles, the old wax congealed on rocks, and the five loadbeast faces of his fellow drivers, he saw with sudden and dreadful clarity that he was about to step into his grave.

Instead he shot out his right hand, seizing the officer by the upper part of his left arm. The man howled and tried to draw his sword, but the action was difficult for Radulescu to complete with Ben's strength pulling him forward, bending him off balance. Suddenly pushing with all his power, Ben sent Radulescu stumbling and reeling into the cave. The force of the thrust propelled the officer right on down the stairs, and if he had managed to draw his sword by now it was not going to do him any good.

Before Radulescu could draw breath for a second outraged yell, Ben pivoted and threw his weight on the great sealing stone. For one heart-stopping instant the sheer inertia of the huge boulder resisted him. Then the mass moved, slowly for the first fraction of a second, faster in the next, then falling with a doomlike thud to close the cave. Ben pulled a foot back just in time to save it from being crushed.

Candlelight had been sealed down into the earth now, along with yells and wrath, but the cold torch lay as brilliant as ever on the ground. Ben, who wanted to pull darkness round him like a cloak, left it where it was. He turned and ran into the night. He had already considered taking Radulescu's riding beast, and had rejected the idea. Where he planned to go his own feet would serve him better.

That mode of travel had its drawbacks too. Almost at once Ben banged his feet on rocks concealed in darkness, and tore his legs on thorns. He had to slow down to a quick walk, to keep from breaking a shin or toe. If he crippled himself now, the damage would very soon become permanent. He was moving, he hoped, south and a little east, trying to angle toward the coastline with its irregular brink of cliffs somewhere not far ahead. Ben had in mind a plan of sorts. It was not an elaborate plan, having necessarily been made on very short notice. That might be just as well.

What he had feared was going to happen next now happened, and almost immediately. Once more the dragon's chiming snort came clearly through the night, this time from right behind Ben, and disconcertingly close. The officer Radulescu, though sealed into the cave and probably injured, had been able to release the binding magic. Now Ben could hear the monster coming after him, the sounds audible through the unceasing wind and his own heavy breathing as he trotted. He heard the crunch and roll of stones beneath the dragon's feet, the breaking of thorny bushes as it trod them down.

Very little of Ben's bulk was fat. And he had been known to dash for short distances at a speed that others found surprising. But running was not really his strong point, and he knew that he was not going to outrun a landwalker; nobody was, not even on a fast and level track, which this certainly was not. Running all out, gambling against the chance of broken toes and shins, he angled more sharply toward the east and the invisible clifftop.

Now those huge feet behind him, terrible in the slow length of stride that gained on him, had settled into what was certainly direct pursuit. The ground-shaking rhythm of that walk grew perilously near, and nearer still. Ben, the experienced dragon hunter, made himself wait until the last possible moment before he tore his trailing cloak free of its last clasp and flung it up into the wind behind him. He dared not break stride or turn his head to find out what effect the action had.

Two of his own strides later, his ears told him that the effort at distraction had been at least a momentary success. There was a thunder-roar behind him that came from a little closer than the sky, and the earth-quivering pursuit faltered.

Ben managed to get in twenty more gasping strides before he could hear the dragon coming after him again. And then he came near running clean off the

cliff's edge before he saw it in the night. Just in time
he managed to throw himself down, clinging to the very
brink. He clambered over it as carefully as possible,
groping with his feet and legs for some kind of solidity
below. At last his sandals scraped on rock, found
purchase of a kind. As he had hoped, the steepness of
the cliffside here was not quite too much for human
hands and feet. Ben let go of his grip on the edge and
found places lower down where he could hang on with
his hands. Then he tried to extend his feet downward
once more.

Now, when he could have used some lightning to
see by, it had ceased almost entirely. Ben clung to one
rock after another that he could barely see, working
his way slowly down the cliff. And even more slowly
he made some progress to the south along its face. For
the present he could no longer hear the dragon. It
might have given up on chasing him. Or it might not.
They were like that, unpredictable.

With no lightning in the sky, the ocean a hundred
meters down was completely invisible. Just as well,
no doubt. But Ben could still hear its waves, rending
themselves on rock. Breathing devout prayers to Ardneh
and to Draffut, those two most merciful of gods, groping for one handhold and foothold below another, half
expecting each moment to be his last, Ben fumbled his
way down the face of the cliff toward the absolute
darkness of the sea.

CHAPTER 2

The tall young man stood on the bank of a small, muddy stream, looking around him uncertainly in bright sunlight. Even in broad day, and even with the distant mountains in the east to give a landmark, he could not be sure that the village he was looking for had ever existed on this spot.

Still, he was almost sure.

He could remember that most of the surrounding territory had once been prosperous farming and grazing land. No more. It was largely abandoned now. And here, where the Aldan had once run clean and fair, this mucky and unrecognizable stream now followed a strangely altered course through a sadly altered countryside. Even the distant mountains bore new scars. So much had everything changed that the young man remained uncertain of precisely where he was until his eye discovered a portion of a remembered millwheel sticking up out of a bank of earth amid the dried stalks of last year's weeds.

Only one corner of one broad wooden blade was visible, but the young man knew what it was at once. Staring at that cracked and splitting wood, he let himself sink down on the ground beside it. This sitting was the heavy movement of an old man, though the youth could hardly have been more than twenty at the most. His tanned face under its ragged growth of beard was still unlined, though from the expression in which it was set it seemed that lines ought to be there; and already the blue-gray eyes were old.

The bow and quiver that rode on the young man's broad back looked well-used, as did the long knife sheathed at his side. He might have been a hunter or a ranger, perhaps a military scout. Parts of his clothing and equipment were of leather, and some of these might once have been components of a more formal soldier's outfit. If so, their identifying colors had long since been cut or bleached away. The young man's hair was moderately short, as if it might be in the process of growing out from a close military or priestly cut.

He now put out a hand, large and tanned deeply like his face, and as rough-worn as his clothing. With it he touched the visible corner of the decaying millwheel blade. He let his hand rest there briefly on the old wood, as if he were trying to feel something in it. Meanwhile he raised his eyes toward the eastern mountains.

There was a faint sound behind the young man, as of someone or something moving through the thicket there to the west. He turned quickly, without getting up, then sat still, watching the thicket carefully. In his position he was half hidden by the rise of the earthen bank.

Presently a half-grown boy dressed in ragged home-spun emerged from the scrubby growth of bushes. The boy was carrying a pail crudely fashioned out of bark, and was obviously coming to the stream for water. He was almost at the water's edge before he caught sight of the motionless young man watching him, and came to a vaguely alarmed halt.

An Emperor's child for sure, the young man thought, surveying that small dirty figure in wretched clothing. "Hello, young one," he said aloud.

The boy did not answer. He stood there holding the empty pail, shifting his weight from one bare foot to the other as if uncertain whether he ought to run away or try to go on about his business.

"Hello, I say. Have you been living around here very long?"

Still no answer.

"My name's Mark. I mean you no harm. I used to live near here myself."

Now the boy moved again. Still keeping a wary eye on Mark, he waded into the stream. He bent his head to fill the pail, then looked up, tossing back long greasy hair. He said: "We been here a year now."

Mark nodded encouragingly. "Five years ago," he said, "there was a whole village here. A big sawmill stood right about where I'm sitting now." And he moved a hand in a vague gesture that ought to have included the village street. Only five years ago, he marveled silently. It seemed impossible. He tried without success to visualize this boy as one of the smaller children in the village then.

"That's as may be," the boy said. "We came here

later. After the mountains burst and the gods fought."

"The mountains burst, all right," Mark agreed. "And I don't doubt that the gods fought too . . . what's your name?"

"Virgil."

"A good name. You know, when I was your size, I played here along this stream. It was a lot different then." Mark felt a sudden need to make someone understand just how totally different it had been. "I swam here, I caught fish . . . "

He broke off. Someone else was coming down through the thicket.

A woman emerged, as ragged and dirty as the boy. Her walk was the walk of age, and much gray showed in her disordered hair. A dirty bandage covered both her eyes. Mark could see the ends of scars showing past the edges of the cloth.

Just at the edge of the thicket the blind woman halted, one hand touching a bush as if by that means she could assure herself of her position. "Virgil?" she called out. It was a surprisingly young voice, and it carried fear. "Who's there?"

"One lone traveler, ma'm," Mark called in answer. At the same time the boy replied with something reassuring, and came out of the water with his filled pail.

The woman turned her face in Mark's direction. There were indications in that face that she was still young, even evidence that a few years ago she might have been called pretty. She called toward Mark harshly: "We don't have much."

"I don't want anything you have. I was just telling the young man that I used to live nearby."

Virgil put in: "He says he was here five years ago.

Before the mountains burst."

Mark was on his feet now, and approached a little closer to the woman. "I'll be going right along, ma'm. But could you tell me one thing first, maybe? Did you ever hear any word of the family of Jord the Miller? He was a big man with only one arm. Had a wife named Mala and a daughter, Marian, real blue-eyed and fair. Daughter'd be in her twenties now. They lived right here on this spot, five years ago, when Duke Fraktin was alive and claimed this land."

"Never heard of any of 'em," the woman said at once in her hard young voice. "Five years ago we weren't here."

"None of the old villagers were here when you arrived?"

"No one. There was no village."

And the boy Virgil said, as if repeating a lesson learned: "The Silver Queen now holds dominion over this land."

"Aye," said Mark. "I know she claims that. But I suppose you don't see her soldiers way out here very often?"

"I don't see them at all." The woman's harsh voice was no harsher than before. "The last time I saw them was when they blinded me. We ceased our wandering, then."

"I'm sorry," Mark said. In his heart he cursed all soldiers; at the moment he did not feel like one himself.

"Are you one of her army too? Or a deserter?"

"Neither, ma'm."

Virgil asked Mark unexpectedly: "Were you here when the gods were fighting among themselves? Did you see them?"

Mark didn't answer. He was trying to discern in the bandaged face of the blind woman the countenance of any of the village girls he could remember. But it was useless.

Young Virgil, evidently feeling braver now, persisted. "Did you ever see the gods?"

Mark looked at him. "My father did. But I have only seen them in—visions, and that only once or twice." He made himself smile. "In dreams, no more than that." Then, seeing that the woman had turned her back on him and was about to retreat into the thicket again, he called to her: "Let me walk with you, back up the hill, if that's the way you're going. I won't be any bother to you. A manor house stood up there once, and I want to see if anything is left of it."

The woman made no reply, but moved on, groping her way from bush to bush along what must be a familiar path. The boy came after her, carrying the pail of water in silence. Then Mark. The three of them climbed more or less together along the path worn through the hillside thicket.

When they reached the top of the little hill Mark could see how little was left of Sir Sharfa's manor house. The great stone hearth and chimney remained, and almost nothing else. Against the chimney a crude lean-to shelter had been built from scraps of wood. From inside the shelter came a snoring sound, and a man's bony hand and wrist were visible in the muddy doorway, their owner evidently lying on the floor inside. The snore sounded unhealthy, as if the man emitting it were drunk or dying. Maybe he was both, thought Mark.

The boy, who had put his pail down now, was not ready to abandon the subject of the gods. "Mars and

Draffut had their fight right over on those mountains,"
he resumed suddenly, pointing to the east. "And the
twelve magic Swords were forged right up there. Vulcan
kidnapped a smith and six men from a village, to help
him make 'em. Afterwards he killed the six men, and
he took off the smith's arm . . . " Virgil stopped rather
suddenly. He was looking at Mark, with the expression of a boy who has suddenly remembered something.

"How do you know how many Swords there were?"
Mark asked him. It amazed Mark how knowledge
spread—or how, sometimes, it seemed determined on
remaining secret. It was almost twenty years now, he
knew, since the twelve Swords had been forged, and
half a dozen years ago still only a few people in the
whole world had known about them. And now it
seemed that the whole world knew.

The boy looked at him, as if Mark had asked how it
was known that a woolbeast had four legs. "Twelve
Swords, that's how many there were. Everyone knows
that."

"Oh."

Virgil's eyes were intense, his voice hurried. "But
Hermes played a joke on all the other gods. He gave
the Swords only to mortals, and he scattered them all
across the world. Each Sword went to a different man
or woman to start with, and none of the gods got any
themselves. And each Sword gave whoever got it a
different kind of power."

"Oh." It was true, for the most part anyway. He
didn't want to appear to possess superior knowledge,
and he didn't know quite what to say. "Why would
Hermes have done a thing like that?"

"Part of the game that the gods play with each

other. Aye, he scattered them and gave them all to people. I wish I could have got one."

Mark was looking at the woman, who stood leaning with one hand on the shelter, blindly listening. The man inside snored on. Suddenly Mark felt a great necessity to do something for these people; maybe he could at least shoot them a rabbit or two before he left. And then—yes, he had decided now. There was something much more important that he was going to do for them, and thousands like them.

Virgil asked him: "Did you say that the miller only had one arm? Was—he your father?"

Mark studied him a moment, then put another question in return. "If you had one of those Swords, what would you do with it? Hide it away somewhere?"

The boy's expression showed he thought that question was insane. "Whoever gets all those Swords into his hands will rule the world."

"Aye," said Mark. "But if you had one? Coinspinner, maybe. What then? What would you do with it? Try to rule a twelfth of the world, or what?"

Neither of his listeners answered him. Maybe he had scared them now. But now that he'd started he couldn't stop. "What would you say about a man who knew where one of those Swords was hidden? Maybe Dragonslicer . . . a man who could go and get it, but he just let it stay hidden. When there's so many wrong things in the world, like . . . when there's so much that needs to be set right."

The woman's scarred and blinded face turned slowly back and forth. She was shaking her head. "You'll straighten out the wrongs of the world, young man? You might as well set out to serve the Emperor."

CHAPTER 3

In darkness Ben continued his methodical struggle to work his way down the face of the cliff. Whenever he could he made a little headway south along its face as well. The plan he had in mind required that he go south. It was a simple plan, basically. It was also madly dangerous—or he would have thought it so, had he not found himself in a situation where every other course seemed suicidal.

Anyway, he had now acted on his plan. He had rebelled, assaulted an officer, deserted, and there was nothing to do now but go on. From handhold to foothold he moved down, and slowly south.

At least he was able to see a little more clearly now, by the light of a horned moon that had recently come up over the eastern sea. The sky was gradually clearing after the storm, but low fog still shrouded the ocean and its shoreline, which were still at a frightening and discouraging distance below him. The sound of breakers still came drifting up, weaker now, almost indistinguishable from the weakening wind. And Ben had certain bad moments, in which he thought he was able to hear another sound as well—the voices of six men trapped and howling in a cave. One of the six was armed with a sword. But would that do him any good, when the great white hands came reaching out for him?

Ben fought down the images springing from his imagination. Then another kind of sound reached his ears, and was enough to drive imaginary terrors away. He heard the steps of the dragon. It was coming back for him, walking the flatland now some uncertain number of meters above his head. Ben continued to descend, a few centimeters at a time. There was nothing else for him to do.

The dragon must have been able to sense his presence, for it came to the clifftop immediately above him. Looking up, Ben caught one glimpse of its head, a lovely silver in the moonlight, and saw the red glow of its breath. After that he kept his own head down.

The dragon bellowed at Ben. Or, for all he knew, it might be the horned moon that drew its wrath. Stamping with table-sized feet along the brink, it shook down stones and clods of earth. Ben's helmet saved him once from being stunned. The dragon projected fire out into the night. Ben saw the glow on the rocks around him, and he felt the backwash of the heat, as if a door had opened briefly to some tremendous oven. But either the creature could not bend over the cliff far enough to breathe at him directly, or it did not care to try. Ben was confident that it lacked the intelligence to try to trickle fire on him along the rocks.

Presently, as he continued moving down, the hail of dirt and stones abated. Then the stamping moved away, until he could no longer feel it in the earth. Ben heard the chiming snort again, this time from some considerable distance, and almost drowned in wind.

As if he had never had any other goal in life, and could imagine none, he kept on moving. Mechanically he went down, and south. And presently he found to his relief that the slope was no longer quite so steep. He began to make real progress.

His way now took him round a large convexity of cliff, and out of most of the remaining wind. Looking to seaward now, from a level only a little above the tendrils of the fog, he saw that he was confronting a long but possibly narrow inlet of the sea, a fjord that stretched inland to the west for some indeterminable distance. Ben could just discern high land across the water, but in fog and intermittent moonlight he could only guess at that land's distance and its nature.

According to the mental map that he relied on for guidance, he had to continue south if he was to have any hope of leaving Blue Temple land behind him before daylight. But now continuing south meant some-how crossing this arm of the sea. There was no choice. Unless he stumbled on a boat when he got down to the shore—and he had no reason to think he would—he was going to have to trust his fate to the powers of the deep, and swim across.

As he worked his way lower and lower, getting into patchy fog, he kept trying to estimate the height and distance of those opposing cliffs. But under the conditions he could not. He was not even certain he was not looking at an island. All he could really be sure of was that if he stayed where he was until morning, he would be discovered by Blue Temple searchers who would be out in force. He had to assume that they would have flying creatures out looking for him at sunrise. And if they found him on this cliff he would do well then to hurl himself to speedy death. . . .

The land flattened briefly at the cliff's foot. Ben moved among fallen boulders, able to feel the spray now from invisible waves. He moved onto a shingle of coarse rounded stones, and was granted a dim vision of the sea at last. There was no boat, of course, nor any sign of one. Not even a scrap of log.

Uttering silent prayers to Neptune, he crept forward onto a jutting rock, with sea-foam bubbling at his feet. He stripped off a few more garments, and threw his helmet out as offering to the sea. Then, not giving himself time to think, he entered the water in a bold leap.

He surfaced gasping with the salt chill, and struck out boldly. How the tides and currents might run here he had no idea. His fate was in the hands of the sea gods, but drowning was hardly the worst fate that might overtake him in the next few hours.

Ben was a strong swimmer, and all but impervious to cold. The water was not warm, but he doubted that it was cold enough to kill him. Glimpsing the horned moon through ragged clouds as he swam, he tried to keep it on his left. The waves were strong and regular. Once he got out a little from the shore, it was hard to tell if they were helping or hindering his progress. Patches of fog closed in at times, obscuring the moon and making him doubt whether he was swimming in the right direction. But always the moon came back, and he was never very far off his chosen course.

Eventually he thought that the moon was higher. Had he been swimming for an hour now? For two? It couldn't have been for very long, he told himself, or there'd be signs in the sky of the coming daylight. . . .

He tried to hold his thought on how difficult it was going to be for the Blue Temple searchers when they came looking for him. They'd find his cloak right away, up on the cliff, if the dragon hadn't swallowed it whole. They'd think that it had swallowed him . . . they'd never find him in this kind of fog.

He was wondering seriously whether he was going to make it, when a mass of land loomed vaguely ahead, and from the same direction he heard the sound of waves on rocks again.

The dawn rising grayly out of the sea seemed to carry Ben up with it, lifting him onto land.

On a small strip of sandy beach he lay quietly for a few minutes, breathing heavily, having a little difficulty realizing that he was still alive. He was nearer exhaustion than he had realized. But he did not forget a prayer of thanks to Neptune.

A few meters inland, the foot of an unfamiliar cliff confronted him. As soon as he felt able, he got to his feet and began to climb it. The mist from the sea seemed to rise with him as he climbed, like some demonic substance seeking to escape the depths. Even though he still moved through fog, the movement dried and warmed him.

When he'd gained what he thought was a considerable height he paused to catch his breath and look back. Across the fjord, the headland that he'd fled was hard to make out. Clouds shrouded it from the first direct rays of the morning sun. The search for him had probably already started over there, but he couldn't see it. He trusted that so far they hadn't been able to see him, either.

What he had to do now was get himself off this exposed cliff, get inland as rapidly as possible. Climbing now at the fastest pace he could sustain, Ben saw with alarm that his tough hands were starting to bleed from their prolonged struggle with sharp rock. If the Blue Temple's flying scouts should come to visit this cliff as well, would they be able to trail him by those tiny flecks of blood?

If so, there was no point in worrying about it. He was doing all he could do to survive, he told himself. If he'd gone meekly down into the cave that last time as he'd been ordered, he'd be quite meekly dead by now. That much he was sure of. He was convinced that the five other drivers were dead by now . . . unless, he thought suddenly, they had somehow been kept alive for questioning about the plot. The higher-ups were sure to think that there had been some kind of plot. Probably even Radulescu, if *he* was still alive, was being questioned.

Excuse me, sir, there wasn't no plot, sir. Just Big Ben, Slow Ben, doing his best to stay alive.

He thought about that as he climbed. Certainly, last night when he'd started running, there'd been nothing more on his mind than keeping himself alive. And even now, climbing rapidly, he was willing to settle for that.

But now . . .

Now, with the possibility of escape looking more real with each passing moment, other ideas were inviting themselves into Ben's mind. True, he hadn't been *trying* to carry away any important secrets. But, since they were going to hunt him anyway . . . well, he'd be a fool not to try to get some chance to benefit out of this, as well as the chance of getting killed.

Twenty-three years' experience had taught Ben that the life of a poor man was not much of a life. It was too bad the world was like that, but so it was. He wanted money, enough at least to promise some kind of minimal security. Once a man had a little gold in his pocket, he could be somebody, could have some kind of chance for a decent life. Ben had joined the Blue Temple service a year ago only because he saw in it the possibility at least of modest success, security—in a word, of getting a little money. A man had to have a certain minimum of that. At least he did if he was ever going to attract and keep a woman whose own yearnings were for prosperous stability.

Once Ben had enlisted, given his size and strength and lack of other education, there was little doubt about which branch of the Temple service he'd be assigned to. Not for him one of the easy desk jobs, tallying and re-tallying the Temple's wealth in all its categories, figuring up the interest on all the loans they had outstanding. He'd seen the rows of busy clerks, scribbling at the long desks. That looked like an easy life. But he himself had been sent into the Guards.

For Ben, already accustomed to a hard, poor existence, and not expecting much from his new career right at the start, the life of a military recruit had not seemed too unpleasant. He had already taken part in more actual fighting than he had ever wanted to see, but he had managed to live through it; in the peaceful Blue Temple garrison where he was first assigned, he really did not expect to be called upon for more. Adequate food and clothing were regularly provided, and a man who did what he was told could usually keep himself out of trouble.

It had turned out, though, somewhat to Ben's own surprise, that he was not the kind of man to always do what he was told.

He might have enlisted in other organizations than Blue Temple, sought jobs under other conditions of service, in other places, that would have offered him just as good a chance of security. It was easy to realize that now. Now, he saw that he had picked Blue Temple really because the idea of its great wealth had attracted him. He hadn't been quite naive enough to imagine that he was going to become personally rich as soon as he signed up—as the recruiter had somehow managed to suggest. No. But still Ben had known that all the money, the wealth, the gold of the Blue Temple, was going to be around, and the idea of it had attracted him. At the time he'd told himself that he'd chosen to join Blue Temple because it lacked the reputation for gratuitous oppression and cruelty that was shared by so many of the world's other powers. The Dark King, for example, or the Silver Queen of Yambu, or the late Duke Fraktin.

Blue Temple were the worshippers of wealth, the harvesters and heapers-up of gold. Somehow they usually contrived to extract the stuff from everyone who came in reach, from rich and poor, devotees and scoffers, friends and deadly foes alike. In the process they also somehow financed and indirectly controlled much of the world's trade. Ben's bunk in the guardhouse had been remote from the inner chambers where financial matters were seriously discussed, but information, as always, had a way of seeping through walls. In the morning the Temple accepted a rich man's offering, in return insuring him against some feared disaster; in the afternoon it levied a tax on a poor widow — making sure to leave her enough to sustain life, that next year she would be able to pay some tax again.

And incessantly the Temple complained about how inappropriately poor it was, how much help and protection and shelter it needed against the financial dangers of the world. Always the Guardsmen were exhorted to be ready to lay down their lives in defense of the last shreds of assets remaining. It was never actually stated that the wealth was almost gone — any more than the location of the main hoard was revealed — but the general implication was that it had to be dwindling fast. Always the soldiers were reminded how much their meagre pay, their weapons and clothes and food, all cost their poor masters. And how essential it was, therefore, for the soldiers — especially those who hoped someday to be promoted, and those too who wanted to eventually draw a pension — how essential it was that they return some generous fraction of their pay as a Temple offering.

If a man were to serve in the ranks for twenty years, investing a substantial part of his pay as such an offering each year, he would be able to retire at that point with a pension. Exactly how much of a pension was a little vague.

The recruiter had mentioned generous pensions to

Ben, but had somehow neglected to explain just what
a soldier had to do to qualify for one.

So, there were financial as well as other reasons
why the enlistment hadn't been working out for Ben
as well as he had hoped. Even before last night's crisis
he had been ready to get out. Of course he could have
bought out his enlistment at any time, if he'd had the
money to do so—but then, if he'd had that much
money he never would have joined up in the first
place. Barbara would have been willing to marry him,
or live with him permanently anyway. The two of
them could have stopped their precarious wandering
about with shows and carnivals, a life that kept them
usually very little better off than beggars. They could
have bought themselves a little shop somewhere, in
some prosperous strong city with high walls. . . .

It was a year now since he'd seen Barbara, and he
had missed her even more than he'd expected to. He
didn't want to go back, though, until he'd accom-
plished something at last, got a start in some kind of
life that she'd want to share. He'd sent her letters from
his garrison station once or twice, when the opportunity to do so had arisen, but he hadn't heard from her
at all. For all Ben knew, she'd taken up with someone
else by now. There had been no promise from her that
she would not.

Ben's reason for enlisting had, of course, been to get
himself established in some kind of secure Blue Temple
post, something that would pay well enough to let him
send for her . . . looking back at it now, it seemed a
very foolish hope. But then, at the time he'd enlisted,
every other hope had seemed more foolish still.

Now, in the gradually brightening daylight, Ben continued his climb. This cliff was not quite so steep, he thought, as the one he'd had to come down in the dark. Or it might just be that having some daylight made things that much easier. Anyway, he was making good progress, and quite soon reached a place from which it was possible to look up and feel sure he'd be able to make it all the way to the top. He had not the slightest idea of what he was going to find up there, except he expected and hoped that he'd no longer be on Blue Temple land. He might, of course, be wrong. . . .

When he had climbed a little farther still, Ben paused to look upward again. Yes, from here on the slope was definitely gentler, and he had no doubt that he could climb it. He could even see a short stretch of what looked like a genuine trail, up there near the top.

Ben climbed another hundred steps and stopped to scan the way ahead again. This time he received something of a shock. Right beside that upper trail, in a spot where no one had been a few moments ago, a man was now sitting on a squarish stone, gazing out to sea.

The man appeared to be taking no notice of Ben, and as far as Ben could tell he was not armed. His body was wrapped in a plain gray cloak that effectively concealed whatever else he might be wearing. The cloak at least didn't look like part of any soldier's or priest's uniform that Ben was familiar with. Maybe the watcher was not a sentry, but he was in a place that a sentry might well choose. And, should he be minded for some reason to dispute Ben's passage up the steep slope, his position would give him a definite advantage.

There was nothing for Ben to do but climb on, meanwhile thinking what he ought to say to the man when he came near. It occured to Ben that he might represent himself as a shipwrecked mariner, just cast ashore at the foot of these cliffs after clinging for days to a bit of wreckage. No notion of where he was—yes, that was the idea. A story like that might well be accepted; the gods knew that Ben was wet and weary enough for it to fit him.

The man who sat alone on the rock did not look down at Ben until Ben was only a few meters below him. But when he did look it was without surprise, as if he'd known all along that Ben was there.

"Hello!" the watcher called down then. He was a nondescript sort of fellow in appearance, smiling and openly cheerful. At close range his gray cloak looked old and worn.

"Hello!" Ben called back. Something in him had wanted to respond at once to the lightheartedness of the other's greeting, and as his voice came out he thought it sounded too cheerful for the tale of woe he had to tell—though on second thought he supposed that any shipwrecked sailor who came to shore alive might have good reason to sound happy.

Ben climbed closer. The man continued to regard him with a smile. Not quite, thought Ben, like an idiot.

Drawing even with the man at last, and no longer at the disadvantage of the steep slope, Ben felt confident enough to pause to regain his breath. Between slow gasps he asked: "Whose lands have I arrived at, sir?" He was ready now with some details of his shipwreck, should they be required.

The man's smile faded to friendly seriousness. "The Emperor's," he said.

Ben stood there looking at him. If the answer had been seriously meant, Ben could derive no sense from it at all. The Emperor was a proverbial figure of fun and ridicule, and hardly anything more. Of course, if Ben thought about it, he supposed that a real man afflicted with that title might still exist somewhere in the world. But . . . a landowner? The Emperor was a clown-masked caperer through jests and stories, a player of practical jokes, the proverbial father of the wretched and the unlucky. He was just not someone that you thought of as owning land.

With a small shake of his head, Ben climbed on a few more steps, just high enough to let him see inland over the final sharp brink of the cliff. He warily kept half an eye on his companion as he did so.

He didn't know quite what he had expected, but the view inland surprised him. Beginning from the barren cliff-face's very edge, a lush meadow sloped inland, knee-deep with dewy grass and wildflowers, to end in an abrupt semicircle where a stately grove or forest began, about a hundred meters inland. Neither meadow nor forest showed any signs of human use.

Ben said: "Well, the cliff here is certainly poor enough to be the Emperor's wall. But someone else must lay claim to this meadow, and to the wood yonder."

The fellow sitting on the rock looked quite grave when he heard this. He gazed back at Ben but did not answer. Ben, deciding that he did not need the complications of a debate with some stray madman, climbed the last three steps to stand gratefully in soft grass. He saw now that the meadow formed a rough triangle, and he was standing very near its seaward point. Not enjoying this exposed position on the cliff's edge, he at once walked inland, heading for the baseline of the woods.

After the long struggling climb, it was a joy to take swift steps through soft grass on almost level land. Patches of mist were rolling up over the edge of the cliff, as if determined to accompany Ben inland. Field-nesting birds, clamoring as if they were unused to disturbance, flew up from almost under his feet.

He reached the trackless grove, and entered it. There was little undergrowth and he moved swiftly. And now, almost before he'd had time to wonder how far the wood extended, he was confronted by a high wall, constructed roughly of gray fieldstone.

The wall stretched left to right as far as Ben could see, losing itself among the trees. But it was so rough-surfaced that climbing it proved easy. Raising his eyes cautiously above the top, Ben observed that on the far side of the wall the woods soon petered out, and innocent-looking countryside began, with a narrow, rutted road winding across it from left to right. In the distance Ben could just discern the top of a tall white pyramid. That was the only building in sight, apart from a couple of distant cottages.

Ben observed that pyramid with relief, taking it as proof that he'd put Blue Temple lands behind him — or, at the worst, that he was just about to do so. In another moment he was over the wall and trotting toward that winding road. As he passed through the last of the trees, with patches of mist still hanging about them to lend an air of mystery, it struck Ben for

the first time that the grove had the look of some kind
of shrine. For what god it was meant he couldn't
guess. He didn't think it was associated with the
Temple of Ardneh—that looked too far away.

He should really stop at Ardneh's temple, he told
himself, and make some thanks-offering for prayers
very recently answered. He certainly would do that, if
he had anything left to offer, but he was practically
naked as he was. On second thought he would stop,
and try to beg some clothes. Also, now that he thought
about it, a little food. Yes, definitely, food.

Less than an hour later, a white-robed acolyte of
Ardneh was ushering Ben up a long flight of white
steps.

When Ben emerged from Ardneh's temple a short
time later, he was dressed in warmer garments. They
were third- or fourth-hand pilgrim's garb, and patched,
but they were clean and dry. And he was no longer
ravenously hungry. But he was very tired, and frowning
thoughtfully.

Again he strode along the road, still heading south.
He'd have to stop somewhere soon and get some sleep,
but right now he wanted to make distance, to get as
far from the Blue Temple as he could. He had a better
knowledge now of where he was, and he'd known all
along where he was heading for.

Sometime this month the carnival that he and
Barbara had been with ought to be making a spring
move to Purkinje Town, if it kept to the old schedule. If
she was still with it, he would find her there.

Ben made the long journey almost entirely on foot.
It took him approximately a month, so spring in these

parts was well advanced when he arrived. And the journey was not without adventure, though if Blue Temple were on his trail, as he thought they must be by this time, he saw no signs of them. Gradually his fears receded, and he began to believe that they thought him dead.

By the time Ben reached Purkinje Town, or rather the place outside the town's crumbling walls where the small carnival was encamped, he'd worn out and replaced his sandals, and had had to replace some of his pilgrim's garb as well. He had also begun a beard, which was coming in a dull, bleached brown to match his hair. He had acquired as well one of the packs and something of the appearance of an itinerant peddler he'd fallen in with early in his journey. The peddler, once convinced that Ben meant him no harm, had been glad to have the strong man as an escort, had cut a sturdy quarterstaff for him to carry, and had rewarded his companionship with food and clothing.

But their paths had diverged, many kilometers back. Ben was alone when he arrived outside Purkinje's half-tumbled walls toward evening on a clear, late spring day. Those walls were no longer a very impressive defense. The city, though, was still flying its own flag of orange and green, evidently still managing to maintain a measure of independence from the brawling warlords whose armies endlessly came and went across the land.

The carnival still looked independent too, though in the past year it had grown even shabbier than Ben remembered it. The tents and wagons that Ben could recognize had endured another year of wear and tear, and he found it difficult to discover among them any

traces of repair, new paint, or fresh decoration. And
there were now a couple of wagons that he did not
recognize.

The crude painting on the cloth side of one of these
vehicles caught Ben's eye, and he paused to look at it.
Large, somewhat uneven lettering proclaimed Tanakir
the Mighty. Tanakir's painted portrait showed him
expanding biceps and chest to break great iron chains
that might have held a drawbridge.

Ben delayed only for a moment to look at this.
Then, with a strange feeling inside his own chest, he
went on to Barbara's recognizable small tent. As usual
she had the tent set up beside her wagon. If she was
keeping a small caged dragon inside her conveyance as
usual, it was hidden by cloth coverings, and made no
sound at Ben's approach.

The flap of her tent was closed, but Ben could see
that it was not tied shut. Ben threw down the wooden
staff that the peddler had given him. Then, obeying
the traditional rules of courtesy, he cleared his throat
and scratched on the tent wall near the flap—there
was of course no way to knock. He waited a few
decent seconds then, and when there was no response
he lifted the fabric gently and stepped in.

At a small table near the center of the tent sat
Barbara, wrapped in the shabby familiar robe that
she often wore around camp. Despite the poor light
in the tent she was trying to do something to pret-
tify her fingernails. She looked up sharply at the
intrusion, her small, spare body coiled like a spring.
Between the two black sheaves of her hair, her round,
expressive face showed anger, even before she had
time to recognize Ben and be surprised—she had

been keeping her anger ready, he thought, for someone else.

"You've got a look in your eye, Ben." That was how she greeted him after a year's absence, uncoiling the spring of her body slightly. Barbara was very nearly the same age as Ben, though not much more than a third his weight. They had known each other for a number of years. He saw now that her straight black hair had been allowed to grow a little longer since he'd left. Otherwise she looked just about the same. She went on: "Fuzz on your chin and a look in your eye. What are you up to now? I don't suppose you rode back here in a golden coach pulled by six white show-beasts?"

"Thinking," he replied, choosing to answer the one halfway sensible question in her speech, letting the rest of it go by. It was a way he had. He thought it was one of the things that she did like about him.

"Thinking about what?"

"About certain things that I've found out." Ben slid off his peddler's pack, looked about for a place to put it, then dropped it on the floor and kicked it under the small table, conserving floor space.

"It sounds like you've managed to addle your mind somehow, whatever else you've done. I suppose you're hungry?" Barbara gave up the pretense of continuing to fuss with her nails. She turned to give him her full attention and frank interest.

Ben crouched and reached under the table to get something from his pack. His hand rejected a half-loaf of bread that was going stale, and pulled out some good sausage. "Not really. I have this, if you'd like some."

"Maybe later, thanks. Did you go to the Blue Temple and enlist, as you were saying you'd do?"

"Didn't you get either of my letters?"

"No."

That was hardly surprising, Ben supposed. "Well, I wrote twice. And I did enlist." He took a bite off the end of the sausage himself, and offered it again. "Ever hear from Mark?"

"Not since he left." This time Barbara was not so reluctant. Chewing, she regarded Ben for a little while in silence, while he stood there unable to keep himself from smiling at her. He could, as always, see thoughts coming and going in her face, though he was hardly ever sure of what they were. It sounded simple, but it was one of the things about her that gave Ben a sensation of enchantment.

At last Barbara said to him: "There's more on your mind than Mark, or bringing me sausage. I suppose you've deserted. Is that the big secret I can see in the back of your eyes? A Blue Temple enlistment should run for four or five years, shouldn't it?"

Ben's eye had caught sight of his old lute. It was hanging in a prominent place, tied high up on the tent's central pole. Seeing the instrument so honored gave him a good feeling, and seeing it also brought back memories. Ben reached up and took it down.

"I've kept it as a decoration, like."

He strummed the instrument, but only briefly and softly. He could see at once that the strings were in bad shape. It seemed too that his hands were well on the way to losing entirely whatever poor skill they'd once possessed. For years, for most of his life, Ben had nursed deep, fervent dreams of being a musician.

His broad mouth twisted now, under his new beard, remembering that.

Now that he had some form of music in his hands, the tune that had been haunting him ever since that night of treasure and terror and flight came back irresistibly. In his mind the music ran sweet and clear—all tunes ran that way for him, in his mind. It was only when he tried to get them to come out properly through his fingers or his voice that his difficulties started.

He sang the old tune now, very softly and almost to himself, in a voice that sounded as inadequate as he had feared it would:

> Benambra's gold
> Doth glitter coldly . . .

"Gods and demons, what a noise!" judged the harsh bass voice of someone standing just outside the tent. A moment later the entrance flap was whipped aside, this time by no gentle hand. The man who had to bow his head to enter seemed to fill up what little space Ben's presence had left in the small interior.

The newcomer could be no one but Tanakir the Mighty, though perhaps he did not quite do justice to his portrait on the wagon's side. Well, thought Ben, no human figure could do that. Tanakir was almost a head taller than Ben, and his upper body proportionately broad. His shirt, a garment undoubtedly once expensive though now badly faded, was worn halfway open to reveal the carven plates of muscle on his chest. His biceps were more than simply large, and as he came into the tent his movements were ponderous, as if slowed down by equal weights of muscle and of vanity. At second glance he was a considerably older man than Ben. There were a few gray hairs showing in his long dark braids.

Once inside, Tanakir paused, fists on hips in a pose that might well be some part of his act. He glared at the two other people in the tent as if he were demanding an explanation from them.

"We have a strongman now," said Barbara in conversational tones to Ben. "You never wanted that job while you were here."

Tanakir from his greater height glowered down at Ben, who stood with lute in hand, blinking back at him. "So, this is Ben," the strongman rumbled. "He didn't *want* the job? Him? This chubby minstrel?"

Ben turned a little away, to hang up the lute again carefully, high up on the central pole, out of head-knocking range. It was one of the few times in his life that anyone had ever called him a minstrel, and he felt unreasonably pleased.

Tanakir told him: "You're leaving very soon."

Ben blinked at him again, then backed up carefully and sat down on a small chest, which creaked a little with the burden. He sat in a position that left his hands and feet ready if they should be needed. "I haven't decided about that yet."

"I'm deciding for you."

"All right," said Ben mildly. He allowed the other just a beat in which to begin triumphant relaxation, before he added, "One of us leaves tonight, if you feel that way. Well, maybe in the morning. No one wants to start out on the road at night."

Ben paused briefly, then suggested: "Arm-wrestle

for it?" It was impossible not to notice how the other's god-like arms had been circled with bands and bracelets to make them look still thicker, and what pains had been taken with short, tattered sleeves, that they might be best revealed. Ben's own arms, if they had not been hidden in his long pilgrim's sleeves, would by comparison have looked almost as chubby as they did strong.

Tanakir, after having been kept mentally off-balance for a few moments, now looked pleased. All strongmen, thought Ben, are certainly not bright. And this particular one must be a chronic pain to have around.

"Arm-wrestle," Tanakir repeated, nodding. "All right, we'll do that. Yeah."

Barbara, who knew them both, must also have been pleased by Ben's suggestion, for she made no objection to it. When Ben saw this his heart dared to rise again. He smiled at Barbara as she moved quickly to clear the little table for their contest, and he got the briefest of smiles from her in return.

Before the contest could get started there was an outburst of whispering from outside the tent. First, it sounded like some conspiratorial meeting getting too loud; and then, suddenly, like they were greeting someone in surprise.

Then imperturbable old Viktor, who by consent and diplomacy ran the carnival, put his head into the tent. There was an uncommon smile on his face. Ben understood the smile when, a moment later, the head of a much taller and younger man appeared above Viktor's, grinning.

Still it took Ben a moment to make the recognition. He jumped to his feet then, and cried out: "Mark!" It had been two years. Ben would have moved forward, but Barbara was in his way. She had already darted to the doorway to give the tall young man a great hug and kiss.

Tanakir was upset all over again. "What is this?" he roared at them. "Come on, arm-wrestle, or just get out."

Barbara turned to him. "Don't be so eager; you've never managed to out-wrestle *me*." She turned back to Mark. "Look at you, you're taller than Ben."

"I was that when I left. Or very nearly."

"And just as strong—"

Mark had to grin at that.

"Come on!" This was Tanakir again. "Whoever that clown is, he can wait his turn."

So the rest of the reunion had to be postponed. Old Viktor, as usual, kept things moving with a few diplomatic words and gestures. Mark remained in the background, smiling. Viktor, having greeted Ben, nodded sagely when he saw what was developing in Barbara's tent. Then he sent one of his wives on an errand, while he himself stood by, authoritatively twirling his gray mustache.

The wife was back promptly, bringing two stubs of candles into the darkening tent, along with a burning twig to light them. Ben noticed with irrational relief that the candles were not blue beneath their golden tongues of flame. They were set burning on the small table to the right and left of the two contestants.

Barbara gave up her single folding chair to Tanakir. It creaked impressively when he sat down. Ben hitched the little chest around and sat on it, so that he faced his opponent across the table. He noted that Barbara and Mark together were now finishing off his sausage.

Fortunately he, Ben, had not arrived weak with hunger. Mark looked good—but there was something that had to be taken care of first, before he could enjoy the company of friends.

The two big men sat facing each other, their noses a meter apart. The carnival strongman made a show of getting ready, rolling up his right sleeve a trifle more. He managed to ripple the muscles of his arm impressively as he did so.

"Don't fear the flame," said Tanakir, leaning forward to put his elbow on the table. Ben's elbow was already there. The strongman's fierce scowl emanated onions. "I'll not burn you very much. Cry out once and I'll let you go."

"Don't fear the flame," returned Ben, "for I'll not burn you at all." And he reached forward, ready to meet the all-out surge of strength that the other was certain to apply as soon as he could grab Ben's hand.

"Get him, Ben!" called Mark.

Their grips locked in the surge, the table quaked beneath their elbows.

And Barbara, with a greater urgency in her voice than merely friendship: "Win, Ben! Win!"

Tanakir cried out, but not with victory, nor yet with candle-burn. The back of his hand descending had snuffed the flame before the heat could even scorch the hairs. Snuffed out the flame, and thudded on to squash the wax below.

CHAPTER 4

The small man rode the once-paved road upon a fine but almost starving riding beast, and wore at his side a poor scabbard that had the hilt of a fine sword protruding from it. Some things about this man, including his long, carefully trained black mustache, suggested that he might be castle-born. But most of his clothing, and certain other indications, argued for a more humble origin. He was bareheaded, and under the shock of wild black hair his lean, elegant face was grim. He was mumbling to himself as he rode slowly through the warm spring sunshine.

Two more men, on foot, were following the mumbling rider across the grimly peaceful countryside, past abandoned farmsteads and untilled fields. And several paces behind those two shuffled along a lad not quite full grown, though already tall. On the right shoulder of this youth there rode a hooded shape, that under its covering of green cloth had to be that of some trained flying creature, bird or reptile perhaps.

Taken as a group, the four men looked like the token representation on a stage of some defeated army. But the only thing their various costumes had in common was the look of wear and poverty; if this was truly an army, it had no other uniform.

Of the two who were walking together, one carried a battle-hatchet in a kind of holster at his belt, and had a bow slung on his back. His taller companion wore a sword on one side of his own belt, with a sling and stone-pouch on the other. The visible hilt of this man's sword, in contrast to their leader's, was dull and cracked.

The surface of the road they traveled had once been paved and cared for, though like most of its users it was now experiencing hard times. And the land through which the road passed looked as if it might once have been well tended. A feral milkbeast, lean and scarred, stared at the procession as if it might never have seen men before, then leaped a broken fence to bolt into a thicket. The man with the bow, hunger starting in his eyes, made the start of a motion to get the weapon off his back, but gave up before completing it. The beast was already out of sight.

The leader appeared to be paying very little heed to any of this. He continued to mouth words to himself as he rode on, eyes fixed ahead. One of the two men following, he who had the bow, was more concerned than the other by this circumstance. He now nudged his taller companion, and signaled that they should lag back a few more steps behind their leader.

As soon as the gap between the two men and the rider had widened enough to give them good prospects for some privacy, the shorter man whispered: "Why does he mutter so?"

The taller man who wore the battered sword had a long face with an habitually grave expression, that made him look like a solemn servant dressed up as a soldier. And he answered gravely: "I think his woes have driven him half mad."

"Ha. Woes? If that would do it, we'd all be jabbering and snarling as we moved about. I wonder now . . ."

"What?"

"I wonder if I decided wisely, yesterday, when I chose to follow him." The shorter man, whose name was Hubert, paused at that point, as if expecting to receive some comment from his companion. When none was immediately forthcoming, he went on. "He spoke me fair enough — well, you were there, you heard. I've yet to hear, though, just what enterprise he plans to use us in. And you say he's not told you, either. Well, at first I thought there was no need to ask. There's little business of any kind to be transacted on these roads, except for robbery. I've not done that before, but I was hungry enough to try anything . . . and there *you* were, looking sane and tolerably well fed, following him already. You looked as if you might know where you were going. And now you tell me he's half mad."

"Sh!"

"You said it first."

"But not so loud." The taller, grave-faced man, whose name was Pu Chou, appeared for a moment to be annoyed. Then he answered thoughtfully: "I followed him because, as you say, he spoke fair. He's fed me, so far. Not a lot, but better than nothing. And he did promise when I joined him that we were going to find wealth."

Hubert said, flatly: "Wealth. And you believed him."

"You said you believed him, when he spoke to you. He can speak convincingly."

"Aye. Well, we've passed travelers who I thought looked like easy game, and not tried to rob them. He must have some other means of gaining wealth in mind. Well, that sword he's got is certainly worth a coin or two, even if the sheath is poor."

Pu Chou was quietly alarmed. "Don't even think of taking it from him. I've seen him use it once."

"Once? He hauls it out at every crossroad. There's some fine charm of magic in it, or at least he thinks there is, for he consults it to choose his way. Whether it works or not—"

"I meant I've seen him use it as a sword. When I was his only follower, and still unarmed myself. Three bandits thought they wanted it. One of them got away. It's one of the others' sword I'm wearing now."

"Oh."

And for some time after that the little procession trudged on in silence. Hubert glanced back once at the lad who was still bringing up the rear, probably too far back to have overheard the whispered conversation. The name of this youth was Golok, and Hubert had rarely heard him speak at all. Instead he appeared to spend most of his life staring straight ahead as if in abstract thought. Whatever the creature was on his shoulder—Hubert had not yet gotten a good look at it without its cover — it was as quiet as if it were asleep, or perhaps dead and stuffed. Hubert had learned from Pu Chou yesterday that Golok had once been apprentice to the Master of the Beasts at some important castle; some kind of a problem had arisen, and he had had to leave. Whether he was the true owner of the thing that perched on his shoulder now was a question that had not been raised. Hubert had no urge to press for details in the lives of these his new companions, even as he was content for his own history to remain unknown to them.

Now Hubert turned his eyes ahead again. The sky in that direction was darkening, he observed, as if a storm were coming. Especially ahead and off there to the right.

Of more immediate interest was something that now lay only a few strides ahead, namely yet another crossroads. Here the disintegrating pavement of what had once been a king's way intersected another and more common road. This was of hard-packed earth and gravel, and it wound away to left and right amidst the gentle rolling of the land. Like most roads in this time of failing commerce, it was beginning to be overgrown by weeds and grass.

To the left, this intersecting thoroughfare led off into a near-monotony of gradually improving fields. It was possible to see for several kilometers in that direction, and in the distance intact houses and barns were visible, as well as small groups of laborers in those far fields. Maybe, thought Hubert, they had now come to the edge of the Margrave's well-protected lands. That suggested to Hubert that they might expect to encounter some of the Margrave's soldiers shortly, and that in turn suggested to him that perhaps this would be a good point to turn back. But then, he was not the leader.

To the right conditions were different. In that direction the simple crossroad soon became a dismal, muddy, heavily rutted way, almost a sunken road. It lost its way among leafless thickets, and clumps of inordinately tall thistles, that seemed to have grown where they were for no other purpose than to provide some ideal sites for ambush. A chill wind drifted down on the travelers from that direction, where, as Hubert had noted earlier, the sky was growing dark. On the horizon to the right the clouds were really ominous.

The leader had reined in his steed at the very center of the crossroads. Hubert had expected him to draw his fine sword, as usual, as soon as the intersection was reached. But the horseman had not done so yet. He was looking from right to left, and back again, as if considering. At last his mumbled monologue had ceased.

Tall Pu Chou, shading his eyes from local sunshine, was squinting off into forbidding shadows to the right. "What's that, I wonder? I can make out a certain tall structure, almost half a kilometer off. Just at the edge of those trees, beside the road."

The youth Golok had come up close to the others now, and it was his surprisingly deep voice that next broke the silence. "That's a gallows," he intoned.

The mounted leader looked at him, and made a brisk gesture with one hand. Obediently Golok reached up and whisked off the cloth covering the creature that rode his shoulder. It's a monkbird, thought Hubert, moderately surprised. He himself was no expert at handling beasts, but it was his understanding that the small flying mammals were notoriously hard to train, and that few beast-handlers would attempt it. Golok crooned low orders to the beast, as its eyes blinked yellow against dark brown fur. Hubert noticed suddenly how handlike the tiny feet of the creature were, at the ends of its hind limbs.

"Go, Dart, fly," Golok whispered. His voice when he spoke to the animal was much changed.

In a moment the monkbird had risen into the air from its master's shoulder. It flew in a low circle on membranous wings, as if orienting itself. Then it flapped softly off to the right, following a course above the road that led to darkness.

The mounted leader sat motionless in his saddle, gazing after the winged scout, long after distance and shadows had taken the monkbird out of Hubert's effective range of vision. The leader's hand was resting on the black hilt of his fine sword. As if, Hubert thought, he knew that he was going to have to draw it soon, but wished to postpone that act as long as possible.

And now the leader spoke again. He was still talking to himself, but this time Hubert was close enough to hear some of the words. " . . . cursed poverty . . . more real than many another curse. Whether some wizard has fastened it upon me, or . . . "

The monkbird's reconnaissance did not take very long. It reappeared in the shadowy distance and drew closer, until with a final flourish of the forelimbs that unfurled its wings it sat again on Golok's shoulder. Then it shivered slightly, as if it might have experienced a chill under that dark portion of the sky.

"Man on tree?" Golok asked it, evidently confident that it would understand the question.

"Two-leg fruit," the monkbird answered, the first intelligible sounds that Hubert had heard from it. Its voice was tiny but piercing in tone.

"Two-leg is living?" Golok questioned.

"No." It was the single, sharp note of a birdcall.

At this, the mounted leader, with one final muttered comment to himself, drew out his sword, wrenching it from the scabbard with a violent motion and holding it aloft. As Hubert had observed before, when that sword cleared its sheath it negated all the poverty in the appearance of the man who held it. The blade, a full, perfect meter in length, was moderately wide, incredibly straight and sharp. A mottled pattern on the flat side seemed to exist just beneath the perfect polish of the surface, and appeared to extend into the metal, to a depth greater than the blade was thick. The hilt was rich and rough in texture, of lustrous black, with some small design worked on it in white. Earlier Hubert had been able to read this design as the symbol of a small white arrow, point aimed upward toward the pommel.

The lean right arm of the mounted man held out the weighty sword without a quiver. The blade was extended in turn to each of the four roads leading from the intersection. When the point was aimed along the rutty road in the direction of the gallows, Hubert thought that he could see the blade-tip quivering, as if after all there might be a trace of weakness in that determined arm.

"This way," the leader ordered. And his voice was no more unsteady than was the single ringing snap with which he sheathed his blade.

He rode along the rutted way toward that darkened sky, no faster and no slower than before. This time, the two soldiers and the youth all followed closely. And in silence. Their surroundings, once they had turned at the crossroads, were not conducive to unnecessary talk.

A daylight owl fled through a roadside thicket, as if it were horrified at something it had found within. The road here took a winding course among the ugly thickets, making it impossible for the traveler to see more than a few meters ahead at any point. The gallows — if that was what it was — had disappeared from sight for the time being. But it was waiting for them, thought Hubert, up ahead.

When at last the tall skeletal structure came into view again, there was no doubt of what it was. The rude scaffolding had room for three or four victims, but there was only one in residence, though the frayed ends of other ropes indicated that once he had enjoyed company.

One lone, attenuated human shape hung from the weathered crosstree. From the half-face that remained, a single empty eyesocket looked down upon the travelers, and seemed sardonically to mark their progress. Hubert could not keep from looking up at it several times, though their march did not pause as it went by. At last the windings of the road took the gallows out of sight behind a screen of barren trees. All the plants here were oddly leafless, Hubert suddenly realized, though spring was well advanced.

Still the mounted leader rode on in silence, concentrating his attention on the road ahead and the surrounding woods and thickets. Even leafless as it was, the growth beside the road still seemed to promise ambush. No birds sang. A hush held, as if some enemy already lay in wait, and had only a moment ago fallen silent in anticipation. At intervals the leader, as he rode, put hand to sword once more. But he did not draw. His fingers rested carefully, almost caressingly on that black hilt, then slid away again.

When they were a few hundred meters past the gallows, he sighed gently, and appeared to come to the conclusion that any immediate challenge from the roadside was unlikely. He relaxed a trifle in the saddle, and, while still keeping an alert eye on his surroundings, rode forward a trifle faster and more boldly.

Hubert, reassured by this sight, and growing ever more conscious of his rumbling stomach, speeded up the pace of his own feet somewhat until he drew close to the rider's stirrup. Then, when the way ahead appeared to be clear for a little way at least, Hubert dared to speak. "Sir? Will the blade show us where we can find some food? I'm empty, pack and belly both."

There was no immediate response. At least there had not been, as Hubert had half-feared there would, a flash of rage.

Encouraged, Hubert tried again. "Baron Doon? Sir?"

The rider did not turn his head by so much as a centimeter, but this time he answered. "If food were what I wanted," grated the low voice from between his teeth, "what I, the owner and master of this Sword, desired more than anything else in the sweet universe, then Wayfinder would guide us to as great a feast as I desired. But since food is not what I crave at this moment, it does not. Now keep quiet, and follow me alertly. Safety is not what I am looking for either."

Wayfinder, thought Hubert to himself. Wayfinder. I've heard some story about that, some tale of magic Swords. . . . But, having been ordered to keep quiet, he kept quiet.

The four men continued to move forward — again, more slowly, for now the riding beast, well-trained though it was, was giving signs of reluctance to proceed any farther along this road. At a sign from Baron Doon, Golok unhooded his monkbird again, though for the time being he kept it on his shoulder.

The road continued a progressive deterioration, till now it was doubtful whether it deserved that name at all. And now, as if capriciously, it branched again. Again it was the right-hand fork that bore the most unfavorable aspect, even though the left appeared to lead into nothing better than another nasty thicket, this one so overgrown as to almost swallow up the track entirely.

Still there was no doubt that the right-hand way looked worse. Even though — and here Hubert rubbed at his eyes, blinked, and looked again — even though it did appear to lead to a house. Yes, there was an abandoned dwelling down there, right on the edge of an encroaching swamp. It was a large house, or rather it looked as if it might have been large before portions of it had suffered a collapse. The swamp, thought Hubert, had probably begun to undermine it from the rear.

The surviving portion had been sturdily built of timber and of stone, the masonry discolored and weakened now. There might be, Hubert supposed, three or four rooms still standing roofed and usable, counting the fragment of an upper story that remained.

Usable, that is, if the whole thing did not collapse the first time someone walked into it.

The road to the right did not go past the house, but terminated at it, or, more precisely, at a narrow bridge a few meters from the wooden door. The rickety, unsafe-looking bridge spanned a noisome ditch formed by an advanced arm of the swamp. The bridge was fashioned of two thin, round logs, slippery-looking with damp and moss. There was a sketch of a railing on one side, and crosswise between the logs a scattering of short boards for footing. Some of these floorboards already hung down broken.

Again Baron Doon had recourse to his Sword. This time, Hubert observed with a fatalistic lack of surprise, the blade quivered only when its owner pointed it in the direction of the house.

This time Doon did not sheath the blade, using it instead to gesture to Golok. Then he went back to watching the house intently.

Again the flying mammal, after a low-crooning conference with its master, took to its dark, membranous wings. It circled the house first. Then it hovered briefly in front of one shadowed window, but balked at entering that dark, blank space. In another moment it had returned to its master's shoulder, where it sat shivering. When Golok spoke to it this time, it would not answer.

Doon, drawn blade still in hand, dismounted. Then silently, leading his mount behind him, he approached the bridge. The riding beast allowed itself to be led, though unwillingly, its hide quivering with its high-strung nerves. Hubert saw how its feet curved, the hard footpads trying to grip the slippery logs of the bridge where the crossboards were missing.

The others were all hesitating. Hubert swallowed, and crossed second. Once he had made up his mind to follow and serve a leader, he'd serve and follow him. Until the time came when he decided to quit altogether. Provided, of course, that when the time came he was still able. . . .

Firmly he banished thoughts like that. Become a coward, and the world was through with you for good. The bridge under his feet felt more solid than it looked.

Once across the bridge, Hubert shot one glance behind him, and saw that the other two were starting over. He could not help seeing, also, that the world back there, the distant parts of it at least, looked infinitely inviting. Yonder in the background a clear sky spanned fair, green hills, and happy fields. . . .

Such pleasant things were not for the highwayman-adventurer. Hubert turned his back on them. Now the frowning, vacant windows of the house were scant meters in front of him. They reminded him uncomfortably of the empty eyesocket that had seemed to watch him, only a little while ago.

As soon as Golok, the last man, was across the bridge, Doon gestured to him again. In obedience Golok again sent the monkbird forward. But again it refused to enter any of those dark apertures, darker than windows ought to be even on such a gloomy day.

The Sword in Doon's hand quivered, lightly and insistently. It was guiding them toward the single broad door that was set in the front of the building at ground level. Doon led his mount right up to the door, and rapped on the panels with Wayfinder's hilt. Then he tugged to open it. It proved not to be locked, but only stuck; noisily it yielded at last.

The interior revealed was not as dark as the upstairs behind those windows. Hubert, looking past his leader, could make out a passageway, surprisingly deep and broad. And at the end of the passage—could that be some kind of an interior courtyard? Somehow, the closer Hubert approached to the building, the larger it became to his eyes. Yet he was never at any point conscious of observing any unnatural change.

Hubert would have liked to delay the others, to talk over with them in whispers this fact and its implications. But Doon was already leading them forward, into the house. The passage was too low for a mounted man to ride through it comfortably, and he continued to tug his animal after him.

Once Hubert had gotten well inside, he blinked his eyes again. Why, he thought, again it's grown bigger. The passageway, its sides doorless and windowless, went straight on for six or eight meters; and the interior court when they reached it was ten meters square, surrounded by two-story building on all sides. Four doors, one in each wall, were at ground level. Only the door by which they were entering the courtyard stood open. More dark windows showed in the walls.

"Magic," breathed Golok in the rear. He was following Hubert and Pu Chou closely now, as if he feared to get very far from the armed men. His word said no more than they had all already realized. This courtyard, now that they were standing in it, was certainly bigger than the whole house had looked when they had first seen it from the road. There were cloisters cracking into disrepair, and a dry, cracked fountain. There were a couple of long-dead trees, and in the tile paving blank clay places that might once have been meant for flowerbeds. Most of the paving was covered with years of blown-in dead leaves and dirt.

Golok drew in his breath with a sharp sound. The door just opposite that they had entered by was slowly creaking open. In a moment a huge, black-furred, two-legged shape had appeared in the doorway. The figure slouched there, almost of human shape, though it looked inhumanly broad and strong. Bright eyes, of a different blackness than its fur, glittered at the intruders, and white teeth showed sharp in a black mouth.

It was—at least, perhaps it was—no more than a beast, and they were four men armed and ready. Yet three of the four men started back.

Doon had already swung himself back up into his saddle, from which vantage point he now confronted the creature with drawn sword. His mount, as if it were relieved to at last face something in the way of concrete danger, snorted but held steady.

Doon cried, to the ebon beast: "Be warned, if ye have power of understanding! I am not here to be entertained by bogey-games. Nor will I be sent hence without that which I need. Be warned also, that this blade when in my hand is doubly magic!"

The monstrous ape retreated. Hubert could not tell quite how it managed the maneuver, only that one moment the midnight bulk still filled the doorway, and the next moment it was gone.

There was a faint sound from the closed door to the right. As one, the men spun in that direction, to watch that broad door creaking open . . .

. . . pushed by a skeletal hand. The hanged man from the gallows was standing just inside it. Hubert could not be mistaken about that face.

Pu Chou uttered a sound that could not be described as speech. But Doon, wheeling his mount, faced this apparition as coolly as he had the other. As if addressing the same entity, he went on speaking. "I tell you, trickery will not move me, nor will threats. Now do you mean to fight me, or listen to me?"

Again, the thing that he confronted disappeared.

All four men were now turning about, twisting their necks, trying to keep all four doorways under observation at the same time. None of them were taken by surprise by the next appearance, in the doorway that had so far remained unoccupied. The tall, richly robed figure that stood there now was that of an old man, gray but sturdy. His massive bald crown was surrounded by a long gray fringe that matched his beard. Great blue eyes, with something in them as innocent as infancy, looked out from under white bushy brows.

Facing Doon, this man asked in a low, impressive voice: "What seek you here?"

Doon lowered his Sword slowly. He started to speak, then looked down at his mount. The riding beast had suddenly relaxed.

And now the Baron heaved a great sigh, as if he too felt finally able to allow himself the luxury of weariness. When he spoke, his voice was no longer as taut as a drawn bowstring. "What I seek is simply wealth. No, not yours; I suppose your treasure might be considerable, but even so it won't be enough for me, and I don't purpose to take it. I believe that the treasure I want is elsewhere. But for some reason the pathway to it leads through your door."

Now Doon's riding beast had suddenly turned its long, gaunt neck aside, and was beginning to graze on something near the ground. Hubert, with a sensation of blurred eyes, saw that the flowerbeds were still active after all, indeed that they were richly grown with leaves and blossoms. There was a splash from the fountain, where moments ago he had seen a cracked and dusty basin. Doon turned his head in mild bewilderment at this new sound, then shrugged and dismounted, letting his animal graze. But he retained his Sword in his right hand.

When a shadow wavered across Hubert's vision, he looked up to see that a bright sun in a clear sky had been intercepted by a full-leaved branch of a tree that was after all not dead.

The tall old man in the doorway was asking: "What is your name?"

"I am the Baron Doon." The words were a quiet distillation of pride.

The old man nodded. "And I am known, for the present, as Indosuaros. Do you need to ask my profession?"

"No, I think not."

"Nor I yours. Well." A songbird twittered in one of the trees, and the monkbird, Dart, on Golok's shoulder replied in happy mockery. Indosuaros added: "I am pleased to offer you and your men my hospitality. Though, as you have doubtless deduced by now, my usual habit is to discourage visitors."

Doon needed only a moment to think about it. "And we are pleased to accept, with thanks." He sheathed his Sword.

Now Hubert was aware that the house around them was altering even more swiftly than before. Dust and dead leaves had disappeared from the courtyard, as had the cracks from the cloisters and the walls. Beside the burbling fountain a table had materialized, flanked by benches and chairs and covered in snowy linen. Hubert could half-see moving forms, whether human or not he could not tell, moving through the air around the table, juggling plates, setting and arranging. The air held a sudden and delicious smell of food, subtle, yet almost staggering to the hungry senses. And, for one breath-catching moment, Hubert was sure that he beheld the delicate shape of a young servant girl, seductively clad. A moment later, only immaterial powers swirled the air where she had been.

An elderly serving man, whose drab shape seemed real and solid enough, had emerged from the house to stand with bowed head at the side of Indosuaros. The tall wizard conferred with him in whispers, then made a gesture of dismissal. Now the benches that had been placed beside the table were whisked away, to be replaced presently by carven chairs. Dishes and platters of substantial food began to appear, and flagons of wine. The settings were enhanced by cutlery and goblets of precious stone.

"Pray be seated," said Indosuaros courteously. "All of you."

"One moment, if you please," said Doon, equally polite. With a nod to the wizard—it was a gesture, Hubert thought, that did not quite ask permission—the Baron drew his magic blade and consulted it again. It pointed him directly to a chair. He took it. At his gesture, the other men moved to seat themselves, with little ceremony.

Indosuaros took his place at the table's head, in a chair whose carven serpents, Hubert thought, could be seen from time to time to move. The wizard lounged there, nibbling at a few grapes from the banquet, watching indolently while his guests satisfied their thirst and hunger. Delightful soft music could now be heard, from somewhere in the background. The courtyard was now certainly a pleasant place, with the trees placed just right to shade the table.

Doon scarcely relaxed. In businesslike fashion he polished off a plate of food, and a single cup of wine, then signified politely that he had finished eating. Again the form of the serving girl was suggested in the air, and plates began to vanish selectively. Doon scarcely glanced at her. He was watching his host carefully.

Indosuaros helped himself to one more grape. Then he leaned toward his principal guest, and in a low and pleasant voice began what amounted to a blunt interrogation.

"We all want gold, don't we? But what makes you think that, as you put it, your road to wealth leads through my door? Speak plainly, please—as I believe you have, so far."

"Why, I intend to do so," Doon answered calmly. "But first, my thanks again for this excellent refreshment."

"You are welcome. By the way, I am curious, Baron. You ate and drank with no sign of hesitancy or suspicion. Did it never cross your mind, even as a possibility, that . . . ?"

Hubert, who had just mopped up some delicious gravy with a morsel of soft white bread, experienced a momentary difficulty in swallowing.

But the Baron only laughed. It seemed almost too big a sound to come out of his small frame. "Sir

Wizard, ordinarily, of course, if someone of your obvious skill were minded to do me harm with poison, I'd have little hope of avoiding it. But my Sword has led me to your table, and I trust it to lead me well."

"Your sword, you say." The old man sounded skeptical.

"Indosuaros, if you can read the page of magic a tenth as well as I believe you can, you already know which Sword it is I wear. Wayfinder. The Sword of Wisdom. Forged, along with its eleven fellows, by none less than the god Vulcan himself."

Hubert forgot about swallowing altogether.

Doon had pushed his chair back a few centimeters. He had both hands resting on the table's edge, and looked ready to push himself back farther and leap up. "God-forged, it is. And not even your powers, Sir Wizard, I think, are able to turn it away from true service to its owner. No magic that mere humans can control can do so."

"And it leads you where you command it?"

"Where my wishes command it. Aye. On to wealth."

"And it makes you immune to death?"

"No. Oh no. I have not commanded it to seek my safety. But, you see, if you had been trying to poison me, that would have been certain death, and certainly not wealth. No, the Sword of Wisdom would not have led me into that."

The old wizard appeared to be giving all of this the deepest thought. "I admit," he said at last, softly, "that I recognized Wayfinder very quickly. But I was not sure at first that you knew what you were carrying. . . . However, Sir Baron, toward what sort of wealth do you think the Sword of Wisdom is leading you?"

"Why, no less wealth," said Doon, "than the greatest in the world. I speak of the main hoard of the Blue Temple itself. And you may be sure, Sir Wizard, that I know what sort of an idea I am carrying when I speak of that."

Hubert could behold his own amazement mirrored in Pu Chou's face, and in Golok's. *Rob the Blue Temple? Impossible!* was his own first reaction, held in silence. On second thought he had to admit that to a master who could hold his own amid all this enchantment, and sit bargaining calmly with its creator, anything in the world might well be possible.

" . . . so you," Doon was saying to the wizard, "ought to have no objection to my plan. If you'll provide me with whatever it is the Sword has brought me here to find, why then I'll be pleased to share the treasure with you. Or help you in whatever other way I can."

"And if I do not," asked the wizard softly, "choose to provide you with this help?"

Doon considered this, drumming his fingers on the table, as if such an idea had never crossed his mind before. "Then, by all the gods," he said at last, "I'll find some way to hinder you."

Hubert, listening to the steady voice, thought that he had never heard a more truly impressive threat.

The old man at the head of the table was silent for a little time, as if he too might have been impressed. Then he gestured with one large, gnarled hand, its fingers heavy with ornate rings, and Hubert watching felt a pang of apprehension. But the gesture evoked nothing stranger than the old manservant, to hold another whispered conversation with his master. And now the clearing of the table proceeded more rapidly.

Hitching his chair a little closer to the table, the wizard said to the baron: "Let us talk. When you say you mean to rob the Blue Temple, I gather that you mean to despoil it in no trivial way."

"I have spoken plainly, as you wished."

"Indeed . . . you don't mean, I suppose, one of those little vaults, that all local Blue Temples have, for the day-to-day business—"

"I've told you what I mean, wizard, as plainly as I know how. And I understand what I am talking about."

"Indeed." Still looking doubtful, Indosuaros lounged back in his chair again. "Well, I can only say that, coming from anyone less well-equipped and less determined than yourself, such an announcement would deserve derision."

"But coming from me," Doon answered calmly, "the announcement is to be taken very seriously. I am glad you have been so quick to grasp that essential point."

"I think I have. But let me restate it just once more, so there can be no ambiguity. You intend to carry off some substantial portion of Benambra's Gold."

"A substantial portion," Doon agreed, nodding affably. "Yes, that's well put. I'd try to take it all, you see, if I thought there was any chance that my men and I could carry it."

"And do you know," asked Indosuaros, "where Benambra's Gold is kept?"

"Wayfinder is going to lead me to it," Doon answered simply. "And now you know the bare bones of my plan. Before I go into any greater detail, let me know whether you object to it."

The grizzled manservant was still standing close by his master's chair, and the two of them now exchanged a glance. In a moment the old wizard began to make a peculiar noise, and perform little lurching motions in his chair. It took Hubert a little while to realize that their host was laughing.

At last Indosuaros said: "I? Object to the Blue Temple's being robbed?" And he laughed again, and waved a hand about him in a gesture that seemed to take in his whole establishment. "I have secluded myself like this from the world for one reason only: that I may devise the most terrible vengeance possible upon the Blue Temple and all its leaders. For the past . . . for never mind how many years, I have devoted all my energies to that one object. And what worse vengeance could there be, upon *them*, than to rob them of what they hold dearer than life itself . . . hey, Mitspieler? Are we going to throw open those vaults of theirs or not?" And with a gesture that looked somehow out of character, he thumped his manservant awkwardly on the arm.

The servant called Mitspieler looked, if not quite as old as his master, somewhat more worn. His was a workman's face, beardless and lined. His stature was fairly small, his build sturdy, his arms emerging wiry and corded from short sleeves. His hair, short, curly, and dark, was richly mixed with gray.

His dark eyes gazed off into the distance as he answered. "In those vaults lies treasure, truly beyond price and beyond compare . . . aye, we can open them. When we are ready. We have been waiting for the help we need."

"And I have woven spells," said Indosuaros, "that the needed help might be brought to me, for until it was, a robbery on the requisite scale seemed well-nigh impossible." He smiled at Doon. "And you still think that your coming here was a matter of your own choosing?"

"I have told you what it was—the Sword's guidance. But come, I'm interested. Just why are you devoting your life to getting back at the moneybags? Vengeance for what?"

"It is a long story."

"I'll hear one, if necessary."

"Later," said Indosuaros, vaguely. "Baron, will you draw your Sword once more if I request it? And hold it up for me to see?"

Doon pushed his chair back farther, and stood up, to make the motion easier. And yet once more he brought Wayfinder bright out of its sheath. The wizard now appeared to focus his full attention for the first time on the blade; and the servant standing beside his chair gazed at it too.

All the others were quietly intent, watching Indosuaros.

At last the old magician looked away, frowning lightly. "I will admit," he said, "that your Sword is genuine. Considerable power rests there in your hand."

"Considerable?" Doon came near to being outraged. "Is that the best word that you can find for it?"

Indosuaros was unruffled. "My own powers are also . . . considerable. And I tell you that they have been at work for a long time to solve the problems of attacking the Blue Temple. I have set them to bring— someone well qualified—perhaps you—here to help me. So, whether your presence here is actually due to the Sword, or—"

Doon brandished Wayfinder once, then clapped it

back into its sheath, as if to save it from the gaze of disreputable eyes. The Baron cried: "Forged by a god! By Vulcan himself!" It appeared that he could not credit the other's attitude. He seated himself again, banging his chair on the pavement.

"I have admitted that your Sword has worth." Indosuaros was looking at his guest more sternly now. "My chief question now is, what do you, yourself, bring to this enterprise? Apart, that is, from your indisputable greed, and courage—or perhaps fool-hardiness. Are you the man whose help I need? I must seek an answer to this question in practical terms."

"Then seek it."

It was probably Hubert himself who unwittingly gave warning. Doon must have seen, mirrored in Hubert's face, that something untoward was develop-ing behind the Baron's chair.

The door leading into that wall of the courtyard had swung open, to show blackness gathered behind it, an interior as dark as ever. And the ebony ape was there again, as silent as before. As soon as its eyes fell upon Doon, it came hurtling toward him from behind. The rush was swift and noiseless, and made with log-sized arms uplifted to seize the man or deal him a crushing blow.

Hubert was on his feet. But he knew he was too late, too slow, knew it even as he stood there with his own weapon but half-drawn, his chair still in the act of toppling behind him. Doon had meanwhile rolled sideways from his own chair, coming out of the move-ment somehow on his feet even as the great ape's fists crashed down to splinter his chair's back. Hubert had not seen Wayfinder drawn again, but now it flickered in its master's hand, the silver tongue of some swift serpent.

The ape turned with a roar, but not in time. Black fur gushing red that was not wine upon white linen, it sprawled forward among the remaining winecups. Gurgling its death, it slid off the table slowly, dragging cloth and cups to crash down with it.

Four men stood around the table armed, ready for the next threat—but there was none. One man sat smiling at the table's head. Nothing but approval glinted in the eye of Indosuaros.

Once more Doon waved the Sword. "I told you, wizard!" he roared in triumph. "I told you! In *my* hand, doubly magic!"

CHAPTER 5

The three of them, Mark, Ben, and Barbara, had been awake most of the night. They had been busy packing, swapping histories and stories, trading off to the other carnival people things that they weren't going to need. Then they had left the carnival at sunrise, driving in Barbara's wagon, one item she hadn't wanted to trade just yet. Tanakir had bartered them some food and a little coin for Barbara's little dragon and its cage, which he meant to incorporate into his own act. He was staying on with the carnival, seeing that she and her friends were leaving. Viktor waved goodbye to the three of them at dawn, and shouted his hope that they'd come back next season.

Mark doubted that very much. One way or another, he thought, they were sure to be somewhere else.

Purkinje Town and the carnival encampment were

a couple of hours behind them now. The road ahead had already straightened out, entering a long rise of nearly flat and mostly empty country that mounted slowly toward distant mountains that were now only just visible. An hour ago they had paused for breakfast, and Mark, as in the old days, had used his bow to hunt down a couple of rabbits.

Now they were well under way again, heading south by mutual though still largely unspoken agreement. The decision had been arrived at in the camp, surrounded by eavesdroppers, and the reasons for going south had not been discussed as yet.

Ben was driving the wagon at the moment, and Barbara talking.

"Ben, you haven't told us what you're up to. You say you joined the Blue Temple, but you're not with 'em any more. All right, so you deserted. But you've got a look about you. What're you planning now?"

Ben smiled faintly. "I'm planning to marry you."

Barbara looked exasperated. "We went through all that before you left. Nothing's changed. When I marry somebody, it's going to have to mean that I can live like a real person somewhere. No more—" She waved a hand, vaguely indicating the wagon and the road.

"Fine with me," said Ben.

Her curiosity obviously aroused, Barbara looked at him closely. "Have you got any money in your pockets?"

"Not in my pockets. Not with me."

"Hidden somewhere, then?"

"I haven't got it yet. But . . . ."

With a loud sigh, Barbara sat back between the men, folding her arms. One more dream-possibility demolished.

Mark enjoyed listening to the two of them. He was curious about Ben's plans too, but he didn't want to interrupt. Now Ben appeared to be content, for the time being, to look mysterious as he gazed into the distance along the road ahead.

They drove for a while without conversation. Then Barbara said to Ben: "I know what it is. You want to get your Sword back, you're ready to try to sell it."

"I want to get it back, yes. Sell it, no. We got rid of the idea of selling them even before we hid the two Swords. We'd get cheated or murdered for sure. No, I've got a use for Dragonslicer."

Mark asked him: "A dragon hunt somewhere? Even Nestor never made much money doing that, remember?"

They all remembered. Ben said: "Nestor wasn't at it long enough. Anyway, it's a special hunt that I have in mind. There's just one dragon that needs to be got rid of."

"Everyone who's plagued with dragons on his land says that," Barbara advised him. "Get your pay in advance." Now she swiveled her head to look at the two men in quick succession. "Both of you, coming back at the same time like this—I wonder if there's some connection?"

"I want my Sword back too," said Mark. "But I'm not going dragon hunting. And I had no idea Ben had gone off to enlist, or that he'd be looking for Dragonslicer now."

"What do you need Coinspinner for?" Barbara asked him. "Not that I have to know. I'll get it back for you anyway."

"No secret about it. I'm going back to Sir Andrew's army."

"Why do you want to do that?" Ben shot at him.

"I don't know if I want to. I just feel like I've got to. I told you I was with him for a while, and then things got to seeming hopeless, and I left. And then . . ."

"They probably are hopeless," said Ben.

"Then I went back to my old village, Arin-on-Aldan, to see if I could locate my mother and my sister. There . . . wasn't any village any more. Five years since I've been there. Maybe I'll never know what happened to them." Mark paused. "But I'm going back to Sir Andrew now. With Coinspinner, if I can."

"Why?" pursued Ben.

Mark leaned forward to talk past Barbara. "Look, he's trying to help his people. The people who were his, before he lost his lands. Don't you think they want him back? It isn't just the lands, the wealth, that he's trying to recover." Feelings, ideas, were struggling in Mark but he couldn't find the words to let them out. "He keeps on fighting the Dark King," he concluded, feeling even as he spoke how inadequate the words were.

"Sounds hopeless," said Ben, remorselessly practical.

"Everything's hopeless, as long as people don't try." And Mark added suddenly: "I wish that you and Barbara would come with me."

"To join an army?" Barbara laughed, though not unkindly.

Ben just shook his head in silence.

Mark hadn't really expected any other answer, but still the refusals, Ben's in particular, irritated him. "So, you're going to hunt dragons instead? That's as hard as fighting in a war, even if you do have Dragonslicer."

Ben turned. Enthusiasm entered his voice again. "I told you, the hunting's only a small part of it. The dragon is just in the way of something else. I wish that both of *you* would come with *me*."

"I'm no good at riddles," Barbara said.

"What would we do?" Mark asked.

"Gain some money. More than just that. Wealth."

"I'm not out to get wealthy," Mark told him.

"All right. You're out to help Sir Andrew fight for his land and get it back—"

"And for his people."

"All right, for his people. Now you could help Sir Andrew a lot more by taking him a share of treasure, couldn't you? Imagine yourself showing up in his camp with jewels and gold enough to feed his army for a year."

"An army, for a year?"

"Ten years, maybe."

Barbara had turned to look at the huge man with concern. "Are you sick?" she asked him. The question sounded uncomfortably serious.

And Mark asked: "Where's anyone going to find wealth like that?"

Ben was calm. "I'll tell you both if you say you're with me."

This wasn't like Ben, and Mark couldn't figure it out. "Look, Sir Andrew needs real help. Not some scheme that. . . . I'm going to get Coinspinner and take it to him. If it's still wherever Barbara hid it."

Ben was looking stubborn now, maybe offended. Mark added: "I think now that we were wrong to hide them the way we did."

Barbara said: "Then you've forgotten how tired the

three of us were of Swords. Remember? We'd worry that they'd be stolen. Or that somebody powerful would find out that we had them, and an army would come after us, or a demon, or some magician that we'd have no way to cope with. Then we'd think of trying to sell them to someone, and we'd realize that we'd be cheated when we did, and murdered afterwards. Then we'd worry that Coinspinner would get lost of itself . . . remember how it'd move around? We'd hide it underneath something on one side of the wagon, and find it on the other. Or just outside. I'm not sure it's going to be there when we look for it."

"We'll look, though," said Mark. He paused. "Neither of you has ever heard anything of Townsaver, I guess?"

As he had expected, the others signed that they had not. Mark's father, Jord the blacksmith, had been the only survivor among the half dozen men conscripted by Vulcan to forge the Swords. And when the job was done, the god had taken Jord's right arm—and given him, in payment he had said, the Sword of Fury, Townsaver. All this before Mark had been born.

Then Jord, and Mark's older brother Kenn, had died in the fight when Townsaver saved their village—a hollow victory indeed, as Mark had seen for himself. . . .

" . . . recovered from his wounds?" Barbara was asking him something.

With an effort Mark recalled his thoughts, and figured out what she was talking about. "Sir Andrew? You mean his wounds from when his castle fell? That was five years ago. He's had more wounds since then, and overcome them—he does right well for a man his age. Or of any age, for that matter. Keeps his own small army in the field, most of the year. Supports

Princess Rimac, and her General Rostov. Harasses the Dark King. And fights Queen Yambu, of course; she now holds Sir Andrew's old lands."

"Dame Yoldi's still with him?"

"Sir Andrew'd not trust any other seer, I think. Nor she, I suppose, any other lord."

Now again for a time there was silence, except for the plodding of the loadbeasts' feet and the creaking of the wagon. All three people riding in it were examining different but related memories. Ben reached up, unconsciously, to rub a scar that crossed his left shoulder and the upper part of his arm. It was from a wound received in the fierce defense of Sir Andrew's castle, five years ago. . . .

And Mark returned to that day now, as he sometimes did in nightmares. Seeing the scaling ladders nosing up over the walls, the Gray Horde ready to swarm up. And massed behind its hideous ranks were the black and silver of Yambu, the blue and white of the army of Duke Fraktin who was now no more. That had been Mark's first real battle, and very nearly his last.

Barbara said: "Every time I think of that day, I think of Nestor."

"Aye," said Ben. And then again all three were silent. On the subject of Nestor there was no more to be said. Dragonslicer had been Nestor's, as had this very wagon; and Nestor must have fallen at some point in the defense, perhaps with Townsaver still in hand. By inheritance, or at least by unspoken agreement among Nestor's friends, Dragonslicer had come to Ben.

"How large is Sir Andrew's army now?" Barbara asked Mark.

"Even if I knew the numbers, I'd be wrong to tell them. Even to you two . . . anyway the numbers change, with fortune and the seasons. But he needs help." Raw urgency was in Mark's voice as he repeated: "I wish you'd come with me. Both of you."

Barbara laughed again. It was not a mocking sound, but quick and unhesitating. "I'm fed up with armies and with fighting. I'd like to try the opposite side of life for a while. Live in some peaceful town, and be a stodgy citizen with my own house and my own bed. A solid bed with four legs, one that doesn't roll. Let the world do its fighting outside the city walls." Again she looked quickly to her companions on left and right. "The last time that the three of us were in a fight, you two had to carry me out of it—that should have been warning enough for all of us."

"And I," said Ben, "have had enough of armies too. March back and forth to no purpose, take stupid orders and sweat and freeze and starve. That's what you do on the good days. And once in a while bad days come along. As both of you know." He faced Mark. "I admire Sir Andrew, but I have to say that I think his brains are addled. He's never going to win his lands and people back."

"So instead," said Mark, "you are going back to something safe and pleasant, like hunting dragons— all right, just one dragon. And that's going to make you fabulously rich. Is that what you said?"

"I didn't say that. But it will."

Barbara made a derisive sound. "The dragon guards a treasure?" That was a situation arising only in old fantastic tales.

"In a manner of speaking, yes, it does." Her mockery had stung Ben. "And I'll tell you something of the treasure. It has at least one more of the Swords in it. I know. I saw it put there myself, down into the earth."

Mark blinked, and suddenly found himself listening to Ben seriously. "One more Sword? Which one?"

"That I don't know," said Ben calmly. "The Sword was well wrapped when I saw it put away, along with six loadbeasts' burden of some other treasure. But I brushed against the Sword once, and even through the wrappings I could feel the power. After living with two of 'em here in the wagon for a couple of years, I know what I felt."

Barbara's face had altered. And her voice, too, when she spoke again. Now it came out in a whisper, almost awed. "You were in Blue Temple service."

"Of course. That's what I've been telling you."

But plainly the implications, the possibilities, hadn't really dawned on her till now.

At sunset they made camp. As so often in the old days, Ben and Mark slept under the wagon, with Barbara inside. In the morning they moved on, steadily and without hurry.

Several days passed in a southward journey. Spring would have shaded into summer around them, except that the country was growing higher. Modest mountains rose up ahead, apparently barring their progress. Mark had never learned the right name for this range, though he had passed this way at least once before.

Next day the road started to wind upward. It remained a comparatively easy way, for a route that traversed a mountain pass. Here at higher altitude the end of winter lingered still, in wasted fragments of snowbanks that survived among the bold spring flowers. The scenery began to tend toward the tremendous.

"I remember this place now. This was where we turned."

There was a small side canyon, that went curving up from the main road that traversed the pass. The wagon could get up the side canyon for a couple of hundred meters, and that was far enough. Suddenly the three who rode in it came in sight of a ruined shrine or temple, built on a small rise. It was a beautiful setting, prettiness nearby in the grass and wildflowers, and grandeur in the distant vistas. What god or goddess the temple might have been raised to honor seemed impossible to determine now. Certainly it was very old.

It was midday when they stood before the ruin. They had left the wagon standing just a few meters downslope, where the drivable surface petered out completely.

"You hid them in here? In the ruins?"

Barbara nodded.

"Why in here?"

"Coinspinner itself directed me to the place. I thought I told you that it had guided me."

The wind sighed through the walls of the canyon, rocks splintered with some ancient heaving of the earth. In the distance, far down the pass, the gentler slopes were beautiful with spring. Mark could see a group of white-robed pilgrims there in the distance, approaching slowly through the pass. If they were chanting a song to Ardneh, as seemed likely, he couldn't hear it at this range.

"Is this one of Ardneh's shrines, I wonder?"

"I suppose the local people would know," said Barbara. "If there were any local people."

But when they went inside the roofless walls and looked about, they found strong evidence that there were. Dried flowers, and freeze-dried fruit, were arranged on a low, flat stone, that might or might not originally have been part of an altar.

Two years ago, Barbara had climbed up to this place alone one night, from their camp a couple of hundred meters down the hill. She had climbed by night, with moonlight to show her the way picked out by the Sword that quivered in her hands.

Once the three had decided among themselves to hide the Swords, Coinspinner itself, in their troubled juggling with it, had shown them how to proceed.

Every time Mark or Ben had taken that weapon in hand, and tried to think of where it and its fellow should be hidden, the point had indicated Barbara.

And then, when they gave her Coinspinner to hold, she could feel no power in it at all. Then she had picked up Dragonslicer too—Mark had been apprehensive lest the two Swords come into contact, and something awkward, or worse than awkward, happen as a result. Then Coinspinner had vibrated almost angrily in Barbara's grasp, pointing out for her a path to follow. But it had ceased its indications whenever the men had tried to follow her.

So they had let her proceed alone. The moon had been the only witness of her climb up to this temple. The ruined structure was not visible from the main road through the pass, and she had not suspected its existence until the Sword of Chance had led her to it.

When the final place was indicated to her, she had hidden Coinspinner and Dragonslicer with a feeling of great relief. After years of hiding them and carrying them about, the nerves of all three people were worn with the strain. At that time their friend Sir Andrew had been a hunted fugitive, hiding they knew not where, and none of them had yet heard of Princess Rimac or her General Rostov, Sir Andrew's potential allies.

Swordless, Barbara had returned to camp. Mark and Ben, both obviously relieved to see her, had started to ask questions.

She had declined to answer. "It's done," she told them shortly. "We can stop worrying. And now I'm going to get some sleep."

And now, almost two years later, they were back.

It was hard to tell, by looking at the temple, what style of building it had been originally. Time and ruin moved all things toward simplicity. If any of the stones had ever been painted, they were now all white again, matching the surface of some nearby cliffs. If there had been carving, it was crumbled now. Architecture had all but vanished, leaving rubbly walls that in places were little more than outlines.

As soon as Ben saw the modern offerings on the flat altar stone, he dug into his pockets until he found a few fragments of bread. These he tossed beside the dessicated fruit and flowers. When he saw the others looking at him, he explained. "Some gods may not amount to much, but it pays to keep on the good side of Ardneh. I've found that out."

Mark was shaking his head. "We don't know it's his temple anyway."

"It might be."

"All right. But Sir Andrew says that Ardneh's dead. And out of all the gods we know are living, there's none whose attention I'd like to attract."

Ben stared at him for a moment, then shrugged and tossed a few more crumbs. "If Ardneh's dead—then this is for the unknown god who means us well, whoever he may be. Or she, if it's a goddess. Can't do any harm, certainly."

"I suppose not," Mark admitted. And, because he could tell that Ben would feel better if he did, Mark dug into his own pockets for some scraps of food, and tossed them on the stone.

Barbara was ignoring them, and had already moved on to more practical matters. "It was dark, before," she was murmuring, more to herself than to the men. "Moonlight, but . . . " And she moved from one angle of wall to another, pausing to look at the ancient stonework thoughtfully. Most of the blocks that were still in place were finely fitted together, without mortar. Few of them were large.

At last she bent, and, with wiry strength, moved aside what looked like a portion of a windowsill. "Come help me. This is the place."

In the men's hands the stones moved rapidly. Presently the old sill had disappeared. The low wall here proved to be hollow. Between the larger stones that made its base, a sizable cavity appeared.

Barbara stepped back, making room for them to reclaim their property. "Reach in," she directed.

Ben pulled up his right sleeve, revealing an arm

that looked almost stubby in its thickness. He thrust it into the hole up to his shoulder, and at once pulled out a sword-shaped bundle. The wrapping on it at once started to fall free, exposing portions of the fabric that had been folded under. Now Mark could recognize the cloth's pattern as that of an old blanket that Barbara had once had in the wagon.

Ben, murmuring something about the feel of power, shook the bundle, and the dusty wrappings fell away entirely. Dragonslicer, unchanged from when they'd seen it last, gleamed forth in meter-long straightness and sharpness. There was the mottled pattern, inside the flat of the bright steel, undimmed by rust. As Ben held the Sword up, cradled in two hands, Mark could see on the jet-black hilt the tiny white outline of a stylized dragon.

Ben made room beside the wall, and Mark knelt and groped into the cavity. He could feel stones and dust, but no wrappings and no blade. He reached farther, extending his fingers slowly and cautiously, in case Coinspinner's blade might be exposed—well he knew the extreme sharpness of the Swords. But still his hand found nothing—no, here was something. An object small and hard and round.

Wonderingly Mark brought out the coin, and held it up and saw that it was gold. The symbols on it were in some language that he could not recognize. The face on the obverse looked to him like that of Hermes, depicted as usual in his cap.

"It ought to be right in there," Barbara was saying to him. "Unless . . . " Her voice died when she saw what Mark held in his hand.

Mark gave her the coin to look at. Then he and Ben

removed more stones, and looked into the wall more deeply. The whole cavity was now exposed, but Coinspinner was gone.

No one sang Coinspinner's verse aloud. But it was running in their minds.

When they were satisfied that the Sword of Chance was no longer there, they restored the half-ruined wall, to a condition at least a little better than it had been on their arrival.

Then Mark sat down on the reconstructed sill, staring at the gold coin that was now in his hand again, while Ben and Barbara stood nearby regarding him.

"The coin is yours to keep," said Barbara.

"Of course," added Ben.

"Worth a good deal," said Mark, flipping it. "But not a Sword. I want to take a Sword back to Sir Andrew."

"Mine does not go there," said Ben. He paused, then added: "But I know where there's at least one more."

Mark, who had forgotten about other treasure for a time, turned Ben's offer over in his mind. He looked up, about to speak, and then was distracted by the oddity of a certain small shadow in the sky. He jumped to his feet, hushing Barbara with a raised hand just as she was about to say something.

High above their heads a creature flew, a small dark shape against the sky. Mark could see that it was a monkbird—that peculiar twisting of the wings in flight was a hard thing to mistake. It was surprising to see a monkbird up here in the highlands, far from its usual habitat.

The creature's flight path was curving in a circle around the zenith, as if it were deliberately observing the ruined temple and the three people who were inside it.

Barbara had scrambled up atop one of the ruined walls, to get a better view downslope. "Some men are coming up the canyon," she announced. "Six of them, I think."

Ben and Mark got into position to see for themselves. On the trail that ascended from the main road, two mounted men led four who moved on foot. Some of them at least were heavily armed.

"Following our wagon tracks?"

"No — maybe not — see the rider's drawn sword? I think he's using it for guidance."

"Coinspinner, then!"

"It could be Wayfinder."

As they watched, the monkbird left off circling and flew down to the approaching procession. It landed on the shoulder of the man walking in the rear, and presumably it could be reporting what it had seen.

Barbara hopped down from the wall. "What do we do? We can't retreat uphill with the wagon."

Ben spat. "I don't feel like just giving them a team and wagon. Six aren't that many, even assuming that they do mean harm." So the three, with good rocks at their back and some advantage in high ground, stood to face those who were approaching.

The leader of the six, he who rode holding a drawn sword in front of him, drew up his mount when he saw the three of them waiting. He was a small man with a large mustache. His gestures at once suggested an imperious manner. And, certainly, it was one of the

Twelve Swords that he gripped, though it was impossible to see at the moment which white symbol marked its hilt.

The second rider was a tall, graybearded man—a wizard, thought Mark, if he had ever seen one. Four more men came tagging along on foot, none of them looking particularly impressive.

When the leader drew up his riding beast some twenty meters or so away, Ben—in response to that brandished Sword—let the wrapping fall free from Dragonslicer. Mark had an arrow already nocked, and Barbara had drawn the sling from her belt and slipped a smooth stone into it from her small pouch. Now she was holding the weapon in expert readiness, letting the weight of the stone swing gently on the thongs.

The armed men in the other group began to draw their weapons also, but without any great appearance of eagerness. He who was so obviously a wizard, however, was frowning and shaking his head. "Peace!" he cried out, in a huge voice, and held up an open palm toward each side.

Ben made no move to put down Dragonslicer, nor Mark to lower his bow. Having weapons out and ready was probably the best move that non-magicians could make to ward off spells.

"Oh, aye, I'll have peace, if I can." The voice of the mustached man was easily loud enough for those confronting him to hear, as he replied to the wizard. Then, when Ben brandished his own Sword again, the man rounded on him and added: "But peace or war, I'll have my treasure. Unless it's Shieldbreaker that you're mishandling there so awkwardly, young man, I'll be able to take it from you if I try."

Mark chose to answer that. "And if that's Coin-spinner in your dainty hand, you'd better know that it belongs to me, and that I mean to have it back. If it's Townsaver, the same. That's mine by inheritance."

The rider controlled his mount. "Ha, we've met an owner of two Swords, by Hades! Neither of which he happens to have with him at the moment, unfortunately . . . since you appear to be so well-versed in the lore of Swords, I'll tell you that I hold Wayfinder here. It's guided me to this place, and now I must determine why." Again the rider had to struggle briefly with his high-spirited mount. He added then: "I am the Baron Doon, and this at my right hand the wizard Indosuaros. And who are you?"

"Mark," said Mark, touching his chest with his free right hand. Then he gestured to his side: "Ben, and Barbara."

"Ha, a notable economy of names. And a lack of pretension in the way of titles. But why not?" And now the mustached one heeded his wizard, who had jockeyed his own mount, a pale loadbeast trained for riding, closer to speak to him in a low voice.

After a short whispered conference, the man who had called himself Baron Doon looked up again. "So. What you have there is Dragonslicer. Doubtless the very implement I need, to break the second sealing." He spoke like a man making his private plans aloud.

There was a moment of ominous silence. Then Ben said in a calm voice: "Why, I have heard of a dragon-sealing, in a song. An old song, about treasure, where the sealings are numbered up to seven."

The Baron—Mark was beginning to believe that he might be such, for he looked proud enough to be a king—the Baron studied calmly the three who faced him. "It may be," Doon said at last, "that I will have use in my enterprise for some of you, as well as for that Sword. We had better talk."

Barbara spoke up, as bold as he. "Use for us in what enterprise? And at what rates of pay?"

The Baron looked at her appreciatively for a moment. Then he said: "I mean to have Benambra's Gold. You say that you know the old song; then you may know as well that it is more than a song, much more than a story. It's real, and those I choose to help me are going to share in it generously."

There was a silence, broken only by the wind feeling its way down the pass to mourn in the stones of the ruined temple. And now the wind brought with it the faint voices of the distant pilgrims, chanting to Ardneh as they drew slowly closer.

Mark exchanged glances with Ben. Then he called to Doon: "We might be willing to join you. We'll have to hear more, first."

And Ben, to Doon: "Whether we agree or not, this is my Sword, and it stays with me."

The Baron called back to them: "I want to consult Wayfinder on which of you, if any, I ought to enlist. You'll pardon me if I come nearer to you with it drawn."

And Barbara: "As long as you'll pardon us for holding our own weapons ready."

Doon now rode slowly forward, while the rest of his group stayed where they were. At a distance of no more than three or four meters he halted again, and now he pointed with the blade in his hand at Mark, Ben, and Barbara in turn. Mark could see the tip quivering, lightly and rapidly, when it was aimed at himself and at Ben. But it remained steady, he thought, when Doon leveled it at Barbara.

Doon told the two young men: "Your young piece there is not going to come with us. Can you trust your lives to her ability to hold her tongue?"

And Ben again: "Speak of the lady gently, or you might get Dragonslicer where you don't want it."

Doon raised an eyebrow, a signal more elegant by far than his attire. "Your pardon, I'm sure, your ladyship. I meant only that I decline to invite you to take part in this enterprise. And I most strongly advise that you say nothing to anyone about it."

She flared back at him fearlessly, "It's well that you decline to invite me, for I'd decline to go. And if my two friends are going, my tongue'll not put them in danger." Her manner softened just a little. "You don't know me, or you'd spare yourself the worry."

Doon slid his Sword back into its poor sheath. Suddenly he appeared somewhat diminished, though still vital and flamboyant. He sat his mount in silence for a few moments, looking over the three people who faced him. Apparently he was satisfied by what he saw, for he smiled suddenly; it was a better smile than any of the three confronting him expected.

"If there are any farewells to be said among you," he told the three, "say them now. My men and I will be waiting for two of you a little down the slope." With that he turned his back and slowly rode away, signing to his men to put their weapons up. They fell in behind him, and without looking back proceeded down the canyon.

The three who were left behind looked at one another.

Ben drew a deep breath, and addressed Mark. "Well, then. I take it we are going?"

"Benambra's Gold," Mark marveled softly, shaking his head.

"And Swords," said Ben, "for Sir Andrew."

"Aye, you tell me there's a Sword."

"Or maybe more than one."

"I'll have to go," said Mark. "I'll have to risk it then."

"And I know you're going too," said Barbara to Ben.

Mark went to her, and put his golden coin into her hand. "What do you have to say," he asked, "about our leaving you? I see no way around it."

"Nor do I, I suppose." If Barbara had any strong feelings in the matter she was keeping them well concealed. "There are some pilgrims moving through the pass, and I expect they'll be glad to have someone with a wagon join them, for a time at least." She tossed the coin once, then put it away inside her garments. "I'll keep this for you. It's less likely that I'll lose it than you will, where you seem to be going."

"Spend it if need be—you know that. It won't buy you a shop in a walled city, but—when Ben comes back, perhaps you can." Mark paused, aware of Ben waiting his turn to say goodbye. "Are you going back to the carnival, then?"

"I didn't think so when I left it. But now—what else? First, though, I'm going to watch from a hilltop, to see if that gang tries to murder you both right off."

"We'll scream for help," said Ben. He took her in his arms and kissed her roughly, swinging her off her feet. "I'll find you with the carnival, then, when I come back with a fortune. And listen. Tell that strongman, if he's still there, that—that—"

"I can manage him. I have so far."

And Mark heard no more, for he walked apart a little, to let the two of them say goodbye alone. Presently, looking back, he saw Ben lifting Barbara into the wagon. She waved her arm once more to Mark, and then drove off.

There had evidently been an old scabbard in the wagon, for Ben was fitting Dragonslicer into it, and belting it round his waist, when Mark caught up to him.

"Let's go get our treasure, comrade."

Following the swiftly driven wagon down the hill, they saw Barbara drive past the place where Doon and his men were loitering, waiting for their two recruits. Moments later they saw her pause, looking back, watching from a small hilltop as she had promised.

CHAPTER 6

Doon welcomed the two of them briskly when they came striding downhill to him, and the combined descent to the main road got under way without delay. Introductions went round among the men while they were moving.

When they reached the place where the trail from the side canyon rejoined the main road through the pass, Doon drew and consulted his Sword again. Barbara's wagon was now out of sight, around the curve of the main road; and the pilgrims' chant was faintly audible from that direction.

Doon's Sword pointed back to the north, in the direction from which Ben and Barbara and Mark had come. Dismounted now, leading his animal, the Baron set the pace in that direction, and motioned for Mark and Ben to walk close beside him.

Now Doon began a conversation by posing them a few cautious questions about their background. He seemed glad to hear that they claimed some minor experience as dragon hunters. Their claim was more readily accepted, thought Mark, because they made it modest.

"And what about yourself, sir?" Mark countered.

"What about myself?"

"How do you come to be leading this expedition?" Mark asked bluntly. "It seems to me that qualifications beyond the ordinary are required."

Doon did not appear to object to being questioned in such a way, but smiled at them graciously. "True," he agreed, "and my qualifications have already been tested, in more ways than one. But it is chiefly a matter of will."

"How's that?" Ben wanted to know.

Doon smiled again. "You see before you, gentlemen," he began, "a man almost devoid of what the world calls wealth. The powers that rule the universe have determined, for what reason I do not know, that pauperism is to be my lot. Whereas I, on my own behalf, have made a different determination. I will have wealth." He said it with majestic sincerity.

"I am impressed," said Mark.

"You should be, young man. If I am willing to defy gods, demons, and unguessed-at powers, think how little likely I am to be turned aside by any merely human obstacles."

"The gods must favor you somewhat," said Ben, "or you would not have a Sword."

"They can never all agree on anything, can they? Tell me —"

"Yes."

"Why were both of you disposed to believe me so quickly, when I mentioned Benambra's Gold? Most folk of any wit would be more skeptical."

"I was a minstrel once," said Ben. "I knew the old song."

"More than that."

"Yes." He looked at Doon steadily as they trudged along. "A couple of months ago, I helped to bury part of it. I've seen it with my own eyes."

"Ah. What have you seen, exactly?" The Baron's question was calm, reserving judgement.

"The gold of the Blue Temple, I'm telling you. Six loadbeasts' burden of it. It was wrapped up in bundles, but there was no mistaking what it was."

"You helped to bury it, you say."

"To put it into a cave, and I know where that cave is."

"What I have heard," said Doon, "is that the men who do that work are always slain, immediately afterward."

"There were six of us, and I think five were killed. I didn't wait to make sure."

"Ah."

The wizard was riding close behind the three of them and doubtless listening. The four other men were keeping close as well, taking in every word.

Doon said: "Wayfinder of course can lead me to the site. But it will be good to learn the location from you in advance, so we can begin to plan more carefully."

Ben squinted up at the sun and got his directions. "I'll tell you this much now. Your Sword is taking you in the right general direction."

"Ah. But you see, for the past month it has been leading me on a zigzag path. I wondered about this when I first realized it, but the reason quickly became clear. When I began I was alone, and I have been gathering the necessary tools and helpers. The Sword has led me to different people—as to you—and to other necessities. But it has been up to me to gain them for my cause, by one means or another."

"I see," said Mark. "And when will your expedition be finally complete and ready?"

"It may be so now, for all I know. Your friend says that we are now heading toward the gold."

"There are a few more things," the wizard put in suddenly, "that I could wish we had, before we reach the hiding place and try to breach it."

Mark turned to look at him. "Such as?"

"You—or your friend—spoke of the sealings, back there. Do you truly know what all six of them are?"

"The song says seven—doesn't it, Ben? And they must be the various protections of the treasure."

Doon meanwhile was looking round, and appeared to be considering the extent of the train of men and beasts he now had following him. In an aside to himself, he muttered: "A few more, and I'll have to form them into companies, and start making out duty rosters . . . well, there's good as well as bad in numbers. The more of us there are, the more treasure we'll be able to carry out. When I know the location, I'll be able to make some better plans on that as well. The gods know there'll be enough for all of us. No need for greedy squabbling."

"No need at all," agreed Ben. And Mark murmured something similar. Then again he looked back at the tall gray man who rode behind him. "Sir Wizard, what are the other things you wish we had?"

"D'ye know the song?" the wizard asked.

In answer, Ben sang it lightly:

> Benambra's gold
> Hath seven sealings . . .

He let it die there.

Doon chuckled. "I already know what the next lines are, I'll not be frightened if you sing them." He pressed on, though, without pausing for any such performance. "Indosuaros and I have pooled our knowledge, and we make it but six sealings that guard the gold, the number seven being merely a poetic convention." He glanced back at the gray man.

Indosuaros nodded confirmation. "The song does not name seven individual barriers."

"No, it doesn't," Ben agreed.

"All right, then," asked Mark, "what are the six?"

"The first," said Doon, "is the location of the place — pretty well impossible to rob it if you don't know that. The secret of the location has been kept for a long time, and with incredible success. But since your friend knows where it is, and we have Wayfinder, that should present no problem." If he had any doubts about the veracity of Ben's claim to knowledge, he was not expressing them.

Mark said: "I suppose the second barrier is some kind of fence or patrol, or both, around the area where the cave is."

"The fence," said Indosuaros, "is made of dragon's teeth."

"A landwalker," said Doon. "I suppose that you, my big friend, may have seen it — ?"

Ben only nodded. "With Dragonslicer I think we can get by. Though it still won't be easy."

"We have another trick or two that we can try as well," Doon assured him.

Ben said: "And the third sealing, I suppose, is something that I saw inside the cave. Just a glimpse, in darkness, of giant white hands. They were grabbing the sacks of treasure as we put them down into the floor, and they looked — well, dead — but at the same time very strong and active. The song doesn't mention anything like them, but —"

The tall wizard, his frame bobbing with the motion of his loadbeast's walk, was signing disagreement. "No, I think not, I think not. Those huge pale creatures are no more than laborers and clerks. They can be trusted by their Blue Temple masters, because they never emerge into the light of day, and have their only contact with the upper world through the Blue Temple priests themselves."

"They're very large and strong," Ben repeated doubtfully. "What are they called?"

"I have knowledge of them from other sources." And the wizard glanced back suddenly over his shoulder, as if someone or something of importance could be following him. " 'Whitehands' is as good a name as any," he concluded.

Ben repeated, stubbornly: "Whatever they are, their hands are very large."

"Well, so are yours," said Doon. "And my hands are well-armed, as are your friend's, who walks beside you. And we have sturdy company."

"I am only trying to be clear about what we face."

"An admirable plan. No, the third sealing is something else. The researches of my learned friend here" —and he nodded toward the wizard, rather formally— "confirm some small investigations of my own. The third sealing is in fact a subterranean maze, and, as might be expected, one of no little danger and difficulty. But I have a long key here at my side to open it." And again he fondled Wayfinder's hilt.

The eight men trudged on in silence for a while. In the distance, past the mouth of the pass, flatlands stretched for many kilometers, greening here and there with crops or only with onrushing summer. Beyond, more mountains, very far away and barely visible.

"And the fourth sealing?" Mark finally prodded.

"A kind of maze again," said Indosuaros. "But this one of pure magic. I have been preparing for more than a century to breach it, and you may depend upon it that the key to it is also with us."

"And then, the fifth?" asked Ben.

"There is an underground garrison," answered the magician, "who guard Benambra's wealth. They are human soldiers, yet not human as you and I."

"What does that mean?"

"We will have to discover exactly what it means. But I am confident that we can pass."

Mark put in a question: "Who's Benambra, anyway?"

Ben, who had undergone some indoctrination in the history of the institution he had once joined, could answer that one. "He was the first High Priest of the Blue Temple. From him, all who worship wealth still draw their inspiration."

Doon was closely studying the huge man who walked

beside him, no doubt revising a first impression of his recruit.

"So," said Mark, "let's try to complete this inventory that we've begun." It came to him as he spoke that his own attitude had already been revised. He had entered this conversation to learn what Doon's plans were, but now he found himself taking part in the planning, as for an enterprise he had already joined. "Whoever these guardian soldiers of the fifth sealing may be, they appear to stand in our way. What means do we have of getting past them?"

Doon said briskly: "Wayfinder will point one out to us, when the time comes. Of course we are going to face risks; but what prize could be worth greater risks than this one?"

"So we come to the sixth sealing," Ben urged. "You said that there were six."

Indosuaros answered shortly. "The sixth—and last —is apparently some kind of demon. You need not be too much concerned, young man, only do your part to get us through the others. I've dealt before with demons, as you and your friend have with landwalkers."

Ben did not appear entirely satisfied. "I don't suppose you have this particular demon's life in hand? No? Then you have words of magic certain to command him?"

The ghost of a fearful murmur could be heard among the listening men. The wizard appeared to be making an effort to restrain his temper. "I have not his life in my hand, no. His name, yes, though I should not speak it now. I have said that there are things I wish we had. But what we do have is sufficient. Else I should not be here now."

"Whatever we may truly need," Doon said firmly, "Wayfinder will bring us to it."

Wherever it might be bringing them now, they passed four more days in the process, entering lands that none of the men knew very well.

Ben warned them all, first Mark in private and then the others, that Wayfinder's last few crossroad choices were in fact taking them farther and farther from the place where he knew the gold to be. Doon did not argue the point, calmly insisting that there might well be something else they had to obtain first. Nor did he press Ben to reveal the location of the hoard.

Ben had already given that information to Mark, privately. The two of them continued to meet frequently, apart from the others, to assess their situation. They were doing this late one afternoon, on a hillside covered with a wild orchard of tall, almost tree-like bushes, covered at this season with fine pink and white blossoms that had drawn innumerable bees.

The two sat on a patch of grass, in conference, and Mark was asking: "Doesn't it come down to this: How long can we trust Doon?"

"As long as he needs us. Which ought to be till we've got past the dragon, at least."

"Of course after that, he's still going to need all the help that he can get, to get past the other sealings. . . . "

"And after *that*, if we win through, there'll be more treasure in our hands than we can carry, if we were eighty men instead of eight. No reason for us to fight over it then, that I can see."

Mark still marveled, silently, every time he thought about it. If he could bring Sir Andrew two Swords, possibly, or even three.... "Blue Temple won't be watching the area, you think? I have trouble believing that."

"If they are watching, we should discover the fact when we get near. Then ... I don't know. But I don't think they're watching. They probably think I'm dead, as I've told you. Even if they doubt that, they won't believe that I could be coming back so soon, with a band as well-organized as this one is."

"I suppose. You know, Ben, about Doon ... "

"Yes?"

"Indosuaros wouldn't have joined up with him, would he, if Doon didn't know what he was doing? I get the feeling that the wizard definitely knows what *he's* doing."

"Me too. Good point." Ben stretched his arms, then lay back on the grass, staring at the sky. "I hope Barb made it back to the carnival safely."

"We could ask the magician to send one of his powers to find out."

Ben shook his head. "I don't want to draw his attention to her."

"Hm. Yes. I wonder why he hates Blue Temple so?"

"Hah, why not?" Ben reared himself up on an elbow. "If ever I meet someone who doesn't hate them, then I'll be puzzled and ask why."

Their talk was interrupted by a small black shadow, that darted toward them among roseate blossoms. The monkbird had plainly not come spying on them, but had been sent to summon them to rejoin the others. It clung for a moment to a nearby branch with its handlike feet, whistling at them with soft urgency. Then next moment it was gone, back in the direction it had come from, keeping its flight below the tops of the bushes.

Wordlessly Mark and Ben grabbed up their weapons. As silently as possible they scrambled after the messenger.

Doon and the others were gathered at the edge of a slope, peering downhill between branches toward a road not much more than a hundred meters away. The Baron pointed. "Look."

A slave caravan was passing on the road, from right to left. It consisted mainly of short columns of people chained together, men, women, and children in separate groups. They were being watched over and prodded along by mounted spearmen wearing the red and black of the Red Temple. There were a few litters in the procession too, some of these borne by male slaves and some by animals.

Mark, hearing a drawn-in breath from the Baron, turned his head. Wayfinder, in Doon's hands, was pointing straight downslope at the caravan. There was a fierce vibration in the blade's tip.

Suddenly the monkbird flew among the men at head height, yammering. Then it sought shelter on its master's shoulder, just as a new sound arose from a little distance uphill among the trees and bush.

The men had their weapons drawn, but little time to accomplish more in the way of readiness, when the mounted Red Temple patrol burst shouting out of the bush and onto them, sabers leveled and scarlet-lined cloaks flying in the charge.

CHAPTER 7

The charge was clumsily planned, coming as it did through the awkward bushes where it had to be both slow and noisy. The men who were its target had plenty of time and plenty of places in which to step aside. Still the long cavalry swords were formidable weapons. Mark saw Pu Chou go down before that first rush, amid a blizzard of pink and white blossoms. Golok also had been struck down, or had thrown himself flat, while his creature Dart howled, and managed to hover like a hummingbird in the air above its fallen master. Indosuaros and Mitspieler were crouching under showers of blossoms, presumably doing as much as they could with their magic given the conditions. Ben, like Mark himself, had taken shelter behind a bush. Then Ben had stepped out at the right moment to use Dragonslicer to good effect on a trooper thundering by. Doon and Hubert had adopted the same tactic, and both had done damage to the foe.

Mark nocked an arrow to his bow while he avoided that first rush. Stepping into the open again to shoot, he got his first clear look at the face of the Red Temple officer who had led the attack. The man's countenance was flushed and glassy-eyed, as he fought to wheel his mount around between constricting bushes, presumably with the idea of making another charge. That charge was never ordered, never made, for Mark's arrow took the officer in the throat an instant later.

The other riders of the patrol were circling in the bushes, milling around in what looked like complete confusion. Mark saw one man scraped from his mount by projecting branches; a stroke from Hubert's battle hatchet finished him off in an instant. Many of the mounts were already riderless, thrashing and crashing in panic through the wild orchard, and the snowstorm of delicate petals did not slacken.

Doon, back in his own saddle now, parried a saber-slash and killed a rider in his saddle. Dragonslicer hewed at human flesh. Red-and-black capes lay crumpled and twisted on the ground, amid the blossoms and the blood. Hubert's bow twanged. The last survivor of the patrol had dropped his saber and turned his mount to flee, when Mark's second arrow of the skirmish struck him in the back. The rider screamed and fell.

Even more quickly than it had begun, the crash of combat ceased. Mark turned to look for Ben. The big man was on his feet and apparently unhurt, and gave Mark a salute with bloodied Dragonslicer.

Now there was almost silence. Mark could hear the

blood in his own head, his own panting, gasping breath, the loud thrashing of a downed and wounded riding beast. Doon, prevented by the noise from listening, set his foot on the animal's neck and cut its throat.

Golok had risen to his hands and knees and was crawling toward the animal, evidently with the intention of giving it some kind of help. The youth paused, transfixed in horror and disbelief with his eyes on Doon.

His leader was paying him no attention. But now Doon started to relax. There were no sounds of any more enemies approaching, or of any who might have gotten away to alarm the other troopers with the caravan.

Indosuaros and Mitspieler were both on their feet again, apparently unhurt, their four arms spread, their two mouths chanting softly.

A quick look at Pu Chou was enough to show that he was beyond help; a heavy saber-stroke had caught him full in the forehead. Of all the fallen men, only the enemy commander still breathed, with Mark's arrowhead protruding from the side of his neck. A good arrow, that one, Mark found himself thinking distantly. If the shaft's not cracked, I'll have to retrieve it before we go on.

The officer's lips were moving. Doon bent over him, trying to hear whatever the man was trying to say, then sniffed and straightened up, frowning with contempt.

"Stoned blind," Doon muttered scornfully. "You can smell it on him." He looked round at the human wreckage of what had been this officer's command. "Probably his whole patrol was in the same shape. Typical Red Temple."

Hubert looked up from his self-assigned task of going through Pu Chou's pockets. "But usually they're not this hot to get into a fight."

"Usually," said Doon, and bent to wipe his Sword before putting it away. The fallen officer was not going to mind this misuse of his cloak, for he had now stopped breathing altogether.

Wayfinder, thought Mark, heightens risks. One more flower petal drifted down past his eyes, and sideslipped, just missing a landing on another dead man's face.

And now Wayfinder, already gleaming clean again, was pointing in the direction of the passed caravan.

"Well, we must overtake it," said Doon, moving on quickly to the next order of business. Briskly he climbed a tree, trying to see more of the hillside and the road below. "This slope is all ravines below us — we could hardly have jumped on their caravan from here. Very poor operation on their part. Well, Golok, get your little monk up in the air, bring us some news of the caravan — I can't see it from here now. Indosuaros, now that swords are put away again, see what you can do to calm these riding beasts and bring them to us. We'll need six new mounts — no, Pu Chou's gone, five will be enough."

The magician and his aide began a process of soft soothing magic, summoning the hurt and frightened animals to submit to strange human hands. Golok, as the riding beasts came within his reach, touched and spoke to them, using beast-master's lore to soothe their hurts and make them tractable.

Doon watched this process impatiently, and meanwhile issued orders to his other men. "We're going to dress ourselves in these Red Temple uniforms — in parts of them, anyway. It's all right if we look sloppy, half out of uniform, that's typical Red Temple too. If we look totally like swine, they'll take us for some of their mercenaries. Or maybe even regulars. I want to be able to get close to that caravan without another fight."

Golok and Mitspieler had to physically treat the hurts of a couple of the animals before five mounts were ready. By then, all the men had replaced some of their garments with those of the dead enemy, and helped themselves to choice weapons here and there. Very shortly afterward, what now indeed looked much like a Red Temple mercenary patrol was on its way.

The caravan had had no very great start on them, nor was it moving any faster than a weary slave could be compelled to walk. But Doon's men had to master their new mounts and nurse them along. And there was the difficult hillside, that had to be negotiated before they even got down to the road. By the time they had managed that, the caravan was long out of sight; but Dart brought back word to Golok that it was still on the road, proceeding no faster than before.

Still, dusk was falling before the mounted men caught sight of it again. If Doon had been seeking an opportunity to attack it in isolation on the road, that chance had now slipped away. The caravan was traversing a busy crossroads now. And, only a couple of hundred meters farther on, the gates of a large Red Temple complex were standing open to receive it.

Doon gestured, slowing his troop's progress, that they might have a chance to look over the Temple complex as they approached it. It was, as the first glimpse of it had suggested, of considerable size. The walls surrounding it were not much more than head high, but armed with jagged projections along the top that would make a climbing entry difficult. Within the walls were several large but low-built buildings. Buildings and walls alike appeared to be constructed mainly of earthen bricks. The colors of red and black were prominently displayed.

The main gate remained standing open after the caravan had entered it. The entry was flanked by torches, that at dusk were just now being lighted. A brief period of observation was enough to show that the flow of traffic in and out the gate was fairly high, as might be expected of a Red Temple near the intersection of two well-traveled roads.

"A lot of customers," Golok commented. He had evidently got over his outrage now. "There must be a busy town or two nearby. Maybe a large castle, too."

"Aye." Hubert chuckled. "Red Temple always does good business."

"I think," said Doon, "we're going to be able to ride right on in without being challenged."

"And if we are challenged?" asked Indosuaros. He had contrived a black-and-red cap for himself, suggesting a minor wizard working in Red Temple pay.

"We'll see," said Doon. "Be ready to take your cue from me—get that, everyone? Let's go."

The guard post at the main gate was manned by a single sentry. He was sitting with his head slumped, half asleep or perhaps entranced by drugs. He paid little or no attention to the passage of what might well have been a mercenary patrol.

The compound seen from inside was as large and

busy as its appearance at a distance had suggested.
This main portion of it, generally open to the public,
was well lit by torches. Spaces and hitching racks
were provided to accommodate customers' vehicles
and animals. On three sides of this broad open courtyard were the several houses of pleasure that made up
the usual Red Temple layout. To the right, as Doon
and his men rode in, were the Houses of Dancing and
of Joy. Gaming was on the left, and Drink and Food
were straight ahead — music, like the smell of drugs,
seemed to be everywhere once the main gate had been
passed.

Passages led between buildings, to what would be
the non-public parts of the compound. Mark was able
to catch just a glimpse of one of the caravan's litters,
disappearing down one of these alleyways, before a
closing gate cut off the sight. The gangs of slaves who
had been driven in on foot were probably already back
there, in some kind of pens.

Doon drew his Sword briefly, and found that it
guided him to the right. A couple of passing customers
looked at him curiously before he put the blade away
again.

He turned right, then signed to his men to halt their
animals and dismount. They tied their riding beasts at
one of the hitching racks nearest the entrance of the
House of Dancing. So far, no one else in the compound
appeared to be paying them much attention.

"Golok," the Baron ordered quietly, "stay here and
keep the animals quiet. Be ready for a quick start
when we come back." Golok nodded; the hooded monkbird was resting behind his saddle now.

Doon left his Sword sheathed, but unbuckled the

whole apparatus from his waist, and carried it in his hand, pausing now and then to feel his way forward with it, almost like a blind man with a cane. It still looked odd behavior, thought Mark, but it was not going to draw as much attention as the Baron would have by waving a meter of bare blade.

The entrance to the House of Dance was watched inside by fee-collectors, who, as Mark had expected, let the red uniforms pass in free. Red Temple mercenaries were probably not paid very much in coin, but there appeared to be certain compensations. Inside the House of Dance, drum music throbbed in thick, warm air. Most of the interior was a single vast, low room. Scantily clad girls and young women, with a few boys and young men mixed among them, sat round the edges of the room. These were slaves of the Temple, waiting for the personal attentions of some customer. Some couples were dancing, and in the center of the large floor a professional group performed, dancers and musicians mingling.

Doon moved at first as if to cross the floor directly, then evidently thought better of interfering with the dance, and led his men around the edge. Now, in the distant corners of the hall, Mark could recognize the traditional four Red Temple statues: Aphrodite, Bacchus, Dionysus, Eros. Here at one side was a broad stairway, going up, probably communicating on an upper level with the House of Joy next door. A painted young man was just ascending, giggling, supported on either side by two customers, man and woman. Meanwhile on the far side of the dance floor, four men were just emerging from some back room. They were all uniformed in blue and gold, and though they paid attention to the dancers as they strolled, Mark thought that probably they were here on business rather than on pleasure only. It was no secret that connections existed between the Blue Temple and the Red, particularly on the upper levels of organization.

In the corner of the dancehall farthest from the entrance, broad open steps led down. As Doon led them down the steps, following the discreet guidance of the Sword, Mark began to realize that some large part of the whole Red Temple complex was probably underground. Different musicians were playing down here, from somewhere out of view; and the sound they made was different, having a disconnected anguish in it. The air was thicker too, with more torch-smoke in it, as well as heavier fumes of incense and of drugs.

For a few moments Doon and his followers tramped an empty corridor in silence. Suddenly Mark thought that he knew where the Sword was taking them. It was a part of the usual Red Temple installation that he'd heard about, but had never seen on the few occasions when he'd visited other branches of the Temple as a customer.

The corridor branched. And still the Sword of Wisdom led the way unhesitatingly.

"Are we going to the worm-pit?" Hubert grumbled quietly. "What's in *there*, or who, that we could need?"

No one had an answer for him. Soon the Sword would tell.

Still the path chosen by Wayfinder led through the public precincts of the Temple, and they were not challenged. It guided them at last through a heavily curtained doorway, into another large, low room, this one much darker and worse-smelling than the dance-hall above.

Here only a few candles were burning, to illuminate what looked at first glance like some barracks or dormitory. Or perhaps a ward in some hospital-dungeon, if such a combination could be imagined. The place was almost too long to be called a room, too wide for a corridor. It was lined on both sides with bunks and couches, about half of which were occupied. A few bent figures, those of male and female attendants, were moving about in the gloom. As one of these passed before a candle, Mark could see that she was carrying a small saucer-shaped tray of earth, and tools that looked like a pair of tweezers and a large, fine-toothed comb.

The light was a little better near the curtained doorway where Doon and his men had entered. Here some of the customers were conversing from couch to couch, and sipping at winecups. Men and women alike could be seen to be for the most part naked under their beds' sheets. One or two were currently in the phase of ecstasy that the pleasure-worms induced. These sobbed or groaned on their cots, executing jerky motions, kicking aside coverings, scratching at their skin with combs, now slowly and now in rapid frenzy.

As Doon, still trying to hold his sheathed Sword unobtrusively, led the way slowly forward between rows of beds, Mark saw the attendant with the tray of earth stop at the side of a recumbent customer. From the saucer of earth the attendant lifted, in the tweezers, a tiny pale gray worm—weight for weight, Mark knew, worth more than gold. The creature was inconspicuous, and would have been unnoticeable except for the attention that was focused on it. The client, a stoutish woman with an obviously well cared for body, turned beneath her sheet, exposing her wide back in the candle's light. The attendant applied the tweezers near the customer's shoulder with one hand, and quickly brought a candle closer with the other. The small worm, released by the tweezers, promptly disappeared. Mark knew, though he had not seen, that it was gone into the skin, driven by its burrowing instincts and the painful light. Worm-pits were always underground, because the creatures had to be cultivated away from daylight.

An attendant approached Doon as he led the way forward, but the Baron shook his head in silence and pressed on, his men following him closely. The attendant appeared momentarily puzzled, Mark thought, but then went on about his tasks. Like the others working here he looked thin and vaguely unhealthy.

Here was another client, a man, recently infected with one worm, or several, and now crying out with the full sensation. His trembling hands went scratching back and forth, all ten fingernails working on the skin over his left ribs. The worms followed the paths of nerve-tissue in their hosts, inducing pleasure in exchange for food and shelter inside a mammalian body. Sometimes the pleasure shaded into unendurable tickling, hence the work for fingernails and combs. Mark had even heard once that the worms were used in Red Temple dungeons as tools of torture, with the victims simply infected and kept from scratching.

On succeeding couches, people tossed and scratched and moaned. Attendants were at work on some of them with combs. As he got farther toward the rear of the room, Mark decided that it was probably arranged by classes of addicts, with beginners or occasional users near the front, those more enslaved by the habit near the middle. In the dimmer reaches of the rear, where Mark and his companions now walked among them, were people who by appearances never left their cots at all. The bodies back here tended to look starved and wasted, marked with old scars and not-so-old dried blood. Here attendants gave less attention. Sometimes —inevitably, Mark had heard—the worms turned inward from the skin toward the spinal column and the brain.

In the room's farthest recess was an inconspicuous door. It would be the way out, thought Mark, for customers who could either not continue paying or not walk. The Sword led Doon directly to this door. It was not locked, and swung open at a touch, revealing a dim passage. In a side room off this passage, another attendant moving amid trays and racks of earth looked up in dim candlelight as six armed men came tramping through. But he made no protest or even comment.

The service corridor soon branched. Wayfinder chose the left-hand way, which quickly ran into a strong grill-work door, tightly closed and probably locked. Beyond the door, a red-helmeted soldier was on guard, and beyond the guard Mark could see what looked like the doors of individual cells lining the corridor.

"Open up," commanded Doon, rattling briskly at the grill.

But the soldier was not in a mood to be intimidated. "No passage through here without a written order. What do you want in here, anyway? You field troops think you can come in here and have fun any time, without any—"

Wayfinder, still sheathed and belted, hit the floor stones with a muffled thud. It had been replaced in Doon's right hand with a dagger, handier tool for such close work. Meanwhile Doon's thin left arm had snaked through the grill to seize the guard by the front of his garments and snatch him sharply forward. Instantly the Baron's right hand shoved the dagger home, up beneath the breastbone. The soldier's eyes bulged, then glazed. If he made a sound at all, it was too faint to be heard over the now-distant music.

"Keys," said Doon laconically, supporting his victim against the grill. The man was wearing a ring of them on his belt.

Mark reached in through the bars, detached the keys, and brought them out. One part of his mind was protesting that this had been cold murder, while another part exulted in the triumph, the demonstration of Doon's proficiency. War required capable leaders, and this was war, a part of Sir Andrew's fight against the Dark King and the cruel Silver Queen. This robbery was meant as a stroke of war against the allies of Sir Andrew's foes, the Temples Red and Blue.

The grill-door was opened, and the dead man propped sitting in a corner, his presence made as inconspicuous as possible in the restricted space. Apparently none of the other Temple people had noticed anything wrong as yet. The music went on as before, behind doors in the distance. Somewhere nearby, around a corner, the clashing of pots and the slosh of water told of a kitchen of some kind functioning.

Bundled Wayfinder in hand again, the Baron led

his small troop of armed men down the corridor lined with cells. All of the doors were closed.

The Sword paused. "This one, here. Try the keys."

The ring held six of them. Mark fumbled past one key that did not look meant to fit this crude lock, tried another that looked as if it might but didn't. The third try was lucky, and the brass-bound oaken door swung back. The space behind it was very dark, as one might expect the interior of a cell to be.

Quick reflexes ducked Mark safely under an on-rushing metal blur. He recognized the missile as a brass chamber pot, as it clanged and spattered on the opposite wall of the narrow corridor.

"Keep away from me!" The voice coming out of the dark cell was certainly a woman's, but forceful enough to have served an infantry sergeant. "You putrid collection of loadbeast droppings, do you know who I am? Do you know what'll happen to you if you touch me?"

Doon, who had started in at the open door, recoiled now, swearing by several demons, as another missile of some kind flew past his head. The cell's sole occupant was now visible in the light from the open door. She was a tall young woman, sturdily built, her pale skin streaked with dirt and her red hair matted. Her clothing was rich, or had been once, long ago before it approached its present state of wear and dirtiness. Her height overtopped Doon, who now moved into the cell again, by a good measure, and indeed came within a few centimeters of matching Mark's, who was tallest of the men present.

Doon, murmuring something no doubt meant either to frighten or reassure, took her by the arm and tried to tug her from the cell. She would have none of it, but cursed at him again. Her white hands and arms, emerging from torn sleeves, grabbed at him and fought him off.

The little man, unwilling to use deadly force, struggled ineffectually in the grip of the big young woman — the big girl, really, Mark realized, for she was very young. The Baron's momentary predicament would perhaps have been comic, at some other time. It was not, now.

"I am Ariane!" the girl was shouting at them all, as Mark moved forward to try to help his leader. Her cries had awakened an echoing clamor from some of the other cells, so that the corridor reverberated with unintelligible noise. The girl was yelling: "I am the . . ."

Her voice faltered, at the first instant when she looked Mark full in the face. And when it came back, it was vastly changed, a dreamer's whisper to match the sudden wonder in her eyes. "My brother," she breathed. And in the next instant Mark saw her eyes roll up. He stepped forward just in time to help Doon catch her slumping body. She apparently had fainted.

Doon was supporting her, but turning his head, looking for his wizard. "Indosuaros, what—?"

"Not my doing," said the magician, incongruous figure of power against the shabby background.

Doon was not going to puzzle over it now. Leaving the girl to Mark to hold, he had his Sword in hand again. "It points us back the way we came . . . bring her, and let's get out."

Mark, impeded by the longbow still on his back, had to struggle in the narrow corridor to carry the heavy girl along. Ben stopped him and wordlessly relieved him of the burden. Without effort Ben hoisted her body over one shoulder and strode on. Long red hair, even matted as it was, still fell nearly to the floor, and strong white forearms dangled.

As they tramped past the dead guard, his fixed eyes seemed to gaze at Mark.

CHAPTER 8

The Blue Temple furnished itself elegantly here on the upper levels of the central office, especially in the chambers where the members of the Inner Council met to talk business, among themselves and with other folk of comparable importance in the world. The clerks and administrators who worked on the lower floors might have to make do with worn furniture and blank paneled walls, but up here there was no stinting on slaves and fountains, marble and gold, tapestries and entertainment.

Not that Radulescu had been provided with any entertainers to keep him company as he cooled his heels in the High Priest's outer office, actually an anteroom of one of a suite of offices. But he could hear string music in the distance somewhere. He could distract himself, if he liked, by getting up from the luxuriously padded couch from time to time to pace the floor, and gaze out of the curtained window. That window overlooked walls, and parapets, and some lesser towers belonging to folk of somewhat less importance, affording a clear view above rooftops all the way to the inner side of the city walls themselves. Those walls were even higher—designedly so. They were famed for their height and strength, and this city for its impregnability—indeed, many people believed that the central hoard of the Blue Temple was concealed in some subterranean vault beneath this very building.

Radulescu of course knew better. But only he, the High Priest, and two or three members of the Inner Council—Radulescu was not sure which ones—were the only people on the surface of the earth who knew with certainty where Benambra's Gold was kept, and how to reach it.

It was generally understood, among those who knew anything of the world, that the present High Priest was the *de facto* ruler of this city and of much other territory besides, to which he laid no formal claim. But cities, no matter how strongly defended, always drew the attention of money-hungry kings and other potentates; and no, the Blue Temple was not going to put its treasure, the main reason for its existence, in any such obvious place as that.

The whole organization appeared so straightforward to the uninitiated, and it was really so devious. Radulescu's thoughts were on that fact, as it related to his own career, when there was a stir at a curtained doorway, and a bald-headed, gold-garbed secretary appeared.

"The Chairman will see you now."

And Radulescu, as he hurried to follow the aide through one elaborate office after another, allowed himself a small sigh of relief. When the chief functionary of the Blue Temple chose to use that title, the business at hand was more likely to be business than some ecclesiastical ritual—as, for example, the unfrocking of some priest-officer who had been found derelict in his duty.

The final door opened by the secretary disclosed a large room. Among its other luxurious appointments was a conference table large enough for twenty potentates to have gathered at it. There was, however, only one other person in the room, a rather small man with a rubicund face and a head as bald as that of the secretary who served him. This man was seated at the far end of the table, with a bundle of papers spread out before him on the polished wood.

The High Priest—or Chairman—raised his round, red face at Radulescu's entrance. The chief executive looked quite jovial—but then, he always did, at least in Radulescu's limited experience.

"Colonel Radulescu, come in, be seated." The Chairman motioned to a place near his own. "How are you getting along on detached duty? Have you been finding enough work to keep you busy?"

Radulescu, in the months since the ill-fated delivery of treasure, had been reassigned under several formal classifications while his case was being considered and reconsidered by the Inner Council and the High Priest. In the last ten days or so Radulescu had begun to sense a moderation in the official attitude toward him, and had seized on this as a favorable sign.

"I have worked diligently on the problem of finding ways to contribute to the Temple, Chairman, and I hope that I have had some success." Fortunately he had anticipated some such question, and he counted the composition of a good answer for it as part of the work that he had found.

"Fine, fine," said the Chairman vaguely, looking down at his spread papers once again. They looked to Radulescu like reports having to do with his own case. The windows behind the Chairman were windows such as few eyes ever saw, with real and almost perfect glass in them, and round the edges semiprecious stones set to transmit the light like bits of glass. The thought crossed Radulescu's mind that the Chairman was really only a man, and that he had a name, Hyrcanus; but rarely would anyone speak or even think of such an exalted personage by a mere human name. Only a few scurrilous and regrettably popular songs did that.

"Fine . . . good. Now, I see here that more than two months have already passed since you had that — misadventure. Would you say that is a good term to describe what happened?" And the Chairman looked up with sudden sharpness at Radulescu, treating him to eyes of jovial blue ice.

Radulescu had no trouble managing to look properly solemn as he considered the question. "My own understanding of that event has not really improved in two months, Chairman, I confess." He almost sighed. "I will be very pleased if you will enlighten me with yours." Be weary, be puzzled, be not *too* repentant, he cautioned himself; Radulescu had never admitted any culpability in the events of that strange night, beyond the minimum that the officer in charge and on the scene could not escape.

The icy eyes considered him; the red face nodded lightly, and bent again to a consideration of the many papers. "The man is really still unaccounted for," the Chairman mused. There was no need for him to specify which man he meant. "The dragon has now been replaced . . . very expensive, that, in itself. We had the dragon that was involved in the incident killed soon after, so the stomach contents could be examined. The results, I regret to say, were inconclusive. A few shreds of cloth found in the stomach were identifiable as having come from the rascal's cloak— or at any rate from one of our general issue infantry cloaks. As you may remember, his cloak was found between the cave entrance and the cliffs, looking some-what chewed."

"I remember, sir. I of course released the spells binding the dragon as soon as I fully recovered my wits inside the cave, and realized what must have happened."

"Yes . . . yes." Papers shuffled. "So you stated here in your deposition. And at the, ah, debriefing sessions."

"Yes sir." Those interrogations had been hardly less frightening than that first shock of realization in the dark cave, where the physical pain of the enforced tumble down the stairs had soon been swallowed up in the fear of what was going to happen next.

The five drivers, knowing only that they were all blocked in, had set up a despairing noise. Responding as usual to this signal, the Whitehands had started to come up into the upper cave on their usual post-delivery mission, and Radulescu had had to use his sword by flickering candlelight to fight them off. Fortunately he hadn't forgotten to release the spells that bound the dragon. After giving it a little time in which to destroy the villain outside, he had called it with another spell to tilt the great rock open from outside.

Briefly Radulescu had been tempted to try to keep the whole fiasco a secret from his superiors. But when he got outside again and saw no trace of the missing man except a cloak, he knew he'd be on shaky ground in trying to do that.

The animals, terrified by the great dragon raging near them, had broken their tethers and run off. Radulescu pledged his surviving drivers to silence on the journey back to the Temple, by the most terrifying oaths, and then marched them back, sword in hand, to where the cavalry was still waiting, getting restless. No use disposing of the five drivers now, he knew. They'd certainly be wanted for questioning.

The Chairman was moving on, at least for the time being, to another aspect of the situation. " . . . underwater search along that portion of the coastline has turned up one battered helmet, the type of standard issue for our garrisons . . . regrettably, it is not certain whether this is the helmet issued to the missing man."

Radulescu raised his eyebrows. "I would presume, sir, that a magical investigation of the helmet has been attempted?"

"Oh yes. Certainly."

"And—even after that—we still don't know if it belonged to this Ben or not?"

Once again the Chairman gave him his full attention. "Regrettably not. Certain pernicious influences have been at work."

"Sir?" All of a sudden Radulescu found himself totally lost—a feeling that, in the circumstances, would lead almost at once to desperation.

The Chairman looked at him, and appeared to undergo a moment of uncertainty himself. Then he came to a decision. He rose from his chair at the head of the table and went to one of the long walls of the conference room, whereon a large map was displayed. The site of the treasure trove had of course not been marked on this or any other map, but Radulescu's eyes automatically went to that coastline spot anyway.

The Chairman raised a pointer, not to that vital point, but to another place very near it. "Here, this headland, across the fjord—do you see the ownership indicated for this small piece of land right on the promontory?"

It was only a tiny dot of color, that meant nothing to Radulescu until he had consulted the key at the bottom of the map. "Imperial lands," he said then, softly. He hesitated, then added: "Yes sir, I think I begin to understand."

Even that much was a daring claim, and the Chairman kept on looking at him. Radulescu was evidently expected to say more. He began to flounder. "The Emperor is—is then—an opposing force?"

The Chairman carefully laid down his pointer, and posed in front of the map with hands clasped behind his back. "I doubt you truly do begin to understand. Not your fault, really, you couldn't be expected to . . .

you ought to soon, though. A man in your position, presumably ready for advancement to the Council itself at the next vacancy . . . yes, we must have you in soon for a briefing session with our top magicians, on the subject of the Emperor. That is, of course, provided your status is not downgraded at some point in the near future, for some reason." Thus Radulescu's spirits, that had shot up at the mention of promotion, were carefully cut down again to the proper size. "You do know at least that the Emperor is not a myth, that he's still a real factor to be considered?"

Obviously there was only one answer that could be returned to that.

"I'll try to arrange that briefing soon. If nothing arises to prevent it." The Chairman returned to his chair, and his voice to its usual somewhat dusty joviality. "I think we may say that all the direct evidence we have at this time, Colonel, points to the conclusion that this man Ben, Ben of—what was it? Purkinje, it says here—that this Ben of Purkinje leaped or fell to his death in the sea, *if* indeed he did manage to escape the dragon. By all reports he was somewhat slow on his feet, so the probability that he escaped the dragon is perhaps not very great.

"What I would like to ask you now is this. Do you, yourself, see any reason why this office should not consider the incident closed? Take some routine precautions of course, such as changing the spells for the guardian dragon—that's already been done—but then go on, by and large, as we were?"

Radulescu cleared his throat carefully. He did not need to exert much cleverness to sense that the bland question might well contain some kind of trap. "Have the drivers been questioned, sir?" he asked. "I would assume they have."

"Oh, indeed. No indications of any plot emerged during questioning."

Radulescu tried to think. "I suppose, sir, that an actual inventory of the treasure has been taken by now?"

The Chairman nodded. "By myself, personally. It is secure."

There was a pause. "Well, sir," Radulescu said at last. "There are still a couple of things that bother me."

"Ah. Such as?"

"A clever man, pursued by a dragon, might well think of throwing away his cloak to distract the beast. And from what I've heard about dragons, such a ploy might well succeed, at least momentarily."

"This Ben of Purkinje was far from being a clever man, according to the officers who knew him. You know that clever men are not commonly selected for these jobs."

"That's true, sir, of course. But . . . "

"But what?"

"I supervised, as you know, three previous deliveries to the cave, before this ill-starred one. Out of more than twenty drivers involved in the four deliveries I supervised, *he* was the only one to suspect that anything was amiss. Amiss from his own point of view, I mean. At least he was the only one who took any steps to save his own miserable life."

The Chairman was silent for a little while, pondering. He surprised Radulescu somewhat when he spoke at last. "Wretched life those fellows must lead. I really don't know why they would object too much to having it ended for them—ever think of it that way?"

"No sir, I can't say that I have."

After meditating a moment longer, the Chairman said: "However that may be—I daresay you were warned, before you started making deliveries, that other officers have had to deal with recalcitrant drivers in the past?"

"I was told about the possibility of some such trouble, yes sir. I got the impression that all actual instances had been in the fairly remote past."

"And did they tell you that the officer in charge had always, in the past, managed to deal with it successfully? That's why we see to it that you are armed, you know, and they are not."

Radulescu could feel his ears burning. "Yes, Chairman, I certainly got that impression too."

"What do you think we ought to do now, Radulescu? You've had a couple of months to think about it. What would you order if you were in my position? It may, but it shouldn't, surprise you to hear that I have enemies on the Council, people who would love to see me make a grave mistake and have a chance to bring me down."

Radulescu had thought about it indeed, but his thinking had been of doubtful benefit, as far as he could tell. "Well, sir, we might patrol the area more or less regularly for a time. I know that ordinarily we don't do that because—"

"—because of the excellent reason that if the area were patrolled regularly, its importance would soon no longer be a secret. Of course, if we were *sure* that your man had got away, then, yes, we might patrol. At least until we could arrange to relocate the whole depository somewhere else. And how much chance would we have then of keeping the new location secret? And how much would the move cost us, just the move alone, have you any idea? No, of course you haven't. Just be glad I don't propose to take it out of your pay."

A pleasantry, by all the gods.

CHAPTER 9

The little ship looked old, at least to Mark's admittedly non-expert eyes. But despite this appearance of age, and a thick-bodied shape, she had a certain grace of movement. Whether this was due to her construction, to sheer magic, or to the fact that she was steered and driven by a djinn, was more than Mark could tell.

The ship had two masts, and two cabins, and it belonged to Indosuaros, who had summoned it to meet Doon's party at the coastline, three days' hard ride after their rescue of Ariane from the Red Temple. Unmanned by any visible power, the vessel had come sailing into shallow water to meet them, almost grounding itself. And when its eight human passengers had climbed aboard with their slight luggage, it had needed only a word from the wizard to put out to sea again. And all this without the touch of a human hand on line or sail or rudder. The djinn was harmless to people, or at least to Indosuaros' friends, so Mitspieler assured them all. It was visible only desultorily, as a small cloud or vague disturbance in the air, usually above the masts; and sometimes there was audible an echoing voice, that seemed to come from some great distance, exchanging a few words with Indosuaros.

Right now, in the broad daylight of late morning, the djinn could not be seen. What could be seen was fog, not far ahead. There usually was fog close ahead, except when it lay just behind the ship, or between the ship and the coastline, or enveloped the little craft entirely. Except for fog, the coastline had not been out of sight for the three days of the voyage.

The weather occupied a good deal of the attention of everyone on board. It had been good, except for the patchy fog, and Mark suspected that the weather too was at least partially under the control of Indosuaros. Mark and Ben, both landlubbers, had been seasick at the start of the voyage, but Mitspieler had dosed them with some minor potion that effected an instant cure.

Mark and Ben were sitting on the foredeck now. Doon and Indosuaros were closeted in one of the small cabins below, and Ariane was in the other. Golok and Hubert were looking over the stern, engaged in their own conversation; and Mitspieler was coming abovedecks and going below again, engaged in an endless series of observations and reports on the weather, the ship's position, and perhaps other factors that Mark was not magically sensitive enough to appreciate. Meanwhile the monkbird, Dart, was moving about in the rigging. It spent most of its time up there now, having reached a not entirely easy truce with the djinn who ran the ship.

Ben, for approximately the tenth time since they had left the Red Temple, was asking Mark: "Why did she call you brother, do you suppose?"

Mark gave virtually the same answer that he had given nine times before. "I still have no idea. She looks nothing at all like the sister I do have. Marian's blond, and smaller than this girl, and older than I am. This one says she's eighteen, but I'll bet that she's three years younger than that, even if she is large."

"And I'll bet that she's a little mad," said Ben. "Probably more than a little."

Mark pondered that theory. "She says they gave her drugs, in the caravan, to keep her quiet. She was still drugged when we got to her, and that's why she behaved strangely at the start. Fainted, and so on."

Ariane had started to regain her senses as soon as they reached fresh air, before they were out of the Red Temple compound, and Ben had set her on her feet and let her walk the last steps to where their mounts were waiting. She'd regained her wits enough by then to grasp that the men had not come simply to attack her, and she had cooperated with them. Golok had promptly and neatly stolen another riding beast for her to ride. With the men clustered around her, they'd ridden unchallenged out through the main gate.

"Fainting and confusion I can understand," said Ben. "But—the daughter of a queen? And she still holds to that."

"Well—kings and queens must have daughters sometimes, I suppose, like other people. And she looks like—well, there's something special in the way she looks, apart from being well-shaped, and comely."

"And red-haired. And big. Aye." Ben did not appear to be convinced.

"And being a queen's daughter might not be a bad claim to make to brigands like us, to try to get good treatment for herself. You know, sometimes I get the feeling that she's laughing at the rest of us."

"If that's not madness, in her situation, then I don't know what is."

Mitspieler had gone below, just a moment ago, with one of his many reports. And now Doon stepped up on deck, his Sword in his hands, looking as if he wanted to try an observation for himself. When the girl had first told him her story, he had heard it patiently, and nodded as if he might accept it, mad as it sounded. Mark thought that princess, beggar-girl, or queen would be all one to the Baron, provided only that she served in some way to advance his schemes.

From the hour when Ariane had first come into their hands, Doon had grimly warned his men that she was under his personal protection. One of the ship's two small cabins was inviolately hers. Doon himself slept in the passage athwart her door, leaving the other cabin to the magicians.

Now, as Doon was sighting carefully along his Sword, trying to frown his vision through the fog ahead, Ariane herself came up on deck, and talk ceased momentarily among the men. She was dressed now in man's clothing, a clean and sturdy shirt and trousers from the rich store of resources that Indosuaros had provided for the expedition, and a large-size pair of sandals on her feet.

At once she sprang up into the bow, and poised

there, gripping a line for balance. She looked for a moment like a model for some extravagant figurehead as she tried to peer into the fog ahead. Since she had been away from litters and cells her fair skin was growing sunburnt. Her hair, washed in her cabin's privacy, blew free in a soft red cloud.

"Cliffs ahead now," she called out gaily. Her voice was almost that of a child, very unlike that in which she had called out abuse to the men entering her cell. And she turned now, ignoring Doon for the moment, to drop to the deck beside Mark and Ben. She was smiling at them as if this were all some pleasant picnic outing. As far as Mark knew, she had never yet asked where they were going.

Neither Ben nor the Baron seemed to know quite what to say. So it was Mark who spoke to her first. "Who is your mother—really?"

Ariane sat back cross-legged on the deck, and became abruptly serious. "I suppose it is hard to believe. But I really am the daughter of the Silver Queen. I must have been still dazed when I first told you that, but it's the truth." She shot a glance at Doon. "If you have any ideas of getting ransom from her, though, you may as well forget it. She is my deadly enemy."

Doon made a gesture of indifference. "Well, girl— Princess, if you'd rather—I care very little if your story be true or not. Just out of curiosity, though, who's your father? Yambu reigns without any regular male consort, as far as I'm aware. I think she always has."

Ariane tossed a magnificence of red hair. "I wouldn't count on getting any ransom from my father, either."

Doon repeated his gesture. "I tell you that I don't count on any ransom . . . you'd better bind up that

hair, or braid it, or get it out of the way somehow. It
might be a problem where we're going . . . and why is
your mother so bitterly your enemy? Was it she who
sold you into slavery?"

"Indeed it was." Ariane seemed to accept the dic-
tum about her hair without argument, for her fingers
began working at it as if testing which mode of treatment would be best. "Certain people in the palace, I
am told, had the idea of disposing of my mother and
putting me on the throne instead. The heads of those
people are now prominently in view above the battle-
ments. Maybe they were even guilty, I don't know.
They never consulted me. And I've seen very little of
my mother in my lifetime. I don't know . . . "

"You don't know what?" asked Mark, fascinated.

"It doesn't matter. Also, I sometimes have powers—"

"I know you do," Doon cut in. "I count on them, in
fact."

She looked at him again. "Do you? I wish I could
count on them to help me, but as I say I only sometimes have them, and they are unreliable. I am told,
again, that they depend somewhat on the fact that no
man has ever known me. The Red Temple set great
store on my virginity, when their magicians were satisfied that it was intact. They would have sold me for a
fortune, I suppose to someone who had other than
magical concerns about it. And where are we going,
anyway, that I must bind up my hair?"

But Doon had another question of his own to put.
"And why did not your mother simply have you killed,
instead of selling you?"

"Perhaps she thought that going into slavery would
be worse. Perhaps some seer or oracle warned her

against it. Who knows why great queens do the things they do?" Mark had heard the same tone of bitterness, exactly, in the voice of the peasant woman whose eyes had been put out by soldiers.

The Baron had sheathed his Sword now, and was standing with arms folded, eyes probing at his captive —if that was really the right word, Mark thought, for her status. "You say your mother is your enemy," Doon demanded. "Then you are hers?"

Ariane's blue eyes were suddenly those of an angry child. "Give me the chance to prove it and I will."

"I intend to do just that. Now, the Silver Queen has a deep interest in the Blue Temple, does she not?"

As if she had been expecting to hear something else, the girl had to pause for thought. But then she agreed. "Aye, I am sure she must have. Why?"

"Because we are going to enter the central storehouse of the Blue Temple, and rob it of its wealth. My Sword here informs me that you—your powers—are going to be very useful in the execution of this plan. Cooperate with me willingly, and I promise you that when the time comes for sharing out the treasure, you will not be forgotten. And I promise also that in the meantime you'll take no harm from any man." And he cast a meaningful look at the two members of his crew who were immediately present.

And she is so beautiful, Mark was thinking, that there are a lot of men who'd fight to have her. But there was something almost too impressive in her beauty, so that it served as a warning as well as an invitation. And Mark could not forget that moment in which Ariane had hailed him as her brother. Whenever he had asked her about it later, she had said that she could not remember, that she had been drugged when she called him that. He told himself that there was no way he could actually be her brother. Still . . .

Doon was speaking to the girl again. " . . . and how would you like to find yourself, when we part company, with a purse full of Blue Temple jewels and gold as dowry? Or for any other purpose. You need be dependent upon no prince or potentate then, if you don't want to be."

Ariane mused. "*Her* gold and jewels, in my hands — I think I would like that." She seemed to be accepting without difficulty the prospect of getting into the Blue Temple vaults and robbing them. Mark and Ben exchanged a glance, and Ben nodded slightly; the girl must be at least a little out of touch with reality.

Mitspieler had come up on deck again, and was hovering in the background trying to get Doon's attention. As soon as he had done so, Doon went below again, to consult with the magicians.

The moment the Baron was out of sight, Hubert, with Golok trailing behind him, came forward from the stern. Mark had noticed before now that Hubert was fascinated by Ariane, and could not keep from approaching her when he had the opportunity.

But something that the soldier saw in the sea or fog ahead of the ship appeared to distract him, and when he came up to the others he was frowning. The first thing he said was: "I hope we'll not go near those cliffs."

Ben, still sitting on the deck, leaning back against the rail, looked up at him curiously. "Why not?"

" 'Why not?' the big man asks. Because of who might be up there, that's why not. I've heard our masters talking—all right, if you don't like to call 'em that, our leaders, then. And I know a thing or two about this part of the world myself, without asking them."

"And who is so important, up on the cliffs?" asked Ariane. Suddenly she appeared to be intensely interested, though she usually care nothing for Hubert's talk.

Hubert chuckled, pleased at having made an impression for once. "That's the Emperor's land up there, young lady. Those cliffs ahead of us, beyond the fog."

Ariane almost gasped to hear this. "No, not really!" Though Mark was observing her as keenly as he could, he still could not tell if she was really impressed, frightened, or subtly mocking Hubert.

The short man, at least, had no doubt about what kind of an impression he was making. He seemed to swell a little. "Oh aye . . . did you think that the Emperor was only a story? That's what most people think. A few bright ones know better. I've heard about this place. Down below those cliffs there's a grotto, and in that grotto the Emperor keeps a horde of his pet demons. Oh, he owns other lands too, scattered about the world, but this place is special. I've heard about it from those who've seen it.

"Maybe you thought he was only a story, or only a joke? Ah no, lass, he's real, and no joke. He likes to sit up there on a rock, wearing a gray cloak, and looking like an ordinary man, waiting for shipwrecked folk or anyone else to land and come up to him out of the sea. And when they do, he likes to whistle up his demons. And the victims are dragged by demons down into the grotto, where for the rest of time and eternity they wish that they could die—why, what's the matter, big man, seasickness come back on you?—that's the Emperor's idea of a joke . . . oh, you don't believe me, lass?"

Mark glanced curiously at Ben, who did indeed appear to be upset about something. But Ariane certainly did not. Far from being upset or even impressed by Hubert's tale, she had burst out laughing.

It made Hubert angry to be laughed at, and his ears reddened. "Funny, is it? And if anyone resists, or tries to run away, all the Emperor has to do is throw open his gray cloak. Underneath it, his body's so twisted away from human shape that anyone who sees it will go mad. . . ."

The girl's laughter did not sound to Mark as if it sprang from madness, but from a healthy sense of the ridiculous. Hubert was glaring at her, and his fingers worked. But Mark and Ben were one on each side of her, and watching him; and Doon had spoken his warning. The short man turned and retreated quickly to the stern. And Golok still hovered nearby, watching.

Presently Doon was back on deck, Indosuaros with him. Shortly afterwards the ship changed course, and was bearing in toward land, though not toward the cliffs where the Emperor was said to lie in wait. The wizard was now muttering almost continuous instructions to the djinn. The other humans stood out of the way as much as possible, as the vessel was maneuvered by the invisible power, in through breakers to a small scrap of sandy beach. The ship was brought to a stop just before it ran aground, in water so shallow that it was possible to disembark with no worse effect than a wetting.

Ariane, with her hair already tied up neatly, took part as one of the crew in passing packs and weapons safe to shore.

In a few moments they all stood on the beach, dripping—all but Indosuaros, whose robes had refused to absorb any water even when immersed. The wizard stood conferring cryptically with his djinn, which was visible only as a small cloud of troubled air above the ship.

Meanwhile Doon, gazing up at the towering cliffs, asked Ben: "This is where you climbed down?"

Ben had not yet told anyone, even Mark, the details of his escape after getting away from the dragon and starting down the cliff. And, with Hubert's lurid story still fresh in his mind, he felt reluctant to start talking about them now. He looked at the cliffs uncertainly, and then to right and left. "A little farther south, I think it was. It's hard for me to tell; it was night then, of course. All this cliff looks much the same."

"Aye." Doon studied the face of it to north and south. "Then you worked your way south along the shoreline, I suppose . . . how'd you get across the fjord?"

"Swam. Where it was narrower."

Doon nodded his acceptance. And now, like some infantry commander about to set out on a dangerous patrol, he ordered all packs opened and the contents spread out. In addition he checked the water bottles and skins, making sure all were full and fresh. There was a coil of rope for each member of the expedition. Food supplies were in order—Ben had heard the tale of the feast magically provided by Indosuaros at his headquarters, but there had been no indication of any such service being available on the road. There were weapons, climbing and stonecutting tools. Hubert appropriated a crossbow from Indosuaros' armory. Ariane was given a pack as a matter of course, and, when she spoke to Doon, a knife and a sling to wear at her belt. The magician and his aide had their own inventory to take, and Indosuaros certified that they were ready.

The ship, relieved of its passengers and their modest cargo, bobbed in the water a few score meters offshore, remaining in one spot just as if it had been anchored.

Doon waded out a few steps, to question his magician, who was standing in calf-deep water, gesturing. "What about the djinn?"

"It must stay with the ship, to protect it, move it about as needed, and bring it back to us here when we call."

At another gesture from Indosuaros, the sails emptied, flapped, then bellied as they refilled themselves. The vessel turned away from shore and toward the open sea.

"Wait!" called Doon sharply. When the ship's progress had been stayed by another gesture from the wizard, the Baron added: "I want to know something first, magician. Suppose that when we return to this shore, loaded with treasure, neither you nor your worthy assistant happen to be with us. How do we get the boat to come to us then? And where will it be in the meantime? We may well be gone for days."

"It will be at sea," said Indosuaros, looking down with dignity at the smaller man. "But close enough to be brought back here quickly. And the djinn will maintain enough fog in the area to keep the ship from being very easily observed."

"That's fine. And how do we get it back? There is some small chance, you know, that you will not be here. The place we are going to visit is not without its dangers."

Tension held in the air for a long moment. Then Indosuaros said, mildly enough: "I will give you some words to use for a summoning. And your men should hear them too, just in case *you* are not here, when *they* come back."

If Doon had any objection, he bit it back. The wizard devised a four-word command, and let them all repeat it aloud to be sure they had it memorized. After a trial, in which Ariane successfully summoned the vessel back toward shore, it was dispatched at last, and disappeared into a looming patch of fog.

Doon drew Wayfinder. To no one's surprise, it pointed the way for them straight up the cliff.

The climb began. Doon led the way, as usual, with the monkbird fluttering on ahead and coming back frequently to Golok to report.

Once Doon turned to Ben, who was climbing just behind him. "This cliffside is more irregular than I thought, looking up at it from below. There might be a dozen cave-mouths concealed around here. Do you suppose there could be one, a side entrance to the cave we seek? That would save us from having to face the dragon on the top."

"There might indeed be a dozen such openings, for all I know. It was night when I came down. Your Sword should point out such an entrance if there is one."

"I don't know . . . sometimes I think that there are two ways, and it picks the way of higher risk deliberately."

And they climbed on.

At the brink they paused, peering cautiously over, while once more the monkbird was sent ahead to scout. Wayfinder now pointed directly inland.

Across the rocky headland, a hundred stony hillocks rose, looking like choppy waves frozen in a sea of lava. The thorny vegetation looked even sparser now to Ben than it had on the night of his great escape, when it had seemed to him that he stepped on thorns with almost every stride. Indeed the whole scene, before his eyes now for the first time in daylight, looked unfamiliar. His confidence declined in his ability to find the cave again without the aid of magic.

The monkbird came back to report the way was clear, and was promptly sent out again. The humans climbed over the brink and moved cautiously inland, Doon in the lead.

The black flutterer returned almost at once. Perching on Golok's shoulder, it gave him what sounded like a report of a landwalker inland, almost exactly in the same direction that they were heading.

"How far?"

It jabbered something to its master, something unintelligible to the others.

Golok explained. "Almost a kilometer, I think. Horizontal distances are hard for it to estimate. Dart seems to be telling me that the dragon's eating something."

The Sword was pointing in the same direction still.

Doon chewed at his mustache, a sign of nervousness that Ben had not observed in him before. "You tell me, big man, that it should not be nearly a kilometer from here to the cave."

"Nothing like that far, no."

"Then likely we'll be able to get in, before . . . we'll chance it." Again Doon led the way inland, advancing quickly.

Golok relaunched his airborne scout, and Dart flew inland at low altitude. And returned in a few moments, this time chattering urgently.

"The dragon's moving toward us," Golok translated. "Coming straight this way." Then the youth ran ahead of Doon, who had paused to listen to the warning. "Let me get out in front of you," Golok urged, "and try to manage it. It's accustomed to being managed, from what you tell me."

"Manage a dragon?" But Doon let Golok get out ahead, then led the others in a quick advance.

Ben, even as he trotted forward, drew Dragonslicer from its sheath. Beside him he saw Mark pulling his longbow off his back and reaching for an arrow. Hubert paused for a moment, to throw his weight on the crossbow, cock it, and set the trigger.

You had to hit a big landwalker right in the open mouth, Ben was thinking, or in the tiny target of its eye, to do yourself any good even with a crossbow bolt . . . and now already he could hear the first chiming of the dragon. It was out of sight behind hillocks, but no longer very far ahead. It had to be coming on to meet them.

Ben scrambled up the nearest hillock to get a better look. Golok had climbed another mound, some twenty-five or thirty meters ahead, and from its top he was already talking and crooning and gesturing to the monster.

Not the same dragon I saw that night, thought Ben, this one's a little smaller. Some twenty meters beyond

Golok it had paused, leaning with one of its forearms on a mound three meters high, so that for a moment it made a parody of some irate proprietor behind a counter. It was angry at Golok for being where he was; it was probably angered by his mere existence. Ben could hear the anger in the near-musical chiming of its voice. So far it did not appear to have noticed Ben, or any of the others. It bowed its head once toward Golok, as if in some kind of formal acknowledgement of his existence, and then without further warning it came after him in a clumsy-looking charge. Fire sighed and whistled in its nostrils.

People near Ben were scrambling wildly to and from among the rocks. Golok abandoned the useless position of his mound in a surprisingly graceful leap. A few long strides and he had scrambled up atop another, farther from the people and the dragon and a little closer to the cliffs. He was still gesturing and singing, and something in his method took effect. The dragon's movements slowed abruptly, the charge declining into a mere advance. The monkbird was flying like a sparrow round the dragon's head, as if trying to distract it, but Dart received no attention.

Doon, near Ben's elbow, whispered fiercely: "Indosuaros?"

The wizard's whispered answer was just as taut. "We must use no magic here, if we can possibly avoid it. There will be traces of our passage, if we do."

Ben could sense Doon's indecision. The Baron wanted to get his party into the cave as quickly as possible, and if possible without an open combat against the dragon. Yet at the same time he did not want to lose Golok, or even to separate from him.

Golok made yet another sideways withdrawal, leading the dragon still farther out of their indicated path. And again it lurched and lunged toward him, this time punctuating its advance with the sideways sweep of a clawed forelimb against a mound. Rocks scattered, flying as if cast by some giant's sling.

That movement was enough for Mark. His longbow twanged at a range of no more than twenty meters. The straight shaft, driven, Ben knew, by a thirty-kilo pull, struck within a handsbreadth of the moving dragon's right eye. The arrowhead broke on one of the small scales there, the shaft rebounded like a twig. The dragon paid it not the least attention.

Doon was whispering again. "I don't want to lose my beast-master before we even get below. We'll need him there. We've got to save him, kill the dragon if we must."

And if we can, thought Ben. Still the creature was advancing, in fits and starts, toward Golok. The youth with his best efforts was managing to blunt the edge of its wrath for seconds at a time, but not to turn it away. He dodged, retreated, tried to stand his ground, and was forced back again.

Golok was gradually being driven back toward the edge of the cliffs, now only a few meters behind him. Seven other people, working from one rock-shelter to the next, were following as closely as they dared.

"Go over the edge," Ben called to him, trying to make his voice no louder than was necessary for the youth to hear, fearing to startle the beast into another forward rush. "Over the brink, and hang on. It won't see you then. Maybe it —"

Again, abruptly, the dragon charged at Golok, this

time with a thundering full roar. The subtle nets of control, woven of beast-master's lore, had given way totally at last.

Both Mark and Hubert, meanwhile, had maneuvered away from Ben, so that the dragon was charging more or less in their direction and they had a good shot at the roof of the open mouth. Ben, scrambling forward as fast as he could toward the dragon's flank with Dragonslicer gripped in both hands, thought that even so the chance was small that the bowmen could hit the brain, and that even if you hit the brain your problems with a landwalker were not over necessarily. . . . Already Dragonslicer's powers had awakened, and Ben could feel the Sword, hear it, shrilling as he ran.

Golok had fallen, scrambling, near the brink. Longbow shaft and crossbow bolt, simultaneously, entered the open mouth that loomed above him. There was an explosion of fire that gutted the dragon's left cheek outwards; the jolt of liquid hell that was to have been projected at Golok went spewing and sizzling away instead, some of it over the cliff's edge, some to spill upon the nearby rocks. One of the missiles had burst a firegland in the cheek.

Ariane was yelling bravely, and slinging stones at the dragon, whether accurately or not made no difference in the least. The two wizards were sensibly lying low.

Drooling flame, and certainly now aware of pain, the monster turned toward the other people who beset it. Doon, scrambling desperately over and around rocks, behind the enemy now, struck with Wayfinder at one of its hind legs, aiming for a spot where there should be a tendon beneath the scales. The heavy, razor-edged blade rebounded like a toy sword from an anvil. The dragon did not see or feel him.

It saw Ben though, and it heard him. The Sword of Heroes was in his hands, making its shrill sound, and now he felt the more-than-human power of the weapon flow into his arms.

As always, the great damned beasts were unpredictable. At the last moment the dragon turned again away from Ben, and bent to pick up the screaming Golok in its left forelimb. Ben could see the youth's legs, still living, kicking wildly. Ben yielded himself to Dragonslicer, letting the force of it in his hands pull him forward to the attack. The blow struck by the Sword was almost too swift for his own thought to follow it, and it took off cleanly the dragon's right paw as it swiped at him. The severed forelimb thudded like an armored body falling to the ground, the iridescent blood gushing out.

The Sword of Heroes shrieked.

Ben got one more close look at Golok's living face.

Dragonslicer thrust home for the heart, parting hand-thick scales as if they had been tender leaves. The landwalker stumbled backward, leaving the Sword still keening in Ben's hands. The treetrunk legs kicked out in reflex, hurling stones and dust. With a last roar that ended in eruptive bubbling, the beast went backward over the cliff, Golok still clutched to its scaly breast.

Ben had time to scramble forward to the brink and watch the ending of the fall. The two bodies did not separate until they hit the water and the rocks.

CHAPTER 10

The monkbird screamed, on and on. To Ben it seemed to have been screaming for days. With the Sword of Heroes still dripping dragon's blood in his right hand, he clung to the cliff-edge rocks, looking down a hundred meters at the sullen surge and smash of waves below. It was a fine day, and the sea wore delicate shadings of blue and green over most of its vast surface. The fall on rocks had pulped the huge beast's body like a dropped fruit, but the waves were already sorting and sifting and dispersing the organic wreckage, on the way to accomplishing a tidy disposal of it. And Golok's body had already disappeared completely.

Mark had come to Ben's side, had taken him by the left arm, was pulling him back from the brink.

Doon was frothing angry. "The bird, the demon-damned bird!" He looked up at Dart's small, frantic shape flying not far above his head, as if he were about to strike at it with his Sword. Dart's voiceless keening mingled with the racket of a cloud of seabirds that had been startled up from the shoreline rocks. "How are we going to be able to use it now?"

As if intentionally answering his question, it came down suddenly, down in an abrupt swoop to Ariane standing nearby. Her left arm was extended in the traditional gesture of beast masters to their flying pets. Now, with its fur dark brown against the coils of her red hair, the monkbird huddled on her shoulder, mourning almost silently for its dead master, clinging there with feet and wings like some half-human orphan. Ariane whispered to it and stroked it. When Mitspieler came to her to see if he could help, she sent him away with a gentle headshake, and continued to soothe the creature.

Doon observed this with visible relief. "Good job, Princess. We may not have lost much here after all." He took a quick glance at the sky. "They may think they've lost their dragon over the cliff by accident, chasing a rabbit or some such. Anyway we'll have come and gone, if we do the job right, before the dragon's missed. Let's move."

And he moved ahead himself, Wayfinder drawn. Ben, having cleaned Dragonslicer as well as he could on prickly leaves, followed closely. Mark was near Ben, and the others only a few steps behind.

Ben could still recognize no details of his surroundings, though it looked in general like the same landscape from which he had fled by night. Now, in broad day, it held no sign anywhere of humanity or of human works, apart from the adventurers themselves.

The wasteland stretched away to north, west, and south, kilometer after kilometer, empty and grimly beautiful.

"Where's your local Blue Temple?" asked Mark, sticking his head up over a hillock beside Ben's, to scan the way ahead.

"Somewhere inland, over there. Kilometers away. It took us half a day and half a night to get here from there, even riding part of the way."

And on impulse Ben turned his head to look back across the water. On the other side of the fjord rose the opposite headland, emerging belatedly from the last of the morning's mists to warm itself in early summer's sun. The meadow and the forest on its top were indistinguishable at this distance and in this light. The cliffs, with this side of them just coming into sunshine now, were vaguely blue.

Did I really swim all that way, and climb those cliffs? Ben asked himself. Swimming through the tides at night, with no idea of where I was really going? Someday, he thought, I'll tell my grandchildren all about it. My grandchildren and Barbara's, in our fine house. I saw the Emperor sitting there in his gray cloak, and he looked just like a man. . . . Ben had been on the way to forgetting the incident completely until Hubert had startled him with his tale. But no use worrying now about the real truth of it—there had been no demons in evidence, anyway.

He looked inland again, and moved on, following the others who were getting ahead of him.

Doon, with his Sword in his hands, led them steadily on across the trackless waste. Ben several times murmured to the others that now the proper hillock could not be much farther. In trying to pick it out, he became aware for the first time of how much alike were all these stony knobs. It even seemed that each hillock had on one side an enormous stone, and that each such stone was of a size and shape to possibly form the balance-door protecting the hidden cave. This fact was not immediately obvious, for no two of the huge stones were exactly alike in appearance, nor were they on the same sides of their respective hills. But any of at least a hundred, as far as Ben could tell, might possibly be the one they sought. He wondered silently if this might have been arranged by magic; it seemed impossible that chance alone would be responsible.

Wayfinder was immune to these as to all other distracting elements. Following Doon, who held to an almost straight course, Ben tried to recall in which direction the cave opening had faced. Indelibly he remembered that moment in which he'd turned from the entrance, and, with Radulescu's yell still hanging in the air, had grabbed and pulled the great stone down to bang the doorway shut. Then, himself on the edge of panic, running off into the night, almost blind in darkness, banging his legs on rocks . . . he had run, that night, with the ocean on his left . . .

"Here," said Doon abruptly. He had come to a halt standing in front of a hillock that looked to Ben no more familiar than any of the others standing round it. Facing the side of the mound, Doon stretched forth his arm until the tip of the Sword in his hand touched rock. Now Ben could plainly see the strong vibration in the blade.

"Here?" Ben echoed, questioning; the hillock was

still unrecognizable to him among its fellows. There was one way to make sure, and he slipped off his backpack. "All right. Lend a hand at this end of the rock and help me lift it." And he bent to grip the base of the enormous stone himself. Suddenly, with the feel of it, he was sure that this was the right spot.

But Indosuaros touched his shoulder. "Wait." The magician raised both hands, and rested ten fingertips upon the rock. He stood there for a moment, his eyes closed, then stepped back, glancing at his assistant. "I sense no guardian magic. Lift away."

With Ben exerting himself, Mark and Hubert gave enough help to tilt the great stone back. Ben's remaining doubts vanished; there was the dark triangular opening, just the same.

Doon, his weapon ready, glared into the doorway for a moment, then stepped back, nodding with satisfaction. "Lights," he pronounced.

These, seven Old World devices, were taken out of one of the packs and passed around. They were somewhat different in shape and style from the torch that Ben had seen Radulescu using, but functionally the same. And these had modern, handmade leather straps attached.

Doon demonstrated quickly how the straps could be used to put the light on like a helmet, leaving the wearer's hands free. "For these, again, we have our wizard to thank. We'll see to it, Indosuaros, that your years of preparation were not wasted." He took the helmet off to demonstrate its function. "Press here, and it gives light. Press again and it goes dark. Turn this to make it brighter or dimmer. Twist and push like this, and you can focus the light into a beam. Twist and draw back again, and the glow spreads out to light a room."

"How long will they keep burning?" asked Hubert, who was obviously fascinated. He had probably, Ben thought, never seen the like before.

Doon shrugged. "They're already nearly as old as the world itself. I suppose they may keep burning until its end, so don't fear to use them."

The actual entry into the cave seemed to Ben almost an anticlimax. With the new light shining from his forehead, he noted the old wax candle drippings still on the floor. There was no visible trace of the six men he had shut in here with his own hands. But now the memory of that night came back more sharply than ever, for the cave looked no different now than it had looked then in the beam of the Old World light carried by Radulescu.

Indosuaros, standing by the large opening in the floor, again reported that he could detect no guardian magic. "Not here . . . but far down, yes. There's magic moiling in the earth, well below us. Magic, and . . . "

"And what?" Doon asked him sharply.

The magician sighed. "I think . . . there is something down there of the Old World, also. Something large."

"Is that all you can tell us?"

"Old World technology." Indosuaros curled his lip. "Who can tell about technology?"

"The magic that you sense, then—are you going to be able to deal with it, when we reach it?"

The wizard appeared for a moment to be taking some kind of inward inventory. He stared hard at his assistant. Then he answered, firmly enough: "I can."

"Then," said Doon briskly, "the next order of business is to make sure we can open the outer door here, when we come back." And he trotted back up the crooked stair to scrutinize the great rock carefully. Ben had already explained to everyone how he had used that door to get away.

Now Doon sighed, dissatisfied. He scowled at the rock as if it offended him. "Ben, tell me this. The priests must come here on inspection tours from time to time, to see that their treasure's safe. Don't they?"

"I suppose they must," Ben answered, climbing the stairs too. "But I never heard anything about it."

"Well, you say it can't be opened from the inside. That officer would have opened it if he could, and pursued you. Right?"

"I don't think," said Ben, "that I could lift it alone, from inside, if my life depended on it. And only one person can get at it from inside, there's room only for one."

"I doubt that the priests leave this open behind them when they come. And I doubt they come with half a dozen slaves each time, to wait outside and lift this for them when they want to leave." Again Doon sighed. "Once we are well down and in, of course, we may discover some alternate way out. Or we may not. Now I have stonecutting tools, but . . . " Just looking at the rock, Doon shook his head. Then he made a gesture of giving up. "Indosuaros? I know our plan was not to leave any magic traces of our passage, so near the surface anyway. But to seal ourselves into this cave without a known way out would be even worse."

The wizard had to agree, gloomily. "I fear that you are right." Then Indosuaros held a hurried, whispered conference with Mitspieler, after which the two of them drew objects from a pack. Soon they were standing just outside the upper doorway, rubbing at the huge rock with what looked to Ben like raw slices of some kind of vegetable.

All this time Ariane was content to remain in the lower cave, occupying her time by petting the monkbird and whispering to it soothingly. She showed little or no sign of fear.

When the magicians had finished their treatment of the rock, Doon summoned Ben to pull it down and close the door. It felt to Ben as if the mass of the stone were now greatly diminished; when he tried, he was able to catch it falling, halfway closed, and push it up again very easily. One after another, all the members of the party now tried lifting it open from inside, and all could manage it.

With everyone inside the cave at last, and the outer door closed, Doon gathered his party around the large slot in the lower floor.

"This is where we put the treasure down," said Ben. "And where I saw the Whitehands reach for it."

The wizard Indosuaros smiled, as if he were now determined to be reassuring. "They come this close to the surface only to receive treasure, as they did on the night when you were here."

"How do you know?"

Ben's answer was an arrogant look, that said the sources of the wizard's knowledge were doubtless beyond Ben's grasp, and were not really any of his business anyway.

"It would be a neat trick," offered Hubert, "if we could capture one of those to serve us as a guide. They must know a quick way to the treasure. Trust those who have to carry it to know the shortest way."

"If we meet one of them," muttered Doon abstractedly, "we'll ask him." The Baron had braced his body directly above the aperture, and was looking intently down into it with the aid of a beam from his headlamp. "There are steps carved into the side here," he announced. "And it doesn't look far down. I don't think I'll need a rope—but let me have one, just in case. Two of you hold it up here."

Mark and Ben gripped one of the thin, supple coils, and paid out an end. Doon sheathed Wayfinder and in a moment had vanished, sliding down.

The line went slack in their hands almost at once. "I'm down," the Baron's voice called up to them softly. "Come ahead." Ben, looking down through the aperture, could see the Baron's headlamp moving about just a short distance below. In the augmented light, the series of niches for steps and grips, carved in the side of the short shaft, stood out plainly. One side of the shaft joined with a wall of the chamber below, and the steps went down nearly to that lower floor.

Ben followed his leader, and soon the whole party was down. The chamber in which they now found themselves was about the same size and shape as the one they had just descended from, and again there was a single lower exit. This time, though, the exit was a tunnel mouth, cut in the side of the cave approximately opposite the entrance shaft. The tunnel was narrow, and just about high enough for a moderately tall man to walk into it erect. Ben expected that Mark would have to watch his head.

Again Doon led the way, the others following necessarily in single file. After first twisting to the right, the tunnel bent back to the left, while continuously and ever more steeply descending. As the steepness increased, carved grips and steps appeared again in sides and floor.

They had followed this passage for no more than a few score meters, when Doon stopped, calling softly back to the others that the tunnel ahead turned into a perfectly vertical shaft.

The Baron refused the suggestion of a rope, and simply continued to work his way lower, by means of the plentiful niches provided in the shaft's sides. Ben followed cautiously. Above and behind him, Indosuaros looked down and ahead with eyes half-closed, as if he were groping his way along by the use of senses beyond the normal. After Indosuaros was Ariane, the monkbird riding unhooded on her shoulder, clinging tightly to her shirt. Hubert was next, then Mark, with Mitspieler bringing up the rear.

Again there was an easy egress from the lower end of the shaft. It ended a little more than a meter above a circular dais that was two or three meters wide, and raised perhaps a meter above the floor of the surrounding room.

The lower end of the shaft was finished in what looked like ancient masonry, with hairline gaps showing between blocks, so that Ben marveled as he let go of the last grip that it had not all come crashing down with his weight on it.

But soon all seven members of the expedition were safely down out of the shaft, and standing round the dais. They were in a squat cylinder of a room, perhaps ten meters across, larger than either of the two rooms above. Here the stone wall, floor, and ceiling were all carved quite smoothly into a regular shape. Twelve dark doorways were more or less regularly spaced round the circumference of the circular wall. From near the center of the room it was not possible to throw a beam of light very far into any of the twelve apertures, as the passages beyond all curved sharply after a few meters, turning down or sideways or both. Each tunnel, at the start at least, was wide enough for only one person to enter it comfortably at a time.

"We have reached the third sealing," said Doon. And he raised his Sword in a salute, as if to a worthy foe.

CHAPTER 11

Doon was standing near the round wheel-hub of the dais, turning his body slowly, aiming Wayfinder to determine which of the dark tunnels they ought to follow. Mark, watching the Baron's face, saw him for once frowning at what his guide told him.

Indosuaros, gazing over Doon's shoulder, prodded. "There seems no doubt about it, does there? The Sword says that's the one to take." And the magician pointed with a long, gnarled forefinger at a tunnel.

All the more irritated by this advice, Doon moved the Sword. "But first, a moment ago, it indicated this other passage, over here. I'm sure of it. And now it doesn't."

"It certainly does not," Indosuaros agreed. He paused, then added: "Your hand may have been shaking, man. Or perhaps the light was unsteady for a moment."

"My hand did not shake! And I really don't need any light to feel the vibration in the blade."

Ben chimed in: "There could be a smaller amount of treasure at the end of the passage where it first pointed, and a larger at the end of this one. Anyway, I'd read the augury so."

"Or," suggested Ariane, "one treasure that's being moved about, even as you attempt to get a bearing on it?" There was something like enjoyment in her voice, that did not fade even when Doon glared at her.

"I doubt we're very near to any treasure yet," the Baron growled.

And the magician again: "Either trust your Sword or not, is all I can advise you. If you're going to trust it no longer, then I'll start to try to find our way by other means." Why, he's jealous of the Sword, thought Mark.

The Baron evidently thought the same. "You'll start to try? Why no, I think we'll trust this god-forged metal yet awhile. And we'll take the way it showed me first." The two men stared at each other for a moment.

"Some of us could try one way and some another," Hubert offered, though not as if he really thought it was a good idea.

Doon gave him a brief glare too. "No, I'll not divide my forces. Not yet anyway. We'll take the way Wayfinder showed me first."

Mark, having some experience of using Coinspinner for guidance, thought that the point called for more discussion. But that too would have its dangers, and he kept quiet, and read agreement in Ben's eyes. Mark met Ariane's gaze too, and thought he saw the beginning there of a realistic concern. And in her eyes as well were other things less easy to interpret.

The party entered the tunnel that Doon had chosen. They were moving in single file as before, and once more Mark found himself next to last, just in front of the silent Mitspieler, and behind Hubert. Mark had to stoop his back or bend his neck almost continuously to keep his headlamp from scraping on the roof of the passage as he moved. If this goes on for very long, he thought, I'll have to take the lamp off and carry it in my hand. Or depend on others' lights while we're in here—this passage was at least a little wider than the last one, though it still lacked room for two to go comfortably abreast.

The tunnel curved sharply from left to right and back again, while constantly descending. But here the slope of the descent never became as steep as it had in the previous tunnel, and the rough floor here was enough to provide secure footing. It occured to Mark to look at the ceiling for torch-smoke stains as he scraped his way along beneath it. Surely not all of the Blue Temple people who had come through this maze to reach the treasure would have used Old World lights, and generations of traffic ought to have left stains along the proper route. Indeed Mark thought that he could see some blackening, though on the dark rock it was difficult to be sure.

"Look at that," said Ben's voice, quietly, from a few meters ahead. The procession did not stop. A few more steps and Mark saw what Ben had meant. They were passing what had once been the mouth of an intersecting passage, its opening now completely blocked by a cave-in, filled with jumbled slabs and fragments fallen from overhead. From this mass, down near the floor, there protruded a pair of dead skeletal hands—

Mark found himself taking note that they were of no more than normal human size. Somehow the mute warning seemed all the more impressive because it had no look of having been planned as a deterrent to intruders.

Mark saw Ariane look down at the bones as she walked past. The girl showed no sign of shock or fright. What kind of a growing-up must she have had? Mark wondered to himself. Could it have been as strange as my own, or even stranger? Maybe her powers, if she truly has any, knew me as her brother in that much at least.

There were no more branching passages. Having no real choice now of which way to go, Doon was not consulting Wayfinder. Now they had reached a comparatively straight stretch of the tunnel, where Mark could see Doon's light bobbing at the head of the procession, revealing the tunnel walls—

Which now ended, not far ahead, in a simple circle of darkness. It was as if the passage here debouched into some vast cave. As they grew closer with their lights, vague distant forms as of jagged rock appeared in the opening.

"What's this, by all the demons?"

The tunnel widened somewhat at its mouth, and the intruders crowded together there as best they could to see what kind of a place they had reached. There was indeed a large cave in front of them now, and it looked virtually impassable. The floor of it, if it could be called a floor, was at some distance below the one on which they stood, and it bristled with spiny projections of rock, that gleamed here and there with flecks of brightness but were also heavily stained and coated with what looked in the lamps' beams like some kind of fungus.

And again, behind a sharp outcropping, Mark saw the startling white of human bone. Some kind of bones, at least; these were jumbled and broken, and Mark could not be sure that they were human.

This deadly looking chamber was some twenty or thirty meters deep, and without any other visible entrance or exit. On right and left it extended for only a few meters before its side walls closed in to come close to the wall from which the tunnel emerged; on each side the space between was far too small to admit a hope that people might be able to squeeze themselves through it. Mark, looking upward as best he could out of the tunnel's mouth, could see only the smooth slight bulge of the rounded wall from which the tunnel emerged, and above that, a jagged rocky roof some meters out of reach. Looking down, the prospect was even more discouraging; upjutting corners of stone waited amid shadows at an intimidating distance below. In no direction could he see anything that looked like a practical continuation of their path.

At Doon's urging, Ariane now prevailed upon the monkbird to try a short scouting flight into the cave ahead. The beams of headlamps lit its way, but still it fluttered about uncertainly and had to be encouraged. At last it flew out for some distance, and was near a far unpromising shelf of rock when there came a sudden popping noise from the fungi near it, and a cloud of dust burst up around the flying creature. The monkbird came speeding back to Ariane's shoulder, where once more it clung tight in fear. It brought with it a taste of choking dust, and at the same time an acrid, poisonous odor drifted to the humans' nostrils from the far reaches of the cave.

Doon, muttering demon-oaths between sudden fits of coughing, had his Sword out and was aiming it at various portions of the cave. But he obtained no response until he pointed it back into the tunnel, in the direction from which the expedition had just come. He looked so black at this that even Indosuaros thought it wise to make no comment at the moment.

Meanwhile Mark was looking back into the cave, and something he saw there kindled an idea. He pulled off his headlamp, and, bending down, placed it on the floor, focusing a tight beam of light upon some rocks in the cave that were twenty or thirty meters distant.

"Turn off all the lights but this one," he told the others. "I'm trying to see something."

The Baron, on the verge of issuing new orders, hesitated and then did as he had been told. The other people muttered questions and protests, mingled with their sneezes and coughs. But in a moment Mark's was the only lamp alight.

He straightened up again. "Look. My lamp isn't moving at all, it's resting on the floor. Watch the light."

From a few bright facets of the distant rock, spots of brilliance were being reflected back into the tunnel, glowing dimly on walls and ceiling and on the faces of the people.

"Look."

The spots of light were all in motion. It was a slow movement, steady and concerted. It appeared that the fixed rock, the whole cave out there, was turning past the tunnel's mouth, in a gradual unvarying rotation. Looking closely at the cave, it was obvious that the perspective of it had changed in the short time the party had been standing in front of it.

People coughed in the fading traces of the poison-spores, and marveled.

"That can't be right."

"But it is moving."

"I think," said Mark, "that I know what's happening. Let's get out of this dust, back through the tunnel. I'll tell you there."

The others were ready enough to go, and Doon to lead the way. In a short time they had climbed back through the twisting tunnel and re-entered the large cylindrical room.

There Mark offered his explanation. "It isn't the cave down there that's moving, it's us. I mean all twelve of these tunnels, and the room we're standing in. What looks like the hub of a wheel here"—and he thumped his hand upon the circular dais—"really is just that. And look up here, around the end of the shaft where we came down. You see what look like loose masonry joints. The two parts are free to turn past each other. Indosuaros, when we were still up there in daylight you said that you could sense something huge down here, something of the Old World."

"I did feel that." The wizard tilted back his head and closed his eyes. "And I feel it now. Technology." And as before, he curled his lip contemptuously at the word.

Doon was incredulous. "A whole section of this cliff, with the twelve tunnels running through it like the spokes of a wheel? It would have to be big enough to build a village on."

Hubert chimed in: "A slab of that size, rotating all

the time? Without even making noise, or—nobody could build such a thing. Nobody could . . . " But he let it die away there. He knew, like the Baron and everyone else, that the Old World had made a thousand wonders just as great.

Mark said to Doon: "But it means that the Sword must have been right, both times. If we'd been quick enough to follow the first tunnel that it chose, we'd have come out in the right place . . . don't you see, the rotating tunnels must match up with a fixed one, or some exit, cut in the solid rock somewhere around the wheel. The twelve tunnel mouths probably turn past it, one after another. At least some of them must."

"Actually," put in Ben, "there could be more than twelve tunnel-mouths, depending on how the tunnels branch inside the wheel."

Doon shook his head, as if to clear it. "Let's try what Wayfinder can tell us now."

This time the Sword indicated a completely different tunnel, not the next one in order around the wall.

"I see," said Ben. "They bend and twist, as we've seen, and probably some of them cross over and under each other, within the thickness of the wheel."

"I wonder, then," asked Hubert. "How do the priests who come here ever manage to find their way in and out? Have they some spell to stop the wheel?"

"Technology won't stop and start on spells. They might know, from the time of day when they enter from outside, which tunnel will be properly aligned when they get down here."

"We've not proven this mad idea yet," growled the Baron. "This time we go with Wayfinder in front of us. Come on!"

"Aye, we'd better use Wayfinder," muttered Mark. "I just thought—there may be other tunnel exits in the fixed rock around the wheel, that could lead to something even worse than that cave we just came from."

Again the group filed single into a chosen tunnel. This time Hubert, anxious now to stay close to Doon in this uncertainty, managed to get right behind him.

Again the tunnel twisted and went down. Again its explorers came to one cross passage, but this time the alternate way was not blocked. The Sword made its choice, pointing to the right. Again, after they had followed it a little farther, the tunnel they were in straightened—but this time something different was visible beyond its ending.

Its mouth, as Mark had predicted, was nearly aligned with a matching opening beyond a modest gap. Here, with the stator and rotor of the great system only a couple of meters apart at the farthest, the slow-creeping rotation of the central wheel was much easier to see.

The tunnel in which they had arrived widened out considerably just at the end. The aperture opposite closely matched it in both size and shape; each was equipped with a stone step just at the lip, as if to facilitate the easy leap, no more than a long stride, between them. The intervening space was deep enough to almost swallow up their light beams, but less than two meters wide. The other opening was also equipped with handgrips, elementary metal studs, set into masonry sockets on both sides of it.

The Sword urged them straight ahead, across the slowly misaligning gap. Doon leaped out first, and landed lightly on the step. He at once moved up another step, into the other tunnel, which appeared to slope downward sharply from just inside its entrance. With his hand that did not hold the Sword, he motioned imperiously for the others to lose no time in following.

Ben took a step forward, that would have been followed by a jump, but for the sudden drag of Ariane's hand upon his sleeve. He halted his movement and turned to meet her eyes, saw them for a moment looking entranced and almost sightless.

In the moment when Ben delayed, Hubert, with the crossbow jouncing lightly on his back leaped out and landed—

Under Hubert's feet the first step of stone fell free at one end like a trapdoor, slamming back against the wall. His hands, grabbing in reflex for the iron studs, for anything to hold, clutched at flat slippery stone. The metal projections, moving in concert with the falling stone, had slid back into their sockets. Hubert's fingers banged helplessly at the smooth surface and were gone, as he fell with a maddened scream into the gap between the walls.

Doon had spun around and tried to grab him, but no human being could have moved quickly enough. Nor could any of the people who were still on the inner, slow-turning wall react in time. Mark, looking down into the narrow chasm, could see Hubert's Old World headlamp turning and bouncing, bouncing and turning again, receding with the body that still wore it. The man's screams had already ceased. The light flashed and flickered in its spinning fall, at one instant revealing fantastic rock formations that in the next instant were again plunged into darkness.

The light bounced once more and was still. The beam, as bright as ever, shone steadily now on more sharp rocks, and also on what looked like a boneyard of the fallen, a scattering of white distant splinters and what might have been round skulls.

The survivors had not a moment to spend in pondering Hubert's fate, not with the relentless rotation of the inner wall steadily carrying the tunnel mouths apart. Some internal mechanism had already brought the trapdoor shelf back up into its innocent-looking raised position. Doon, on the far side of the gap, caught one end of a rope thrown him by Ben, and braced himself well back in the descending tunnel. With Ben holding the other end of the rope, Mitspieler was the first to cross with its insurance, gripping a loop as he jumped and landed on the step, which this time held its load solidly. Mitspieler scrambled on to where Doon stood, and helped him to hold the far end of the rope.

"The Sword didn't warn us!" Ariane complained, as if surprised at some friend's treachery. Meanwhile she landed safely in her turn.

"That is not its function!" the Baron snapped at her, as she appeared beside him to help him hold the rope. And in the next instant Mark was safely over.

Indosuaros was next. And Ben, holding his own end of the rope, and with the monkbird fluttering dumbly round his head, was last to cross. The hinged step supported his bulk solidly, as it had done for everyone but Hubert.

The six survivors, gathered now on the side of the gap that they hoped was toward the treasure, looked back to watch the mouth of the tunnel they had just quitted turn slowly out of sight behind a flange of rock.

"We'll not have long to wait for a passage to open when we come back," said Doon. There was great confidence in his voice, as if Mark's idea of the turning tunnels had been his all along; more, as if he, Doon, had proven that it was right, beyond all possibility of doubt. "There are twelve or more of those rotating tunnels, we calculated. So if yon great wheel turns only twice a day, there should never be need to wait more than an hour for an alignment. We can be sure of that."

Whether they were all sure of it or not, no one said anything. At the moment there was only one thing in Ben's mind: with the vanishing of the last crescent of the other tunnel, there was no immediate possibility of turning back.

The Baron added: "When we come back, we might be in a hurry. So before we go on we'd better figure out just how this damned trap-step works." He spoke in a businesslike tone. And he began cautious experimentation, which soon revealed that the step remained rock-solid as long as no one was standing on the step just above it—where Doon himself had been standing when Hubert made his fatal jump. A substantial weight upon the second step evidently released some kind of hidden latch that let the first step swing down the instant it was burdened.

"I suppose the priests and the Whitehands have that little game memorized—or they don't forget it more than once, when they come this way two at a time. Well, we know it now. Let's move on."

Although there seemed to be only one possible way to go from here, Doon used the Sword. It pointed them forward, through the descending tunnel, and they followed it. After that short, steep descent they were plunged into a maze of tunnels, passages interconnecting sometimes by holes in floor and overhead as well as ordinary doorways. There were doors, some closed, some standing open. On doors and walls alike strange symbols had been carved and painted.

Wayfinder ignored the symbols and the doors alike, and chose an open way. Again, as always, Doon led the others with his Sword in hand. He looked more carefully now at the stone floor before he trod on it, and those behind him looked at it again in turn.

Once or twice in the maze the Baron paused, and ordered Ariane to send the monkbird on ahead. Each time it came back soon, and said little. She had trouble interpreting what it said, and presently they gave up trying to use it altogether.

Now suddenly there was only one tunnel again. It curved sharply, first to the right, then back to the left again. From beyond that final bend a light appeared, that looked to Ben like cheerful daylight. Moving forward, he could hear running water, and then the songs of birds.

CHAPTER 12

In the last meters of its length, the curving tunnel's smooth interior gave way to rough rock, so that the passage appeared to be turning into a natural cave. Mark, emerging behind Doon from the cave's mouth, blinked in what appeared to be sunlight, filtered through the foliage of majestic treetops some meters overhead. The air was warm, and a fresh breeze stirred the high branches. Birds flitted among them, and along the face of the red rock cliff from which the cave emerged. The sound of rushing water, as from a small waterfall or tumbling stream, came from somewhere near at hand but out of sight.

The forest grew up close to the cliff. Its grassy, open floor was some meters below the rocky shelf on which the six intruders gathered in front of the cave's mouth. From that shelf a barely discernible path wound down, among boulders of the reddish rock, to disappear as soon as it got in among the trees. The highest portion of the cliff was masked by branches of the towering trees, which also effectively concealed most of the sky; but so bright was that seeming sky that the effect was not gloom, but welcome shade. Mark raised a hand to turn off his headlamp, and saw that everyone else was doing likewise.

"We have reached the sealing of magic," Mitspieler announced, in a deep solemn voice. He spoke so rarely that everyone tended to look at him when he did. "Given the correct password, we could walk through it as easily as the Blue Temple priests must do. Master, do you think it is worthwhile for us to try again to divine what that word is?"

Indosuaros glanced at him, sighed, and shook his head. "We have tried that often enough, and learned nothing."

Doon said impatiently: "The Sword will guide us through."

Indosuaros agreed. "But, as we have seen, it cannot warn of traps. In this sealing, that task will be up to me. It will not be easy, and I want to rest before we start."

The Baron considered. "Agreed. We can all use a rest at this point, if we can find a suitable place."

The two wizards looked out over the scene and conferred together in low voices for a few moments. Then Indosuaros announced: "We can at least go down to the foot of the cliff safely. I suppose no one needs warning that not everything you will see here conforms to reality. I can tell you already that the grass and trees *are* real, at least for the most part, though I suppose they must be magically maintained. We are of course still inside a cave. This is a very large room — just how large I cannot tell as yet — and naturally lightless. What you perceive as sun and sky and wind are all artifacts of wizardry, and just what reality they may conceal I cannot yet be certain. But we can go forward in safety for a little way at least."

"What about the stream?" Ariane asked shortly. They had started down the path, moving again in single file, and already the twisting path had brought them into sight of a small waterfall, which broke out tumbling from the jagged cliff at no great distance from the cave's mouth. The small stream danced down over the lower rocks, then plunged into a flatter bed that led it away among the trees.

"The water is real enough," Indosuaros answered her after a moment. "Whether it will be safe to drink, or even to touch, I cannot tell until we reach it."

That was soon enough. As soon as the party had reached the grass, growing from what looked and felt like rich forest soil, the two wizards moved forward to the bank of the stream and knelt beside it. There they busied themselves briefly with the art, and presently they rose to give assurance that the water was safe.

"I'm not surprised," said Doon. "There are living humans — well, in some sense living — in the garrison, down below. And the visiting priests must have need of water, not to mention the Whitehands. So this comes from some natural spring. We'll rest here, then, wizard, if you can mark out some safe boundary for us."

Again the two magicians went to work. They paced back and forth, mumbling, gesturing, watching things which common human eyes saw not. They walked apart and then came back to the others. Indosuaros warned the group: "Stay within this first loop of the stream, between it and the foot of the cliffs."

The territory so defined was comfortably large, giving six people plenty of area in which to relax. It even contained enough in the way of trees and rocks and bushes to offer a minimum of privacy. People slipped off their packs and laid their weapons down—within handy reach.

Mark bent to drink from the stream, conserving his carried water, and found it clear and cold. Then with a weary sigh he lay back in the comfortable grass, letting his eyes close. Around him he could hear the others seeking ease in various ways.

He meant to get up in a moment, and find Ben and confer with him on the question that now loomed large in Mark's own mind: Was it time to give up and turn back, or try to do so? Already three were dead out of the small group that Doon had started with. The thought of Sir Andrew's struggling army drove Mark on; but going on to certain death was hardly going to help Sir Andrew or himself.

The first question was of course whether it was less dangerous, or even possible, to turn back now. Doon and the wizard would have to be persuaded, and that might be hopeless. Or else Doon, at least, would probably have to be fought—and it was hard for Mark to imagine any course very much more dangerous than that. . . .

Lying in the grass with his eyes slitted open, Mark was aware of the dappling deceptive sunlight far above. If he turned his head slightly he could still see the place where they had come out of the cliff. The boundary of cliff and sky was still obscured, as if designedly, by the massed intervening foliage of the trees. He wondered if it would be summer here all year round.

When he closed his eyes completely, even his dull ability to perceive magic could sense the magic all around him, as steady as the sound of running water in the stream. It was there, but what it was doing he did not know.

It was hard to relax, to rest. He was afraid. He was almost ready to quit, and he would have quit before now, if Ben had not been here, or if the imagined images of Sir Andrew's suffering people did not move before him, hopelessly fighting the Dark King, clamoring for the help that another Sword or even two might give their cause. . . .

Someone was moving near Mark, very near, and his eyes flew open and he started up. Mitspieler was almost within reach, on hands and knees, with his right hand extended toward Mark's bow and quiver that lay nearby in the grass.

The graying, compact man recoiled sharply at Mark's sudden movement.

"What do you want?" Mark demanded.

"O—only a touch, young sir, I bring you only a little touch of something from my master! To anoint your weapons with, that is. See? This!" And Mitspieler held up what looked like a small bundle of dried herbs. "So if you should have need to use your weapons here in the realm of magic, they will not betray you. I fear that before we are through it we may encounter some creatures that are bigger than songbirds."

"All right. Next time say something, don't come sneaking up on me like that." And Mark sat and watched Mitspieler minister briefly to his bow and arrows, then handed over his knife to be given a similar treatment. Meanwhile Mark observed that Ben and Ariane were now seated together, a few meters off, with their heads close together in conversation.

In a little while he was approaching to join them, wiping another drink of fresh water from his lips as he approached. But there was a distraction. Just beyond a nearby bush, Doon was arguing with Mitspieler that *his* Sword needed no extra magical treatment of any kind, and by all the gods it was not going to be given any.

The junior wizard's voice argued with this claim, but took care to do so diplomatically. "Of course that may be so, sir—may I test it to make sure?"

Mark delayed, watching and listening to the confrontation as well as he could.

"What kind of test are you talking about?" Doon demanded.

"If you would just let me hold the Sword for a moment, sir. You need not worry that it will be damaged—ah, thank you." Mark saw that in one hand Mitspieler was now holding a bundle of fresh-cut twigs or withes, tied up with an ornate cord that Mark remembered seeing among the contents of Indosuaros' pack.

Mitspieler went on. "If truly your Sword needs no further treatment to function well inside this realm of magic, then it should repel the twigs when I strike it with them—thus—"

There was a bright flash that startled even Mark, who had been more or less expecting some spectacular effect. Mitspieler yelled, and dropped the sheathed

Sword to the grass. He threw away the twig bundle, which on contact with Wayfinder had burst violently into flame. Then he went after the twigs, and kicked the bundle angrily, to the accompaniment of Doon's loud laughter, until it plunged into the quenching stream.

Mark did not wait to see if Indosuaros might be angry about the burning of his fancy cord, but instead went on to talk to Ariane and Ben. He told them what he had seen and heard of the incident, and it made them smile. But presently they went back to looking grim, as they had when Mark first approached.

Ariane was still taking care of the monkbird, and it sat either on her shoulder, or on a low branch nearby, while she talked.

"It doesn't like this realm of magic any more than I do," Ben observed about the animal.

The girl said: "I wish that I could let it go—I feel that I'm holding it a prisoner, and I know what it is like to be one of those."

"But it has nowhere else to go," said Ben. Then, with a glance at Mark, he asked her: "Why did you delay me at the leap? You put your hand on my arm just as I was about to jump, and I think you saved my life."

"If I did that—I really don't remember why. I'm very glad, of course, if I saved your life, but . . . my powers just work like that. When they work at all."

Mark said: "I'm sure that Doon is counting on them, to help us somehow later on. But I don't know how, or when."

"I wish I could count on them," the girl answered in a sad whisper. "I wanted to come here and look for treasure. I thought it would be . . . I don't know what I thought. Something easy and swift, I suppose, like breaking into a beehive and getting away with the honey."

Mark's face cracked in a smile, as if reluctantly. He asked her: "Have you done that?"

Ariane almost smiled in turn. "I was not raised in a palace. Or even in a house, really. The people who had me in their charge were rough, in many ways. But . . . maybe someday I'll tell you the story. I knew I was a queen's daughter, but mine was not the kind of life that I suppose most queen's daughters have."

They rummaged in their packs and began to share some food. They talked of inconsequential things, until presently they heard the Baron's voice, warning everyone that it was time to get ready and move on.

Doon, in good spirits again, took Sword in hand and determined which direction to go next. Wayfinder directed them promptly into the forest, at an angle to their right, away from the uneven line of the cliffs. There was no path at all to be seen along their route, and Mark routinely began to store up minor landmarks in his memory, to provide a means of finding his way back, as he would have done on entering any unknown wood. They walked through grass and wildflowers, past widely scattered bushes and an occasional upstanding red-rock boulder. The land sloped downward, very gradually, in the same direction they were walking. The stream had sought its own slope, curving away behind them, and was now out of sight. Now there was only the forest, the look of it somehow already monotonous; and now they had put enough of the forest behind them to cover up the last sight of the cliffs.

Presently a sunlit glade appeared, some fifty or sixty meters ahead and directly in their path. Mark looked forward in a minor way to reaching it and being able to take at least a squinting look more or less directly at the sun of the realm of magic. But in approaching the place minor detours were necessary, first around a large stump and its fallen log, then around some trees, and then around a solitary bush. And when they reached the place where he had seen the open glade, there was only the same thick-topped forest around them as before, lit only by small dancing spots of sunlight too small to show you anything but shattered brilliance when you sighted back upward along the ray. Now Mark could see other sunny glades, all of them somewhat in the distance. The Sword led on indifferently.

He was vaguely alarmed by this minor experience, and looked back when they had walked on a few strides past the place. The last landmark he had noted was a large stump with its broken, fallen tree, and already that was nowhere to be seen. Abruptly Mark lost his automatic outdoorsman's confidence in being able to retrace his steps.

Presently they came to the stream again. Of course it might have been another stream of about the same size, but it looked and sounded like the first one, and it came winding its way back across their path from the same general direction in which the first stream had flowed away. The Sword pointed them straight across it, an easy wading.

Ben, walking now behind Ariane, found his attention continually being distracted by the rhythm of her moving body. He had to warn himself repeatedly to concentrate on being alert for possible danger. Though if he thought about it he was not sure there was any point in doing so, because whatever he saw or heard here was likely to be some magical deception. . . .

Somewhere above the trees and the seeming sky there was, he knew, the maze, containing among its other parts the huge turning mass of the Old World wheel and all its nested tunnels. If Mark was right about that, and it seemed he was . . . abruptly, frighteningly, there came into Ben's imagination a picture of Hubert's battered body, bouncing and falling out of this magic sky. There'd be a riffle through the treetops and then instantly a heavy thud—might they be going to come upon it here at any moment, the shattered head still wearing a glowing lamp?

Or would a mangled corpse, here in the realm of magic, look like something else entirely—?

Whatever a man looked at here, or whatever he tried to think about, it seemed that it had to be done in fear.

Doon kept them moving, maintaining a good pace over the almost-level ground. The forest flowed past them, and flowed past them some more. Ben wondered if he should have started counting steps. The sameness of it, he thought, was already starting to make it seem endless.

Once more they approached and crossed the stream. It looked and sounded the same as ever. The ground, Ben thought, was now rising very slightly beneath their feet as they walked on. The sun, as nearly as he could tell from sighting distant clearings, was somewhere near the zenith, making it hard to tell directions that way. But he could have sworn that they were traveling in a straight line, or very nearly so, ignoring the small necessary detours around minor obstacles.

They passed another sunlit glade, off to their right. Birds sang in it, apparently enjoying the vertical sunshine.

Mark called forward to the leaders: "How big is this cave that we're in, anyway? Are we even still absolutely sure that we're in a cave?"

Indosuaros, next to the head of the line, turned his head with an indulgent smile. "Of course we are. But you are not moving through it as fast as you think."

"I'm having doubts that I'm moving through it at all. Can you see the far end yet?"

The magician turned his eyes forward again, and seemed to be gazing off into the distance as he walked. "Even for me," he began confidently, "it is . . . "

His voice trailed off there. In a moment he had stopped abruptly, and in another moment the whole procession had stumbled to a halt. The two wizards went through a session of whispering together, after which both of them continued to stare off in the same direction.

Looking in that same direction himself, Ben could see—or might it be only his imagination—a faint cloud above the trees, or at least a dimming of the sunshine there. The darkening, whatever might be its cause, deepened swiftly and mysteriously. It was passing like a slow wave, from the left of the observers to their right.

All six of the humans could see it now. The monkbird appeared indifferent, but now the people all gave evidence of being able to feel it, too. It was as if the temperature in the forest had dropped, though where they stood the sun appeared to shine through leaves as brightly as before. But leaves hung quiet in motionless air; whatever was passing was not wind. Ben had not the least doubt now that he was underground; the tricks of light and sky seemed poor and obvious shams.

Over there, something...some power...was passing. Passing, yes, thank all the gods! And it was gone.

The first to break the silence was Doon, and his voice was now constrained to a whisper: "What was *that*?"

Indosuaros turned to him slowly. The wizard's face looked disturbingly pale, and sweat was beaded on his brow. "I had not expected this. That was a god."

A murmur went up, as if involuntarily. Most people, including Ben, had never seen a god or goddess in their lives, and had no real expectation of ever doing so. In human society the presence of a deity was somewhat rarer even than that of a king or queen. "Which god?" several voices asked.

The magician answered thoughtfully. "I believe that it was Hades—or Pluto, as most people call him. No one sees him at close range, or face to face, and lives."

"But what is he doing here?"

The magicians could come up with no real answer for that. "Gods go where they will. And Hades' domain after all comprises everything that is under the earth. But he is not worshipped by the Blue Temple,. so we can hope that he is here—somehow as their antagonist—that he will favor our enterprise, if he takes notice of it at all."

Ben was worried. "Then we should make sacrifice to him right away, shouldn't we?"

He had realized for a long time that magicians in general held a low opinion of the efficacy of routine sacrifice and prayer offered to any god; and these two magicians now proved to be no exception. Indosuaros only gave him a look and turned away. Mitspieler did the same, but then turned back to say: "Do something of the kind quietly, for yourself, if it will make you feel any better. I will not. If it had any effect at all, it would only be to draw to myself the attention of a being whose attention I do not want."

Doon was consulting his Sword, which pointed him in the same direction as before, very close to the area in which they had seen the shadow passing. For the first time he hesitated visibly to follow Wayfinder's guidance. Instead he turned to Ariane. "Girl, is that creature ready and willing to fly? If so, send it out ahead."

Ariane whispered to Dart, and in a moment the monkbird was in flight. Its flight path curved slightly to the left, and in a moment it had disappeared among the trees in the very area where the shade of the presence of the god had seemed to linger longest. A few moments later a small cry, faint and mournful, drifted back. It seemed to Ben more a cry of exhaustion than one of pain or shock.

The six people waited, but they heard no more, nor did the monkbird reappear.

"Come, we'll move on," said Doon at last. He looked at Ariane. "It can catch up with us on the way, if nothing's happened to it."

She protested. "But shouldn't we look for it?"

"It has not proved as useful as I had hoped," said Doon. And the tall wizard shook his head. "Not there, not now. If it can come to us it will."

Ariane looked off into the woods on the left for a moment more, but made no further protest. They tramped on, for what seemed to Ben a long time, without further conversation. It was hopeless to try to measure the day by the featureless light that filtered down through the high branches. Ben now had no idea in which part of the sky the sun was, if there was really something like a sun up there at all. It was still full daylight, as it had been ever since they had entered the realm of magic. And it seemed to Ben that they had been moving all that time in a straight line.

At last Doon called another halt for rest. This time he did not sheathe his Sword at all, but sat in the grass holding it and looking at it, and his doubt was plain to read upon his face.

Meanwhile the two wizards had gone a little apart, for what appeared to be one of their regular periodic conferences. But when Indosuaros returned it was to say that he had sent Mitspieler on ahead to scout.

Doon exploded at the news. He scrambled past the other man, looking wildly off in the direction in which the assistant magician had evidently vanished. Then he rounded on Indosuaros. "What's the idea? *I am in command here.* How dare you do such a thing without telling me?"

Indosuaros, instead of lashing back, suddenly looked somewhat ill. He leaned his back against a tree, and then slowly slid down it, until he was sitting in the grass.

"What's wrong with you?"

The graybeard looked up. "It will pass. I advise you to wait for Mitspieler to come back, before you take any action."

"*If* he comes back, you mean. Gods and demons, man! What possessed you to send him off like that without asking me?"

This time Doon received no answer. Indosuaros' eyes were closed, and Ben saw with alarm that the wizard—now the only wizard that the party had available—was slumping down even more, looking as if he were in pain.

Doon gazed round at the other people, as if he were minded to order them to do something, but could not think of what. In a moment he went back to staring after the vanished Mitspieler.

Ariane had sat down too, and her eyes were closed. But she appeared to be only resting or thinking, and not sick. Presently she said softly: "I think it is the magic all around us that makes the old man sick."

"What can we do about it?" Mark asked her the question as if he really thought she might have a useful answer.

"We should get him out of here. But then we can't travel here without guidance."

Doon was looking at his Sword again. Now he swore, and jammed it violently into the ground, instead of putting it back into its scabbard.

Mark and Ben conferred together, but were unable to decide upon a course of action. As they talked, they became gradually aware that the forest around them was growing darker. This was a different kind of phenomenon from the previous darkening. Now the whole sky was slowly dimming, very much as it would at dusk outdoors on a cloudy day.

Indosuaros roused himself a little, enough to assure the others that this was indeed analogous to the natural fall of night outside, and harmless in itself. Then he lay back, putting his head on his pack and muffling himself in his robes as if preparing to go to sleep. Doon approached him as if intending another confrontation, but shrugged and seemed to give the matter up for the time being when he had taken a close look at the wizard's face.

The four people who were still active drank from the nearby stream, and again ate sparingly from their supplies. As darkness thickened under the trees they turned their headlamps on again. In the soft-focused beams the forest around them looked almost reassuringly normal.

Mark wondered aloud if their lights were going to be noticed.

Doon sniffed. "No need to worry about that, I'd say. Anything that's here already knows that we're here too."

They examined Indosuaros again, and as far as any of them could tell, the wizard was sleeping almost normally, though he looked ill. By general agreement it was decided to let him sleep until morning—no one voiced any doubt that morning was going to come.

Night in the forest deepened further, to an utter blackness that would have been unnatural in the world above. The headlamps were adjusted to throw a diffuse illumination and set on the ground spaced around the party, so that they provided light on the surrounding woods while leaving their owners in partial shadow.

The circle included Indosuaros, as well as the four wakeful people who took turns talking and dozing through the night.

It was a long night, and for a long time in the middle of it Ben found himself awake, with Ariane's hand closed tightly in his. The two of them were lying chastely side by side, and her eyes would watch his for a while and then close in rest or slumber. Doon and Mark both dozed, on either side of them, and Indosuaros nearby faintly snored. Ben's right hand kept the girl's right hand enfolded. Her hand was large and strong, and he could feel the calluses here and there on it that testified she had not been brought up in a palace. Most of the time he was not thinking consciously of anything, but was only conscious of her hand, and all the strange miracle of life that flowed inside it. He was glad that she could sleep, and after a long time he slept himself.

When he woke, the air felt a little cooler, and Mark was crawling here and there and turning off the lights. Dawn, or some analogue of it, was once more brightening the sky above the trees.

Presently Doon was sitting up too, and Ariane. In the morning light, swiftly brightening now, they all looked haggard, the men's beards growing untrimmed and unkempt. Indosuaros looked catastrophic. The others took turns trying to rouse him, first gently and then vigorously, but he could not be made to open his eyes or utter anything but moans.

Doon shook him brutally, and slapped his face. "What's the trouble with you, man? What can we do?"

There was only an incoherent mumble in reply.

Doon, more to himself than to the others, muttered: "I don't know whether to leave him here or not."

Ariane protested. "You can't do that."

"We may have to. Do you think we can carry him?"

"And what about Mitspieler?"

"If he's not back by now, I don't think he's coming back."

"The next question," said Mark, "is which way are we going when we do move? Are we still trying to find the treasure, or are we going to turn around and try—"

Doon cut him off. "We are going to find the treasure. We are going to help ourselves to it, and then we are going to find the way out again. I say so, and the Sword is mine, and in my hands. Anyone who says otherwise is going to have to fight me." He glared at them each in turn, and Wayfinder had come into his hands, so quickly and naturally that it seemed to have been there all along.

Ben asked: "And will you fight all of us at once?"

The Baron looked at them, one after another, a long moment for each. "I will fight none of you unless I have to," he said then, in a reasoning voice. "Look here, lads, and you, girl, it's madness for us to talk of fighting each other now. But I think it would be equal madness to split up, or to try to turn back now that we've come this far. For all we know, there may be some easier exit up ahead."

He paused for a few moments, taking counsel with the Sword again, and with himself. Then he said: "The three of you wait here a little longer, with Indosuaros. I'll go alone and scout ahead a little—I have a hunch we may be almost at the end of this damned woods."

"You just said that we should not split up."

"The separation will be very brief. I'll not go more

than a hundred paces before I turn back—see, the Sword now directs me right along the bed of the stream, it hasn't done that before. So, wait for me—unless you prefer to leave the wizard where he lies, and come along."

The others looked at one another. "We'll wait, then," said Mark.

Ben added: "At least for a reasonable time."

"Wait. I'll not go far, and I'll be back." And Doon splashed away downstream, the Sword evidently guiding him, as he had claimed, right along the current's curving course. When he had gone about forty meters the density of the intervening forest hid him from their eyes, and the endless murmur of the stream drowned the sound made by his splashing feet.

The others gathered once more around Indosuaros. "We've got to wake him," Ariane declared. "Or else we really will be forced to leave him here."

The magician's frame inside his robes now looked incredibly wasted, but when they tried to move him he felt abnormally heavy. His breathing was now barely perceptible; his face was wizened and shrunken, and his eyelids as well as his lips had the look of being pinched together by invisible clamps.

Ben turned round suddenly, crouching, motioning the others to be silent. "Someone's coming . . . or something," he whispered. "From upstream. Look out."

They grasped their weapons and waited motionless, concealed in such cover as was immediately available. In another moment, Doon's unmistakable figure had come into view, Sword held out before him like a challenge to the world, splashing toward them from upstream.

The Baron was if anything more surprised than they were. "What is this? What made you come here?"

"We've not moved a centimeter, Doon. Look—the wizard is resting under the same tree as before."

At first, Doon could not believe it. "But—I've kept going downstream ever since I left you." And for a moment Ben thought that the little man might fling his Sword away.

Before any further debate could begin, another approaching figure was sighted. Everyone seemed to discover it at almost the same time. When first seen, in the distance, it appeared to flit and jump among the trees, as if it were part of a mirage. As it drew closer, it could be seen first to be human, and then to be a man; and next to bear in one hand some kind of sword, with which it groped about as if for guidance. And lastly, as it came near, it could be recognized as Mitspieler, walking simply and normally.

Before any one else could say anything, Indosuaros had roused himself, and propped himself up on one elbow. With a faint, glad cry he turned toward the approaching man. "Master!"

Mitspieler's wiry, graying form was unchanged, except that now he wore something that Ben had never seen before, an ornate belted scabbard. At close range it was easy to see that the weapon in Mitspieler's hand was one of the Twelve Swords, but with his grip upon the hilt there was no way to tell which one it was.

As he approached he ignored the first burst of questions directed at him, and at once bent down over Indosuaros, who had fallen back again and was flat on the ground.

A long moment later Mitspieler straightened up

again. "I fear there is nothing I can do for you now," he told the supine man, who did not react and might not have heard.

"What Sword is that you carry?" demanded Doon. His voice was suddenly suspicious. An instant later the Baron's hand grabbed for the weapon at his own side; but that vanished even as he grasped the hilt, turned to nothingness right before Ben's watching eyes.

For a moment Doon stared blankly at the empty claw of his right hand. Then he would have sprung to the attack, with his dagger or barehanded, but for the fact that the Sword, in Mitspieler's suddenly capable-looking fist, was pointing straight at him.

"Do not lunge upon the point, Baron. I may not be able to heal you if you do. Hear me!" And the voice of the graying man boomed out with a sudden authority. "Yes, I have the Sword of Wisdom here. I hope that it will be back in your hand before we leave this sealing, so you can use it when we reach the next — but before I give it back, I require that you hear me."

Doon mastered himself. "Then speak on, and quickly."

"I borrowed Wayfinder a short time ago, under the pretext of testing it. To replace it in your scabbard I left a phantom sword of my own creation — of course the phantom could not really guide you anywhere. But I needed the real Sword to go ahead on my own reconnaissance, and I foresaw that you would not lend it to me willingly."

Doon nodded grim agreement. "In that you read the future well . . . what is your real name?"

"Mitspieler will still do. And his name" — the speaker threw a moment's glance to one side and down — "is really Indosuaros . . . now listen to me, all of you. The god whose presence brushed us yesterday was really Hades. I have just been trying to look for him, to see where he has gone, but I was unsuccessful. I think that he has left the caves completely now. In any case, the way ahead now seems clear for us to go on . . . I take it you are all still ready to go on?"

"We are ready," the Baron told him. "Give me the Sword."

"There is one thing more."

"I thought there might be. Well, speak."

"The treasure *I* seek," Mitspieler said, "is not gold or jewels, and it is not with the gold in the vaults below the demon-sealing, but only on the next level down from this one. I want you to swear, Baron, on your honor and on your hope of wealth, that you will help me get it. I, in my turn, swear now most solemnly and on my oaths of magic, that if you help me I will then go with you and help you however I can, to reach the last level and to prosper there." He swung his gaze away from Doon, to let it rest on Mark and Ben and Ariane in turn. "I swear the same to each of you, if you will help me first."

Doon was shaking his head in doubt. He squinted at Mitspieler as if the man were hard to see. The Baron said: "You and I are now to trust each other's pledges? Now, after you've stolen my Sword? After you've lied to us all along, about—" and he gestured sharply toward the fallen form of Indosuaros.

"I borrowed your Sword, no more than that. Because I had to have it, nothing less would serve. And yes, I'll trust your pledge, if you will swear it as I've said. You are a man of honor, Baron Doon. Swear now, and your blade comes back to you at once. I'll even swear over to you now my share of whatever treasure there may be on the bottom level."

Doon appeared to be impressed in spite of himself by this last offer. "No need to talk of sharing that treasure, man. There's so much—"

"Don't say that until you've seen it . . . as I have, though only in tranced visions. There are certain morsels choicer than the rest. . . . Well?"

Doon made up his mind—perhaps, thought Ben, a shade too quickly. "Very well, you have my word to help you on the level below this one, as long as it does not prevent my reaching my own goal."

"Have I your solemn oath, just as I said it should be given?"

There was a pause. "You have."

And Wayfinder, tossed hilt upward, came leaping toward Doon, so that his right hand had no trouble to pluck it safely from the air.

"Master . . . " The cry was an almost vanishingly faint moan, and it came from the fallen husk of Indosuaros. Ariane was squatting beside him again; she was holding a much shriveled hand, from whose fingers some of the ornate rings had already fallen off.

"There's nothing to be done for him now, girl." Mitspieler, looking down, appeared saddened, but not greatly; he might perhaps have been watching the death of his second favorite pet animal. "Could he have finished this journey, it would have served as his—what is the word that other guilds and professions sometimes use?—his masterpiece. His passport to the upper ranks of magic . . . but he will never be a master now. He simply was not strong enough."

"But what's wrong with him? What is he . . . dying of?"

"You who are not magicians can pass through this sealing freely—provided you can find the way to pass through it at all. But we of the profession, from the moment that we enter, are engaged by the local powers in a continuous struggle. We undergo a ceaseless assault upon our specially developed senses. I am strong enough to bear it. Regrettably, my faithful helper here was not—not without me at his side to aid him."

Doon demanded: "Why did you let him play the leader until now?"

"Oh yes, that. As you must know, Baron, being a leader has its problems as well as its advantages. It elevates one, but often as a target. I could not be sure at first about you and your men, whether or not you were really just the simple adventurers that you appeared to be. There was a whiff of something subtle and dangerous about you—I think now that it was the Sword, no more. . . . Well, Baron, you have it in your hand again. Are we going on, or not? I am ready to follow, if you will lead the way."

Doon, looking half entranced himself, inspected the weapon in his hand. He felt of it, and tried it once or twice in and out of the scabbard. Then like a sleep-walker he raised it ahead of him, moved it to right and left and back again.

"But what about—" Ben, looking down upon the crumpled robes of Indosuaros, began a protest. Then he realized that those garments were no longer tenanted by any human form.

Ariane, reluctant to believe that, lifted the robes

and shook them. A giant spider leaped out and went running away into the grass.

The Sword—the real Sword, for the first time here in the sealing of magic—directed Doon at an angle away from the curving stream. With haggard confidence he followed its guidance again. Mitspieler, having picked up Indosuaros' rings, and taken what he wanted from the contents of his pack, marched second in the shortened line. Ariane was in the middle, with Mark just behind her and Ben to guard the rear.

The real Sword neither followed the stream nor kept to what looked like a straight line among the trees. Instead it subjected its users to sudden and apparently purposeless shifts of course. They walked fifty meters in a straight line, then turned a sharp corner and walked straight in a new direction for forty meters more. This was followed by another turn, after which it seemed to Mark that they moved in the arc of a great lefthanded circle; and yet another change, after which they walked a circle curving to the right. Mark was just beginning to wonder if even the genuine Sword were now malfunctioning, when through the treetops ahead he caught sight of what looked like a familiar line of cliffs.

The rock formation was no more than about fifty meters away when it first became visible; they had hiked no more than a hundred and fifty meters or so from the place where they had seen the last of Indosuaros. Now the Sword guided them rapidly toward the rocks, though their course was still not quite a straight line. Once more the inescapable stream appeared, curving toward the explorers, flowing in the direction of the cliffs. In a few moments they were close enough for Mark to see where the current tumbled precipitously into a cave that opened just at the cliffs' base.

Looking higher on the rocky wall, he tried to locate the entrance through which they had come into this realm of magic, at what now seemed like some time in the remote past. The cliffs looked very much the same, but if the entrance cave was actually here he could not see it.

Doon now led them wading into the shallow water. They followed the course of the stream bed almost to the cave, before stepping out onto a dry path, that switchbacked its way down into the earth beside the stream. The water disappeared now into a jumble of rocks, though the tumbling roar of it stayed with them.

The stream reappeared near the bottom of the dark cliff, its channel now become a complex of artificial basins and waterfalls, followed by a paved ditch at the bottom.

As the false sunlight faded out completely behind the expedition, another kind of light came into view ahead of them. It took them some time to get down near its source.

CHAPTER 13

The reddish light ahead emanated from fierce torch-like flames, flames that sprang from many vents high on the sides of another great cave. These torch-flames appeared to consume invisible fuel, as if they fed on jets of gas flowing somehow from inside the earth. So large was this cave that only parts of it were effectively illuminated by this strange light; its size was therefore hard to estimate, but certainly it was enormous.

Here again the stream vanished. This time its disappearance had an air of permanence, as it dove into a broad pipe or conduit of what looked like ancient masonry, with its intake covered by a heavy, rusted grill; and from this point on even the sound of the stream faded, until soon it was altogether gone.

And here the path completed its descent into this new cave, across a fan of fallen rubble. Mark could make out sections of high wall still standing on either side of the path. It appeared that some defensive works had once stood here, had been breached by some powerful attack, and then had never been repaired. And indeed the dark hillside that the party was now descending looked in the headlamps' beams like some dream of an old battlefield, with fragments of old bones and rusted weapons mingled with the earth and the fallen stones of the wall.

Now, from somewhere ahead, a new sound was suddenly audible. It was dull and thick, heavy and rhythmic, loud as a great slow drum, ominous as a troubled heart.

"Our presence has been noted, I'm afraid," Mitspieler commented on hearing it. "I will do what I can, but I advise you to be ready to fight."

At a distance of twenty meters or so ahead, the cave's illumination was somewhat brighter. There the walls narrowed in, bringing the towering gas-flames a little closer on either hand. At about the same place, the slope of the rubbled hillside gentled, until there ceased to be a slope at all. The drum, if such it was, continued sounding somewhere in the distance. It was accompanied now by other dull, booming sounds, that made Mark think of the stone lids of sarcophagi falling back. He wished that image had not come to him, for now in the middle distance, beyond the narrowing of the cave, he could see long rows of what might be couches, or, in the poor light, elevated coffins. He saw, or imagined that he saw, draped human forms recumbent upon some of these, or perhaps in them. And he thought or imagined that some of these forms were stirring into action as the great war drum quickened its beat slightly . . .

. . . but there were two drums, Mark realized now, and probably no sarcophagi-lids at all. He thought of focusing his lamp's beam into the distance to make sure, but decided not to risk disturbing whoever might be there with a bright light.

Doon and his four followers continued their advance. But now, directly in their path, just at the place where the cave narrowed and the flames were brighter, a limping human form appeared to bar their way. This figure, armed with shield and spear and helmet, was quickly joined by another and another. More appeared, until there were ten in all, all in motley clothing and irregularly armed and armored. Unmatching uniforms, faded or shredded, hung upon unhealthy-looking bodies, some scrawny and some bloated. The thin men were so thin that for a moment Mark feared that he and his companions were about to encounter skeletons animated by some new power of magic; but this impression passed as they drew closer.

The force assembled to oppose them acted more effectively than their first appearance had suggested. When their leader barked a short command it was vigorously executed. Their weapons, drawn and presented now, were in some cases little more than bars of rust, but they were held in firm readiness.

He who acted the part of their officer now slouched a step forward from the center of the patchwork line. "The password!" he demanded, facing toward Doon's advancing group. His voice was a dry croak, as if the throat that formed it might not have been used for a long time. "Give me the password!"

"In a moment," Doon called back, quite calmly. "I

have it here in hand." He brandished Wayfinder. In the near-darkness at Mark's right, Ariane's sling had begun whining its dull song of warning, and the hope passed briefly through his mind that she might be as good as Barbara with that weapon. Mark had his bow in hand already, and had dropped his pack. Now he reached back to draw an arrow from his quiver. He saw Ben's Sword come out. And from the corner of his eye he saw Mitspieler start to raise one hand, and disappear.

The opposing leader snapped out another command, and his ragged rank of followers charged to the attack. They made their move with evident good discipline and determination, though not with overwhelming energy or speed. Mark was able to get off two shots, scoring hits with both, before he had to drop his bow and defend himself at close quarters with his long knife. A moment later the spearman who was menacing him had his thin legs cut out from under him by Ben's Dragonslicer.

Two more of the enemy had already been chopped down by the Baron, and the two struck by Mark's arrows were out of action. From the hands of one of these Ariane had seized a mace, and she was making the air perilous around her with inexpert swings.

The first clash was over, and Doon's party had managed to get through it without injury. Six or eight of the enemy were still on their feet—they must, thought Mark, have received some reinforcement that he had not noticed during the skirmish—and they had retreated now to some little distance, dragging wounded with them. Even as they were trying to re-form their rank, some invisible force began to strike at them. One after another were felled, as by blows from an unseen hand. As the third man went down, the rest scattered in fear and confusion. They cried out alarms as they dispersed back into the shadowed depths of the enormous cave, among the rows of couches.

In the area that they had just quitted, a human form now seemed to materialize out of the air. It was Mitspieler; the wizard was holding a bloodied dagger in one hand as he came strolling back to his companions.

"I think," he called to them, "that the help they cry for may be some little time in arriving. But it will come in great numbers when it does, so we should waste no time. Baron—and the rest of you as well—I now hold you to your pledge. Loan me the Sword again, or else bend your own will upon it, to help me find what I am looking for."

The Baron, like his followers, was picking up the backpack he had dropped to fight. He hesitated only briefly before answering. "And what is that?"

"I am trying to locate a certain member of the garrison, who came here as a robber like ourselves, but more than a century ago. Most likely he is in one of these barracks-beds, but the rows of them look endless, and it could take a long time to find him without the Sword."

"Very well," said Doon resignedly, and gripped Wayfinder with both hands, as if preparing to deal some mighty blow. He stared at the Sword. "Let Wayfinder lead us to him, whoever and wherever he is—and then on to the gold." And he swung the blade's point in an arc, until the power in it signaled to him.

Headlamps probing ahead, the five raced in the indicated direction, between long rows of coffin-couches, and into dim regions that were farther from the torch-flames on the receding walls. Gradually the enormous size of this cavern was becoming more apparent. The bed-pedestals, some of which bore the dead or sleeping forms of warriors, when seen close at hand were not quite like normal beds and not like biers—Mark was suddenly reminded of the worm-addicts' couches in the basement of the Red Temple.

"The garrison is enormous," he commented as they trotted through it. "Where did they all come from?"

Mitspieler, panting as he kept pace, answered. "From parties like our own. Some large, some small, all coming, like us, to pillage the Blue Temple."

"So many?"

"It's been going on for centuries, since before any of us were born. . . . They are bound by strong magic in this portion of the cave, till death releases them. Or until someone brings a stronger magic to their rescue —as I mean to do for one of them today."

"A garrison of enormous numbers," agreed Doon. "But the ones we fought just now did not seem all that tough."

"Some will be tougher." Mitspieler, trotting, panting, shook his head. "Those were only the first pickets. There may well be shock troops here somewhere, an elite cadre . . . though when folk are kept here for centuries, their bodies and minds both must at least begin to deteriorate. That's why I fear what we may find . . . ah, this row now."

They were approaching another angle of the cave wall, where torch flames flared closer and as a result the light was better. Somewhere in the distance the long drum-alarm continued, and Mark could faintly hear the warning cries of the survivors of the first skirmish.

"Too bad," said Ariane, "that our wizard can't make us all invisible." She had discarded her captured mace, and was easily keeping up with the pace set by the trotting men.

"I can do that only for myself," said Mitspieler, "and not for very long." Mark did not think that the strain in the wizard's voice and face was only a result of running. "And it is doubly hard to do when Swords are out. Today I am squandering the saved capital of a hundred years of sorcery. . . . Do not expect more of me in the way of tricks, for I am near the limit of my powers now."

Still the somewhat irregular ranks and files of the couches of the garrison flowed past. The rows seemed to stretch out into a dream-like infinity of gloom, the individual units spaced on the average only two or three meters apart. The pattern of occupation was even more irregular, with whole ranks of unoccupied beds followed by areas wherein most were tenanted. How far could it go on? Mark, tuning his headlamp's beam to a sharp focus, projected it as far as possible into the distance. But it was muffled there by what appeared to be rolling clouds of mist, leaving the far wall still undiscovered.

Doon ordered: "Turn off your lamps! There's some firelight here, we can see well enough without them. No use showing everyone just where we are."

Lamps went off. And then, just as it seemed to Mark that the search might be going to last indefinitely, prolonged by magic like the trek through the forest above, Doon came to an abrupt halt.

"Here. This bed. Whoever he is . . ."

A head of curly hair gleamed darkly in the glow of Mitspieler's lamp when the magician briefly switched it on again. The wizard's hand tore back the rough blanket covering the rest of the recumbent form. The face of the man revealed was very young-looking, and handsome as a god's. The youth's uncovered upper body was compact and muscular, clad in worn clothing that did not appear to be a uniform, and in a few fragments of armor as well.

Mitspieler bent over the young man and took him by the hand. "Dmitry," the magician murmured, in a changed and tender voice. In another moment he had dropped the hand, pulled off his own backpack, and was rummaging in it for magical equipment.

The ritual that Mitspieler chanted now was very brief, and it appeared to have been intensely practiced. The power of it was obvious, for at the concluding words even Mark's dull sense of magic could perceive a passing shock. A convulsion ran through the body of the youth, and in a moment he was sitting bolt upright and blinking blue eyes in the soft glow of Mitspieler's dimmed headlamp.

"Father?" the young man murmured, looking at the wizard. "What are you doing here? And who are these?"

"Dmitry, I'm getting you out of here, bringing you back to the world above. These are my friends, they're helping. The bonds that held you here have been broken. Get up quickly, we must leave. . . . Dmitry, it's been so long. Very long. But you haven't changed."

"Leave? Back to the world? But . . . " Half supported by the older man, Dmitry was already on his feet. In another moment he had pushed the support away and stood alone, though swaying a little on his feet. Like his father he was of low-average height and sturdily built, though otherwise they looked little enough alike. "Wait, I can't leave. Not without my friends."

"What friends? Come on, hurry."

Dmitry lurched back, pulling his arm free again from Mitspieler's grasp. From blankness and confusion, the youth's face had settled into a childish scowl. "They're my friends, I said! I'm not going anywhere without them."

The wizard, his own look of tenderness already gone, glared back at him. "If you mean people from that bandit gang you came here with, forget it. I'm not going to waste—"

"Then I'm not leaving. I mean two men in my squad here, Father, Willem and Daghur. They're both great pals of mine and I can't go without . . . well, hello there." His eye had at last fallen upon Ariane.

Doon had had more than enough. In a fierce muted roar he ripped out an oath. "Who doesn't get moving in the next instant, I'll run him through. Now move!"

Dmitry had by now regained his full balance. He used it to vault back over the bed that he had just left. His weapons, sword and dagger, had been stashed on that side of the couch and he grabbed them up. Smiling happily, he told Doon: "Just who in all the hells do you think you are? I'll move on when I am ready."

Mitspieler, with more than a century of experience to draw on, found gesture and speech to quell them both —at least for the moment. "Put down your weapons, the two of you. Put them down, I say! It would be madness to fight here among ourselves. Dmitry, where are these other two? I'll wake them swiftly if I can."

He turned to Doon and added: "It'll mean two more men with us. Two more fighters."

"All right then. But be quick, demons blast you!"

Dmitry indicated to his father the two nearby couches. The following rituals were if anything quicker than the first had been, but Mark thought that when Mitspieler straightened up from the last one he looked notably weaker than before. "No more," the magician murmured in a drained whisper. "Come, we must move on."

Two loutish-looking men, the latest fruit of his endeavors, had sprung up stumbling to their feet. They recognized Dmitry grinning at them, and pleaded in loud bawling voices to be let in on what was going on. He thumped their backs, and swore at them joyfully. "We're going on to pillage the treasure after all!"

Willem was tall and black, his face a whitened mass of scars as from some old ill-treated wound or wounds. He roared out now in a jumble of oaths that he was ready to follow Dmitry anywhere. "Best squad leader in the whole damned garrison!"

Daghur concurred with this, expressing himself with an eloquent grunt. He was short and pale, with good muscles burdened under a thick layer of unhealthy-looking fat. A horned helmet with one horn broken off sat slightly sideways on his head. His gross arms were heavily tatooed, and many of his teeth were broken.

"But where'd you get the rest of this scum?" he demanded of Dmitry, meanwhile glaring at Mark and Ben and Doon. "What made you think they could keep up?"

"The best I could find on short notice!" Dmitry shouted, hugging the two around their necks. "Never mind them, come on."

"And who's the old one here?" Willem wanted to know.

"Never mind, he'll keep up too!"

"So, it's a revolt, hey, Dimmy? I'm for it, what the hell, let's go." Then Willem broke off suddenly, staring at Ariane. It was as if he had deliberately kept her the last to notice. "Wow. This's yours already, I suppose?"

Mark had observed some time ago that Doon could control his temper very neatly whenever its unleashing or display would not advance his purpose. So it was now. The Baron spoke very quickly and earnestly to Mitspieler, and the wizard, his brow now even a little paler than before, spoke solemnly to his son. Dmitry, with a look and a nod, managed to convey much information quickly to his otherwise obtuse friends. Immediately the little army of intruders and escapees began to move in the direction that Doon wanted them to go, following the Sword. Mark, close behind the Baron now, could hear him murmuring to it as to a woman: "Bring us to the treasure now, my beauty!"

Doon's band was now eight strong, and it followed him at a quick pace. But before the group had gone a hundred strides, muttered warnings were exchanged among its members. Looking off to the right, Mark could now discern another band of people, some forty or fifty meters distant, trotting at comparable speed along a parallel course. The headlamps of Doon's party were turned off, and they could not make out the other group very clearly, but undoubtedly it was there.

Mark trusted strongly in the Sword, and he tended to trust Doon's leadership as well. Mark ran now, keeping up with the Baron, who had accelerated his own strides. But already Daghur and Willem were panting, starting to lag, swearing away in protests what little wind they had. Dmitry too was falling behind, declaring in gasps that he was bound to stay with his two companions — it sounded like a transparent excuse, meant to hide his own poor condition.

Even so they had gained a little on the party running to their right. But now Mark could see yet another force, at about the same distance to the left and also speeding along a parallel course, with torchlight glinting on its weapons. The garrison appeared to be rousing itself piecemeal to meet the incursion. Now someone in the group to the left called out, and Mark realized that those were women.

"Amazons," a voice beside him panted. "Bandits and warriors just like the rest of the garrison. I'd rather face the men."

Doon was not disposed to loiter for the benefit of stragglers, and Dmitry and his two friends kept falling farther back. Mark looking over his shoulder saw that there was now pursuit to the rear as well; whatever they might encounter up ahead, doubling back did not appear to be an option.

And now, directly ahead, another armed, torchbearing contingent was assembling, soldiers moving into position to block the way.

Doon halted, his people stopped around him, all gasping with the effort of the futile run. The enemy array blocking their path was already solidly in place behind its leveled spears, and in itself had some advantage in numbers over the intruders. Certainly the other forces on both flanks and in the rear would have time to close in before any breakthrough could be made.

Now for a little time there was silence in the cave, except for the less and less distant shuffle of many feet, a sound that gradually shuffled into silence; and for the faint sizzle and drip of the torches that a number of the enemy were carrying; and for the slowly quieting breathing of hard-worked lungs.

Now, from the very center of the opposing front line, a grotesquely squat, thick-bodied figure detached itself, and waddled a few paces forward. This man wore an elongated helmet, as if in some preposterous effort to achieve impressive height. His strange, waddling gait made Mark look at his feet, and these also appeared lengthened, by oddly thick-soled boots. Torches on either side of him cast a flickering red light upon his bulbous, red-nosed face. In a hoarse voice this figure bellowed: "Surrender, you scurvy sons of loadbeasts! We have you surrounded!" The sentences were punctuated with waves of a short sword.

Dmitry for once was quiet; Mark from the corner of his eye observed that the youth appeared sullenly downcast. But Doon was equal to the occasion, and put on his best commander's voice and manner: "Who speaks? Where's your captain?"

The squat one bellowed back at him: "I'm captain here! Commander of the bloody garrison of the Blue Temple Main Depository. Field Marshall d'Albarno— ever hear of me?" He rolled a few paces farther forward, into somewhat brighter light, as if he took pride in his bizarre appearance. His face, now more clearly visible, was bloated and spectacularly ugly.

"There's elfin blood in him, I'll bet." The tense whisper came from Ariane, at Mark's side. He looked at her. Elves were only superstition, or so he thought that all well educated people believed.

Field Marshal d'Albarno — Mark, at least, had never heard of either the rank or the name before — was now roaring at them: "So, are you all going to surrender, you bloody lumps of demon-dung? Or are we going to have to hack you all to bits and get our weapons dirty?"

"Aphrodite's armpits!" Doon's answering blast was equally, hearteningly loud. He too knew how to swear, and with some artistry. "Shut your mouth for a moment, wormcast-brain, and listen to me. What's the most important thing there is in life, to you, to me, to any soldier?"

D'Albarno blinked. His almost bestial visage gave evidence of trying to register surprise. "Oh." The enemy commander's voice had diminished to something like mere thunder. "Oh, we're getting to that soon. It's our due whenever we're called up to active duty here, our pay for beating back your damned attack." Again he raised the level of his voice to an inhuman bawling. "Do you surrender, or — ?"

"Vulcan's vomit, man, of course we're going to surrender!" No matter how loud the other got, the Baron so far had been able to measure up. "The only point is this — do we get to keep our weapons, and join you like good comrades in your frolic first? Or do we have to mow down half your company to make you meet our terms? That won't leave you with much strength to enjoy your carousal, will it? And maybe not much time for it either." The last sentence was added in a knowing way, as if to hint at inside knowledge.

The self-proclaimed Field Marshal — he did seem to

wear a number of decorations on his chest—planted his ham-sized fists upon his bulbous and unmilitary hips. He turned his head from right to left and back again, as if calling upon witnesses.

"Now," he mumbled, in a voice again reduced almost to human volume, "there's a man who understands what soldiering's about. It ought to be a joy to have him in the garrison. A comrade I can damned well drink with. I might even be able to endure his stories of his wars and battles. I might even—ho there, put down your bloody bow!" This last injunction was directed at a decrepit-looking archer in d'Albarno's own company who, after much effort with trembling fingers, had gotten an arrow nocked and was not disposed to waste the effort but seemed clearly intent upon shooting into the group with Doon.

"Put it down, I say!" the Field Marshal repeated. "And you, you bloody invaders, fall in with us quickly and come along. I'll send a bloody formal announcement of our victory on to the civilians—but not just yet. The damned joyless slugs have gone into hiding, as they do whenever there's an alert, and for all they know, or need to know, we're still locked in bloody combat. As soon as they realize that you've surrendered, they'll come out of their holes and start preaching to us all, and close the party down. We who have faced death to guard their metal will have our fun restricted, and we'll all be stuffed back into our shells until the next excitement starts. Are you with me?"

Doon pressed him to make sure. "We keep our weapons, then? Until the victory party's over?"

"Aye, all right, until the bloody surrender is made

official. But try to use them, and we'll chop you into
bloody hash!"

Doon signed to his own people to put down their
slings and bows, and sheathe their blades. He put
Wayfinder back into its sheath himself. D'Albarno
gave the same orders, and with a flourish put his own
sword away. Ranks melted. Slowly, suspiciously at
first, the confrontation turned into an awkward, then
a less awkward, march.

What is this? thought Mark. Have we surrendered
or not? He caught Ben's eye, but got no help from the
big man's expression of bewilderment. Doon was
marching beside d'Albarno, the two already conversing as if on terms of old acquaintance. And Mitspieler
seemed to have disappeared again.

The hard-faced Amazon warriors rushed to encircle
Ariane, and welcome her as a new recruit. Mark caught
a last frightened look from her as she was swept away.

At least they were all going in the same direction.

On to the party!

CHAPTER 14

The place of revelry was not completely walled off
from the surrounding cave with its gloomy appearance
of half barracks and half cemetery. Instead it was only
partially separated by head-high partitions, constructed
of stacked barracks-beds, and of piled-up barrels, crates,
and kegs. These containers, Mark deduced, held the
supplies necessary for proper celebration. D'Albarno
had evidently already sent ahead this far at least the
word of his triumph in the field, for the bar was
almost ready to open when his combined force of troops
and prisoners, now mingled almost indistinguishably,
arrived. The bar itself was a crude three-sided enclosure,
built up of barracks-beds, some upside down, stacked
lower than the walls. Smaller stacks made tables nearby,
and single beds simply uncovered served as benches.
The scene was lit by mounted torches.

The only halfway permanent-looking structure in sight was a crude stone fireplace, its sides so low that it was not much more than an open pit. One of the garrison, who was either a minor conjuror or thought he was, was waving his arms to create a spell in hopes of making the smoke rise straight up into the unfathomed darkness overhead. There was a pile of ordinary-looking wood for fuel, brought perhaps from the magic forest on the level above. Over some newly kindled flames a large four-legged beast of some kind was being roasted virtually whole. Turning the spit, and bustling around on various other lowly tasks, were a few of the scroungier and weaker-looking members of the garrison.

Inside the three-sided enclosure of the bar, and setting about more prestigious work, were three beings of a type that Mark recognized at once from Ben's description, though he himself had never seen the like before.

Ben nudged him. "Whitehands," the big man murmured. Indeed the main distinguishing feature of the beings leaped to the eye at once: the huge, pale hands, now at work setting out kegs probably of ale, bottles of wine, crocks of something that might be mead, to judge by the sudden sweetish smell in the air. The strength of those large hands was being demonstrated, yet they looked soft. The rest of the beings' physical appearance also varied from that of common humanity. They had large, staring eyes—the better, Mark supposed, to see in darkness—set in pallid faces. Large ears as well, and worried, thin-lipped mouths. Hair was mostly worn or withered away, and skin was wrinkled. Stature varied, among the three now present, but the average of this small sample was on the short side for humanity. All were in uniform, wearing high-necked blue shirts and smooth short golden capes. Their clothing was immaculate, as compared to the scruffy patchwork garb worn by the military garrison.

The commander of that garrison, the conductor of its most recent successful defense, waddled straight up to the bar. Before he could speak, the tallest of the creatures behind it pounced upon him verbally, asking whether the fighting had been extensive. "It sounded bad, from here. Was there much damage? Costly?"

The Field Marshal roared back at him: "With me and my best people on the job? Not bloody likely! Now bring on the booze, we've earned it. And start the food. And how about some music?"

A shout of approval for this speech went up from d'Albarno's followers, who were already massing just behind him and along the bar. This noise left audible only the last words of the next anxious question from the Whitehand leader: ". . . the prisoners?"

"Of course I've got the prisoners under control! Who's commander of the garrison here, anyway? Not you, you damned white-handed, white-livered blob of money-fat!"

The one who stood behind the bar looked perfectly secure in his own superiority to such behavior, and only distantly offended. "As soon as First Chairman Benambra shows up, I'm going to speak to him about this."

Mark thought that this threat had an effect on d'Albarno. But the Field Marshal was not going to let it show if he could help it. "Speak away," he thundered at the other. "But, until then, you're going to serve us BOOZE!"

Another explosive expression of support burst up behind him. Men and Amazons surged forward to the bar. Those weaker, or perhaps only less desperate for drink, were pushed aside. The Whitehands who had been speaking to d'Albarno nodded fatalistically to his fellows, and he and the others began to pour and serve.

Ben, appearing more bemused than ever, looked over at Mark and asked: "What was that about 'Benambra'?"

Another man answered him before Mark could speak. "Most of the people we get in here recognize that name." This was from one of the garrison, a comparatively healthy-looking specimen, who had been forced close to the prisoners in the increasing crush. (And were we really facing *this* many of them out there? Mark wondered silently. If so, Doon had certainly been wise to do what he did.)

The trooper who had just spoken had by some legerdemain already gotten a filled mug in his hand. He added now: "The first High Priest. You know. There used to be an old song about him, when I was still topside. He's still here, though I bet the cave's changed a lot since he first started hiding Temple treasure in it. You better push your way up there and get a drink while you've still got the chance."

Mark and Ben exchanged another look. Together they began to force their way through the crush, working toward the bar.

The Amazons had come to the party in a group, and this segregation still persisted, though it was beginning to fray out around the edges. Ben kept peering toward their company, trying to catch sight of Ariane. He could obtain occasional glimpses of red hair and a pale face, and from what little he could see of her she appeared to be all right. If she wasn't all right next time he looked, he wasn't sure what he could do about it. Starting a fight would probably be suicidal. So far Doon's strategy, whatever its ultimate goal, was keeping them all from being killed, or enslaved, or even disarmed. But . . .

The talkative garrison man had come along, pushing his way with Mark and Ben toward the bar. He still had his drinking mug in hand, almost full, so he probably had something besides another drink in mind. Standing beside Ben now, he reached out casually for Dragonslicer's hilt. Ben knocked the reaching hand away.

"Neat sword," the man commented, unperturbed. "You might as well hand it over now, and save trouble later. I'm claiming it as spoils. No use my trying to get that headlight of yours, the priests or the Whitehands will latch onto that for sure."

"They will?" Ben couldn't think of anything more helpful to say.

"Sure. Whatever weapons prisoners are captured with are forfeit. After you go through your basic training for the garrison, you can draw new arms from the armory, anything they have available."

"A pile of rusty crap," complained another man nearby, overhearing at least the tail of the conversation.

The first man shrugged. "Maybe you can get something better from the next batch that comes in to rob and gets captured."

"When'll that be?" Ben had now adopted his stupid look. He figured that he ought to keep on talking, while he waited for a chance to do something. He might even be able to learn something useful.

"Who knows? Who can keep track of time down here? Hey, what's going on topside these days? Is Blue Temple in a war? Wish they'd get into a real one, we'd get a lot of recruits down here, I could get a promotion. A war with the Amazons, maybe. The bunch we have is getting a little old." He licked his lips and looked in that direction.

Ben, who before today had never heard of Amazons outside of an old story or two, looked that way again also. Ariane now appeared to have mastered her fears. She was telling some kind of a story, accompanying the tale with sweeping arm-gestures, and had a small audience of warrior-women around her more or less interested. Not far from the slowly dissolving group of women sat Willem and Daghur, who did not in the least look as if they thought of themselves as prisoners, recaptured deserters. They were fraternizing with other men who had to be their old buddies from the garrison. And Dmitry, laughing fit to burst at something, was sitting in the lap of one of the larger Amazons while she drank from his mug.

Doon and d'Albarno, now showing an indefinable but strong similarity despite the disparity in build and features, were sitting with others at a head table, elevated upon some kind of dais. Mark saw the first platters of food, meat sliced nearly raw, were being served there now by garrison youngsters, mostly frightenable-looking Amazon girls. Musicians had now appeared from somewhere, and were at work in their own seats a little below the head table. Whether they played well or badly, or indeed if their instruments made any sound at all, it was impossible to tell amid the general din.

D'Albarno was now obviously telling Doon a story, and from the mammary shapes that the Field Marshal's large hands were sketching in the air, it was easy to guess what kind of a tale it was. Mugs and flagons were passing in profusion everywhere now, and with incredible speed. Kegs and barrels were being appropriated from the Whitehands by main force, and hoisted onto tables to be broached and tapped, as the regular troops impatiently took over the duties of tending bar. Somewhere in the midst of the melee a woman screamed, loud enough to be heard, but more it seemed in delight than in terror.

A man who had been standing on one end of a table fell off, clutching as he went down for the barrel that he and others had been trying to open. The container swayed, wobbled, and fell from the table in its turn, hitting the stone floor with the sound of doom. Liquid and fumes burst forth together in an overpowering flood. People fell and scrambled, and some went down on hands and knees, lapping at the floor. The crush shifted, and the man who had reached for Dragonslicer was borne away in the press of bodies.

Ben had not seen Mitspieler since their capture, and had started to take vague hope from this fact. Now he did see him, seated at the head table, but so inconspicuously slumped among garrison officers that Ben realized his searching eye might well have passed him by before.

Ben fought his way around to the head table, Mark getting slightly separated from him in the process, and approached Mitspieler to try to learn what was going on. At Ben's approach the wizard raised his head, looking exhausted. The small, half-finished drink that sat before him appeared to have knocked him out already.

There was no need to worry about being overheard. Mitspieler had to shout to make himself audible to Ben's ears a matter of centimeters away.

"I went around, invisible . . . tried to wake up everybody . . . thought if we got the whole garrison . . . escape in the confusion." He glared at Ben as if he thought Ben were to blame for the scheme's failure. "Then I lost invisibility."

"You tried your best."

Part of the wizard's reply was lost in the ambient noise. " . . . tried m'best. Tried hard, for a hundred years and more. And there he is. There he stands. So why bother? Never become a father, lad. Never become a parent. It's a great . . . a great sorcery, that's what. Turns your whole life inside out."

Mark, who had managed to get near the leaders at the other end of the head table, now came working his way along to Ben, coming close enough to communicate through the uproar. "We're not yet disarmed. Doon says to bide our time, wait for his signal."

"To do what?"

"That's all he had a chance to say. I'm going back, and stay near him for a little, if I can."

"And I'm going to Ariane." Ben pushed himself away from the dais, into the press.

The Amazons by now were widely dispersed among the general population. They were heavily outnumbered, but even so there was not really that much direct competition for their favor. In truth most of the male garrison seemed more interested in drinking, falling down, and bellowing about their prowess sexual and otherwise, than they did in actually coming to grips with the women. Great bragging songs were going up toward the invisible ceiling, but some of the singers were already flat on their backs.

Between the dais and the place where Ben had last glimpsed Ariane, the floor was even thicker than before with bodies. Mitspieler's tactic might be working, or at least it might help when Doon moved to implement his own plan, whatever that might prove to be. Of course Doon himself might have a hard time getting away from the head table without rousing suspicion. In that regard, one urgency was always possible to plead when a drinking bout was on—there, a few meters past the partitions, away from the center of revelry, floor stones had been taken up to improvise a cesspit, soldiers standing round it in a ring and others waiting for their turn.

A drink was thrust into Ben's hand, and to be a good fellow he sampled it before moving on. The taste was horrible, whatever it was supposed to be, but the potency was certainly above reproach.

Ariane was not really hard to locate. It seemed she had a persistent suitor, a garrison man who was not to be discouraged by smiling appeal, either from her or from Ben, and who went for his dagger when Ben put a hand on his arm a second time. Ben twisted the arm enough to hold the fellow still, then clubbed him on the temple with a fist. Distastefully he lowered the limp body into a sticky mess below a bench; Ben disliked fighting all the more when it had a personal basis.

"I've lost my pack," Ariane told him distractedly, shouting so that he could hear.

"That's all right. Never mind. We're going to try to get out soon. Doon will give us a signal." And somehow she was sheltering in the curve of his arm, though normally she was a centimeter or two taller than he was.

Now she was shouting something else at him. "I'll knife the next one, if he won't listen."

"Not yet. Hold back. Start no blood-fights in here, if you can help it. I'll stay with you. Better yet, you come with me."

With Ariane still muffled part of the time in Ben's protective grip, they struggled back to a place close to the head table. The floor just below the dais was newly awash with booze; maybe, quite likely in fact, at least one more barrel had been dropped and broken. One at least must have been mead. And it was like walking in glue. If they ever did succeed in getting away, thought Ben, it would be impossible for anyone to lose their trail. If there was anyone in shape to try to follow it. . . .

The leaders were sitting pretty much as before. Doon looked up haggardly, but his glance at Ben conveyed nothing of import. At the Baron's side, d'Albarno was at the moment boasting loudly about his capacity for drink, and how he was today going to demonstrate it as never before. In mid-sentence he lost first his train of thought and then his consciousness; few around him paid much attention as he released his grip upon his destiny, and slid already snoring to join a cadre of old comrades who were already nested beneath the table.

Ben, Mark, and Ariane quickly gathered around

Doon, who passed the word succinctly: "Leave here, but separately. We'll meet two hundred strides away, in this direction." And inside the cupped fingers of one hand, held close against the table's edge, the Baron pointed with one finger of the other, indicating a direction that Ben assumed he had somehow managed to determine with the Sword.

The small group split up immediately. Doon himself worked his way along the table to speak to Mitspieler. The others pushed themselves away in various directions through the crush. Ben parted from Ariane with a fierce hand-squeeze, and from Mark with an expressive look.

Ben worked his way through a gradually thinning crowd out to the cesspit. From thence he moved on a curve that took him gradually farther from the celebration. Stumbling as if with drink, he lurched along from one barracks-bed to another. A few of these were tenanted by collapsed celebrants, the others empty.

He paused now and then to try to see if anyone was watching him. As far as he could tell, nobody was. He continued moving in his erratic curve, aiming to reach the rendezvous point from a direction at right angles to the party. After a while he dropped to all fours. He was far from being the only one in that condition, and he hoped to progress even less conspicuously in that mode.

Now all the couches that he passed were empty, and still more garrison troops came streaming and straggling in from the outer reaches of the cave toward the uproar near the center. Of course the noise alone, he thought, ought to be enough to wake anyone within a kilometer, be they asleep, dead, or enchanted. No one paid Ben any attention, and he crawled on.

He was beginning to wonder if he might have misjudged the distance, or the direction of Doon's pointing finger, when he came upon Mark and Ariane, sitting huddled under an empty barracks-bed. From underneath the next bed the bearded head of Doon protruded fiercely, and the Baron motioned Ben to take shelter also and lie low.

He did so and waited. Presently Mitspieler came into view, not crawling but stumbling along in a way that gave an even more convincing portrait of defeat. Approaching together, some meters behind Mitspieler, were Dmitry, Willem, and Daghur. The wizard of course had not been able to leave without telling his son. The son and his two friends were proceeding with exaggerated gestures of caution, preserving a silence that now and then erupted with half-smothered drunken giggles.

Doon's face, as he emerged from his hiding place to survey them, was a study. But, Ben realized, there was not much that the Baron could do. He was still determined on going on—he would not have come this far without a truly fanatical determination—and he had to have the wizard, some kind of wizard, with him on the next level down when it would be necessary to confront at least one demon. And Ben was ready to go on. Now, when he was directly faced with the prospect of unending slavery in the garrison, he himself could not find any distant and still unseen demon all that terrifying. He was not only ready, he was eager.

Almost no words were exchanged. The reunited party slunk off in the direction indicated by Doon, moving directly away from the noise and the crowd, and into regions empty of waking people. Some of the party had lost their packs during their captivity—Mitspieler,

Ben noted, had somehow retained his—but all were still armed. And all had their headlamps, though Doon ordered that they not be used for the present.

Little by little, as the scene of celebration fell farther behind them, they stood up straighter in their march, and became more an advancing group, less a collection of individuals sneaking along in the same direction. Still there was little said among them.

Presently Doon paused, evidently intending to have out his difficulties with Mitspieler; but the wizard urged him on.

"Not here, not now. I know what you want to say, and I am sorry for it. But we must reach the next level before we can pause to talk or argue. And then I must rest, before we can go on."

Doon, after a brief silent struggle with himself, had to agree. The small procession went on quietly. Even Dmitry and his friends were quiet, for the time being. Perhaps, thought Ben, they were all sick with drink.

Now Ben became aware that the cave was narrowing in around them as they progressed. The change was gradual at first, then swift. Doon continued to forbid the use of headlamps, but still it became possible to see that they were headed straight toward a wall, a wall formed not far ahead by the ceiling of the cave coming down in a great curve. Now the side walls closed in even more drastically, and at the same time the floor of the cave tilted into a downward slope. And suddenly they were no longer in the vast and seemingly unbounded room of the garrison-sealing, but had been funneled into a passage only three or four meters wide.

Wall-flames in the cave behind the travelers still

cast enough light here to let them see their way. Now the ceiling was only a few meters overhead, curving sharply down over the high rock shelves that topped the walls on either side.

Doon led them quickly on. The light from behind them was fading rapidly with distance, and soon they would need their headlamps.

"We've done it," Ben said aloud. And just as if the words had been a signal, rock-weighted nets of rope and cord, cast by concealed hands, sprang out simultaneously from the high shelves on both sides of the passage. One of the falling rocks struck Ben on the shoulder with almost numbing force. He had just time enough to reach for Dragonslicer before his arms were tangled completely in the net, but not time enough to draw clear of the scabbard. More cordage tripped him, and he fell.

Someone else's headlamp shot forth a beam, perhaps in an attempt to dazzle the attackers. It might have been a good idea before the net was thrown, but now it was too late. As Ben thrashed and rolled on the rock floor, struggling to get free, he had a good look at Ariane, and a look at Mark. They were both floundering in the grip of some of the attacking Whitehands, a number of whom now came leaping down like clumsy monkeys from the high shelves where they had set their ambush. Clumsy, perhaps, but also strong; and not nearly as clumsy now as were their victims, tangled in the clever weaving of the cords.

Four more Whitehands, large for their kind, now came trotting up out of the passageway ahead. They wore, strapped to their heads, little golden glow-lamps of a kind that Ben had never seen before, and they bore a litter on their shoulders. It was more like a stretcher, really, a mean, penurious-looking equipage.

Ben didn't wait to see what this arrival meant, but continued to roll from side to side, in a furious but so far futile effort to bring his full strength to bear on any of the strands of the net that wrapped him round and bound him down. If he just seized one of the thin cords and pulled as hard as he could, he'd cut his hands to the bone and disable himself from further effort. Maybe he could get hold of one of the thicker ropes properly —

The litter was set down, a few meters away, and a Whitehands, obviously ancient, got himself out of it with some help, and then came to look at Ben and the other captives at close range. He wore a uniform all of gold, the like of which Ben had never seen before.

"Careful, my Founder! Not too close. This one still thrashes."

"You reported that they were already your prisoners, ha hum?" The voice of the ancient one matched his ghastly appearance. He was so pale that the others with him looked almost tanned by comparison.

"Yes, First Chairman, they are." This was another subordinate, who glanced jealously at the first.

"Ha, hum. I think I shall be First High Priest today. Yes, some function in that capacity may be necessary." He was bent, smaller than the other Whitehands and more wizened. Ben was being distracted, despite himself, from his hopeless efforts to burst free.

"Yes," the old man repeated. He was obviously talking more to himself than to his subordinates — though they were certainly expected not to miss anything. "Yes, that fool Hyrcanus has never run things properly topside." And the old man—he was of course an altered human like the others—with his grotesquely large and withered white hands hanging all but useless at his sides, kicked at one of the fallen prisoners. Too feebly, Ben was sure, to hurt. "Well, down *here*, thank Croesus, the man in charge is still Benambra." And one of the impotent huge hands came up with a gesture to flap at its owner's chest.

Now the Founder, First Chairman, First High Priest, bent closely over another captive. "Ah, a fine weapon here, a treasure in itself." A slow straightening of the curved old spine. "And our famous Field Marshal I suppose is drunk as usual after one of these affairs, making ready his report of a dazzling victory. I'm going to have to replace him, I think, after this debacle. Are you sure we've caught them all?

"And we must send word to Hyrcanus to change the passwords everywhere again. . . . I wonder if they have any conception of duty left at all, up there. Prepare these captives for induction processing and then basic training. Let me see the inventory of their possessions when you have it."

There was more, but Ben heard almost none of it. He heard Doon shouting something, and then another Whitehands, capering before Ben with a wizard's gestures, bent down to blow a dusty powder into his face. With his first sneeze, the world was gone.

He was being awakened, for what must be the first watch of the morning. He was going to have to drag his body out of this uncomfortable but oh-so-welcome bed. . . .

No, it wasn't first watch that he had to get up for.

He had just signed up for Blue Temple service, and he was still in basic training, and he faced another day of that . . . at least his shoulder didn't hurt him so much any more, time had healed it. Ben moaned and grumbled to himself. Today he'd try to get another letter off to Barbara, if there was a caravan going that way, and he hoped that this time she might answer. . . .

"Still sleeping, hah?" *Thud*. The sergeant had come back.

Kicked off his wooden barracks-bed, Ben managed to extend one leg and one arm toward the stone floor, enough to partially break his fall. Picking himself up, feeling bruised, he noticed an odd thing: his bed was a different kind from the one he seemed to remember rolling into the night before. Odd. And, wasn't the sun up yet at all?

Then, with a jolt like that of falling into nightmare, much became clear. Ben realized that he was still in the cave. The horror and fear of the recapture returned. And he understood dimly that this was far from being the first time that he'd been awakened in this way, in this dark place. But whatever had happened to him after those earlier awakenings had already been lost again in the mists of dark magic that fogged and clogged the workings of his memory.

Get dressed . . . no, he was dressed already. It was his own clothing, but now all sadly soiled and worn and tattered. Too much damage, he thought, to be accounted for even by all the things that he could remember happening to him since that unlucky hour when he had followed Doon into the upper cave. . . .

Doon, yes. And Mark, and Ariane. And all the others. Where were they, what had happened to them?

The other figures stumbling and cursing around Ben in the darkness now were all strangers to him. His fellow trainees, or fellow prisoners, but he remembered none of them at all. None of them spoke to each other as they formed a crude queue and groped their way through the darkness, on their way to . . . all that Ben could remember, and that dimly, was that to please the sergeant they were expected to go somewhere and line up in a formation.

Dragonslicer was of course no longer at Ben's side. Sheath and belt were gone too, as were his headlamp, and his pack, and the simple little dagger that had been his only other weapon.

The dead weights of training and of fear were back now, hanging on him as a compelling burden. Ben stumbled into the formation with the group of unfamiliar men. Somehow he knew which place in which line was his. In a flash of something like clarity he realized that all of these could hardly be newly taken prisoners. Perhaps this was some kind of a punishment company . . . but it hardly mattered.

Their drill-ground was quite small, a space lighted by torches at its four corners and cleared of barracks-beds and other obstacles. Here in their small formation they practiced marching, and drilled with clumsy wooden spears.

The sergeant wore no badge of rank, but there was no doubt of who he was. He acted like a sergeant, striding through the ranks, barking commands, inspiring terror, yelling and kicking at anyone who displeased him. The drill went on unendingly. It had always been going on, thought Ben, and it always would be, and even that last sleep from which he could remember being awakened was really only one more illusion born of magic. Nowhere could Ben find the foothold of hope that he would have to have to be able to rebel against the sergeant's orders.

He didn't know where he was, except that he was still inside the cave. Which way was out? And where were the other people who had been captured with him? Were Ariane, Mark, Doon all dead? He tried once to ask a question of the sergeant, and got a curse and a kick for answer.

The drilling and the marching went on and on. There was a mindlessness about it that precluded even sadism as a motive. It was, like most basic training, utterly pointless except that it instilled the habit of instant obedience to command, and it filled the time.

At last there came an end, or at least an interruption. Ben was allowed to return to his barracks-bed and rest. But it seemed to him that as soon as he had closed his eyes, he was aroused again, and made to stagger back to drill some more, this time for an even longer period than before. He felt beyond exhaustion, as if his body and mind alike were struggling through thick cotton padding. He was caught in some mesh of magic, so that he hardly knew any longer who he was, or had been, or whether this existence constituted suffering or was only the standard of the universe, with nothing else left in the universe to judge it by.

March and rest. Drill and rest. Then march again. The real merged with the unreal. Ben told himself that he was dreaming this horror, he had to be. Or else all the rest of his life, before his entrance with Doon into the cave, had been a wonderful but lying dream.

Voices, some real and some fantastic (and no way of telling which was which) taunted him with the thought that never again would he see Ariane. Never ... except, perhaps, just once a century or so, he'd be able to catch a glimpse of her across the battlefield during some brawl, and would see how the long decades as an Amazon had changed her. He would still know her, by her hair if nothing else. And then after the battle he might be able to see her across the hall of celebration, with foulness unspeakable and impassable filling all the space between them ...

... and from time to time he was allowed to tumble back into his barracks-bed to rest. When his eyes closed, he feared to dream, and dreaming he feared even more to wake.

He knew that somewhere, in the real world, whatever that might really be, many days at least were passing.

Benambra, the First High Priest, came in a litter and looked at him once, and said something through withered lips, and smiled and went away. . . .

From time to time Ben was allowed, or perhaps compelled, to sit at a table in a dimly lit space called a messhall, where stuff was put before him on a plate. He really couldn't think of it as food. Slop, worse than anything that the Blue Temple had ever tried to feed him as a recruit topside, his first hitch. This was the second time that he'd been taken into Blue Temple service, and if they ever found out, ever realized who he was and how that first hitch of his had ended ...

But usually Ben was too stupefied to even worry about that.

Just as he was allowed or perhaps compelled to eat,

so it was with his dreams. Sometimes the dreams that were permitted or inflicted were not ordinary nightmares, but instead strange yearning visions in which Ben walked again the sweet fair earth above, and never thought of gold, and saw the face of Ariane. She was free too, and smiled at him. Once or twice there appeared a short man with a clown's painted face, wearing a gray cloak, who laughed and pointed as if it were all some happy joke. Then the next thing Ben knew, *she* was with him, holding his hand and smiling, asking him where he wanted to go next.

. . . and next he would wake up to darkness, and the groans of someone else bound down in magical punishment nearby.

Oh yes, he would be allowed to see her again someday. On the battlefield, as the tormenting voices told him. And after the battle if he still lived (maybe after he'd watched her die) he'd be allowed his drink, allowed to joke and bellow with his comrades, to fall down drunk, gradually to forget that once he had been someone else.

While he was actually drilling or marching, lucid moments were allowed to him more often. And in these moments Ben was able to swear solemnly to himself that he would never fight for the Blue Temple. But even as he swore he feared the compulsions that were being put upon him, that would leave him no real choice when the time came. He might once have sworn that he would never endure the kind of existence that he was enduring now. *When the time comes, you'll fight all right. Or die, and you won't want to die.* Who had said that to him, the sergeant? And truthfully life was precious, even now.

Then without warning there arrived a day and an hour when the mists of magical compulsion were wiped away. Ben was sleeping, then he was awake, and in a moment it was as if those mists had never been, even though when he opened his eyes the cave and the barracks area of the punishment company were still as hideously real as ever.

Ben was allowed to stand up from his bed as his own man again. Two sober Whitehands were standing nearby, holding torches, so that he had to squint in unaccustomed light. Also nearby there crouched a large, gray warbeast, a catlike creature bigger than a man, who hummed an intelligent warning growl at Ben.

Another figure, human, stood beside the beast. It was real also, someone Ben had never seen in dreams.

Not Ariane who had come for him this time.

Radulescu.

"Ben of Purkinje, we meet again. Keep quiet!"

The command at the end was really unnecessary. Seeing this, and smiling faintly, the officer made a gesture. One of the Whitehands moved off obediently with his torch, showing Ben which way to go. Ben followed automatically, thinking as he moved that Radulescu looked good, looked fit and healthy, his small beard neatly trimmed, his clothes and his body clean. Before Radulescu fell into step just behind him, Ben had time to see that there was a sword—the same sword he had once tried to draw, just outside the cave?—at the officer's belt. And he was wearing what looked like the same officer's cloak of gold and blue, though it was dry now and the hood was lowered. Despite all greater considerations, Ben instantly felt the contrast with the way that he himself felt and smelled and must appear.

He was quite clearheaded now, in control of his own body and his own thoughts. But with the warbeast sniffing at his heels as he walked, he was really no freer than before. Unless he wanted to decide to end things quickly now, before Radulescu's interrogation and revenge could start—but no, it was unlikely that the beast would kill him quickly, unless it were ordered to do so. Warbeasts were intelligent enough to handle fine gradations of command.

They had walked for only a hundred meters when, to Ben's faint surprise, they came upon Mitspieler and Doon, looking as shabby as Ben felt, also under guard and apparently waiting for the arrival of Ben and Radulescu. Here another warbeast and two more Whitehands were in attendance. There was enough torchlight now for Ben to see, at some distance ahead, the great curve of the cave's ceiling coming down to make a wall. It looked like the same place where they had been captured—but then, the different sides of this cave might look much alike.

Ben came up to where the others were and obeyed an order to halt. Now he saw with a shock of mixed feelings that Mark and Ariane were waiting nearby also, sitting in what had been the shadow of an empty bed and was now torchlight. They looked up as if they were glad to see him, but said nothing. Ben saw in Mark's familiar eye that there was some news— something important, but not to be told now. For right now, only a warning to play dumb.

And there, sitting in another shadow, were Dmitry, yes, and Daghur and Willem too. Ben thought that he

understood now. All the members of Doon's party
were being transferred to some special lock-up. Their
break-in had been relatively successful, and he, Ben,
was involved in it, and now the priests were going to
conduct an investigation into the whole mess.

Right now, he couldn't help welcoming as a relief
anything that took him out of basic training.

What was happening now? Ben looked round, and
realized that Radulescu was in the process of dis-
missing the Whitehands, all four of them evidently.

"I can manage well enough from here on. I have the
beasts."

One of the pale attendants looked worried. "But
sir—"

"You heard my order."

"Yes sir."

The warbeasts no longer looked ready to pounce on
Ben immediately. He risked a cautious step, that brought
him close enough to Ariane to whisper to her. "Are you
all right?"

"Right enough," she whispered back. He thought
her tone was somewhat sprightlier than it had a right
to be, as if she possessed some encouraging secret. Or,
he supposed, she might still be drugged.

She added: "How are you?" The way she asked the
question indicated that she cared about the answer.

Ben thought about how he was. He felt of his
unkempt beard, brushed back his filthy hair. He was a
mess, hungry and weary, but basically he still felt able
to function. "By Ardneh, how long have we been here?"

"Many days." Still her voice was lively.

"How many?"

She picked up the real meaning of his question.

"No, it's been days only, not months or years. It could have been that. It would have been, except . . . "

Ariane let it trail away there, but not unhappily. Smiling faintly, she looked up past Ben. Radulescu, a torch in one hand, was approaching, while behind him the four Whitehands and their other torches were receding into darkness, going back toward the central cave.

Radulescu with a gesture made his two warbeasts lie down and relax. Grinning crookedly at Ariane, he pointed at Ben and said: "Here he is."

"Thank you," she answered calmly, and got to her feet, brushing mechanically at her filthy trousers as if to dust them off. "Now I am ready to go on."

For Ben, the last to be set free, there were still some moments of confusion. He didn't really understand what was happening until Doon, after a quick talk with Radulescu, had begun to harangue the others again in his old fiery way:

"You all look so astonished! Why? Did you think I was dim enough to come seeking treasure in a place like this without being able to expect help along the way? I'd have had to be as stupid as the rest of you to take a chance like that. The colonel here's been planning with me for more than a year now on how to rob the treasury. He's able to get in by himself, of course, but not to get away again with a proper load."

As Doon spoke, he squatted down and began to unwrap a large bundle that Ben only now took notice of. It had been lying at Radulescu's feet. There were weapons in it, Ben observed dully, and backpacks, and headlamps too. People began to crowd around to help themselves.

Ben took a step forward, and Radulescu was standing just in front of him with a Sword . . . unbelievably, the officer was handing Dragonslicer back to him.

Radulescu said: "I'd not part from this so readily, you understand, if I didn't know there's even better down below. And you and I are comrades, partners now." It almost sounded as if Radulescu himself believed the words. "We are in this enterprise together."

"Aye." Ben swallowed. "It seems we are. I had no wish to hurt you, that time, throwing you into the cave and down the stairs. It was just that I had to get away."

The officer nodded. "I must concede that, the necessity of it from your viewpoint, I mean. Well, I hold no grudge." But it was still an officer speaking to an enlisted man, thought Ben; there had been no offer to shake hands.

Doon, looking large and whole again with Wayfinder back in his grip, was trying out its powers. He conferred briefly with Mitspieler—getting, Ben supposed, confirmation that this was the genuine article that he now held, and not another phantom.

Then the Baron approached Radulescu, and with something of his old testiness wanted to know why Radulescu hadn't warned him about the step-trap in the maze. "I lost a man there, and it came near pitching me into the underworld, in more ways than one. I can understand about the password for the magic-sealing; it would have been changed, and you had no chance to give me the new one. But that step—"

Radulescu waved an authoritative hand. "I would have cautioned you on all the traps, of course, could we have held our final meeting as we planned. But I've spent most of the last three months in what amounted to house arrest. I had no hope of getting word out to you. It would have been suicide to try."

Doon nodded. "That's what I hoped. I mean, that nothing worse had happened to you. When the big man here told me the name of the officer he'd thrown down into the upper cave, well ... but even then I couldn't think of giving the attempt up. Not really."

"I didn't suppose you would. I wasn't really terribly surprised to find you where you were just now."

Suddenly Doon was looking more sharply at Radulescu. "What're you supposed to be doing down here now?"

The other chuckled. "Why, I'm thinking up new ways to protect the treasure, naturally. The Chairman told me to spend some time down here and study the problem thoroughly. He has proven to his own satisfaction, after lengthy investigation, that Ben of Purkinje here and I are not involved in any robbery plot together — ergo, I am not involved in any robbery plot at all, and am therefore the most freshly proven innocent of all his trusted lieutenants. Ergo again, I am the one to be trusted with this job. Hyrcanus wants results; he has virtually put me on probation until I can think up some real improvements for the security system. Maybe I'll leave a list for him when we depart." Now it was Radulescu's turn to ask a sudden pointed question. "Do you have some means of hauling away the treasure? Did you bring a ship?"

"There's a vessel, magically concealed, standing by for us — I hope." Doon glanced toward Mitspieler. "Nay, I'm sure it will be there. But if we have to haul the gold on our backs all the way up from the lowest level, back through the six sealings, I don't know how much . . . "

Radulescu smiled mysteriously. "As to that, we may be able to find some better way, when we get down below."

Ben, wondering what that might mean, exchanged a look with Mark. But they could hear no more of the dialogue. The co-leaders had turned away, to conduct the next part in muffled privacy.

Ben sighed. He noted how Dmitry and his father were glaring at each other. And how Willem and Daghur, giggling together about something, sat waiting to be told what to do next so they could try to make a joke of it.

CHAPTER 15

Armed again, with headlamps glowing and the two warbeasts loping peacefully alongside, the party pushed on. Mark was sure now that they were retracing the path that had previously led to capture. They were moving quickly. Divided into small groups, they were united at least in the wish to leave this level of the cave before Benambra or someone else awoke to the fact that they were again escaping. Radulescu had said that there was a good place to rest not far past the entrance to the next lower level; they would reach it soon, and before entering the area where the demon was usually encountered.

Mark, in hurried conversation with Ben and Ariane, soon learned that their experience in captivity had been much like his own: drug- and sorcery-induced drill and marching. Looking back on their capture, they discussed what they might have done to avoid it, but could come up with no really good ideas.

"At least we have an experienced guide this time," Mark murmured to Ben, who walked beside him.

"Aye. And trustworthy—at least until he gets the use he wants out of us." Ben paused. "He would rather have left me where I was, just now." He looked at Ariane, walking on his other side. "I thank you, for refusing to go on until I was released. That's what happened, isn't it?"

"She did the same for me," said Mark. "And I'll thank her again now. Ben, neither of us was really wanted on this part of the trip—unless Doon's Sword pointed to us again, before he lost it . . . anyway they must have decided that we'd be useful to carry treasure, and use weapons when needed. But they definitely wanted the young lady here, so much so that they brought us along just to please her. They'll take great pains to get her to cooperate. And they seemed much relieved when Mitspieler's magic gave assurance that her virginity had not been lost."

Ariane observed, "They still think that I have powers that are going to help them somehow." She looked to her right and left. "I may require more in the way of thanks, from both of you, before we're done."

"You'll have it." And Ben took her briefly by the hand.

They were passing now under the high shelves, from which, this time, no ambush sprang. The sides of the passage narrowed in on them and the floor turned down. Now they were entering territory that was unfamiliar to all of them save Radulescu. Doon, as if he had some reservations about blindly following the priest's guidance, had now drawn Wayfinder and was using it to make sure he was on the right path, even though the chance of going wrong here seemed remote.

The descent of the passage steepened, and its floor became a stair. The tunnel was fairly well lighted here, by small gas flames set at intervals along the neatly finished stonework of its walls. They might, Mark thought, almost have been inside some fort or military guardhouse on the surface. The walls here showed a different workmanship than that of the maze or the other, upper regions of the cave complex. Of course there was no reason to assume that the whole place had been dug out or finished at one time, or under the direction of a single planner.

The stair was forty or fifty meters long, with most of its length in one smooth descending curve. At its bottom the passage leveled out, and then ran for another forty or fifty meters before branching into two. Here Radulescu with a small gesture directed them to the right.

Doon's Sword must have indicated otherwise, for instead of turning at once he paused, looking at the other questioningly.

"The place of rest," said Radulescu patiently. "Looking at you, I can well believe that you all need it."

The right-hand way led through a constricted doorway into a rough cave chamber, perhaps fifteen meters broad and twenty deep. Large rocks made an irregular litter around the sides; there was a clear area of sandy floor in the center, and a sloping ceiling. Mark could hear water running, and when he turned the beam of his headlamp toward the rear of the room he saw the pool. It was fed by a small stream that leapt from a crevice in the upper rocks, then gurgled away on the other side of the cave to provide drainage. Probably it was the same stream, here somewhat diminished, that they had encountered earlier on the higher levels of the complex.

The warbeasts went immediately to the pool, and began lapping at it thirstily. Most of the human members of the party hung back a little, watching without comment as Mitspieler went to the water. First he touched it, then tasted it, and at last drank some of it himself. Soon the whole party except Radulescu were drinking, filling water bottles, and making an effort to wash up. Mark, able at last to rinse what he hoped was the last taste of messhall garbage from his mouth, began to feel more like the person he had been when he first followed Doon into the upper cave.

After drinking, Mitspieler washed himself minimally. A few seconds later he was stretched out sound asleep, his head pillowed on his pack. His face in repose wore a look of total exhaustion, that brought to it a resemblance to the countenance of Indosuaros in that wizard's last hours. Mark's imagination worked briefly on the question of what kind of basic training a captured wizard might be given in the garrison; but he got nowhere with it and soon gave up.

Everywhere people were opening their packs, in search of real food. Nothing seemed to have been stolen from the packs, or spoiled. To people who had subsisted on prisoners' fare for many days, the field rations seemed like a banquet. Dmitry, who had never had a pack, rifled his father's, taking deft care not to disturb its owner. He shared his loot with Daghur and Willem, but only on demand, and somewhat petulantly.

Mark, sitting on a rock and chewing on some dried fruit from his own supply, found himself gazing into the eyes of Radulescu. The officer, sitting nearby, was wearing an air of patience—rather, thought Mark, like a man allowing his herd of beasts to drink and graze a while before he whipped them on.

Obeying an impulse, Mark asked the officer suddenly: "What made you decide to rob what you were guarding, and join forces with the Baron?"

Probably Radulescu was surprised by what must have struck him as impertinence. But he made no objection, and answered promptly enough. "Have you seen Benambra?"

"Aye. It was he who led the Whitehands who took us prisoners."

"Well, I have seen him too. And it was my first look at him, about a year ago, that made me decide to rob what I was guarding, as you put it. Seeing just what I had to look forward to, if I worked diligently as a good officer, and was clever, devoted, fanatical, and lucky enough to rise to the very top of the Blue Temple hierarchy."

The rest stop went on longer than the leaders really wanted. Doon and Radulescu were soon sighing and fidgeting, walking about nervously. But Mitspieler continued in a deep sleep, and Doon when he looked at the wizard's face decided not to wake him, despite what were evidently the Colonel's whispered urgings that he do so. The others meanwhile were ready to take advantage of whatever time for rest they were allowed.

When Mitspieler did awaken, it was suddenly. And perhaps of himself; Mark, who happened to be watching, thought it was as if some unseen power had whispered into the wizard's ear. The man sat up, alert from the start. His first look, a grim one, was aimed at his son. Then he cast a speculative glance toward Ariane.

Getting to his feet, Mitspieler asked Radulescu: "Have you the password that we'll need to get past the demon?"

"I have, of course. I would not have come down into the caves without it."

"And you're sure it's not been changed since you came down? Hyrcanus on the surface can change it at any time, can't he?"

Radulescu frowned at this. "Of course he can. But he won't, he knows I'm down here. If he had wanted to get rid of me, he wouldn't have done it that way."

"I'm not so sure." Mitspieler looked at the officer meditatively. "The Whitehands don't need a password, naturally."

"Naturally not. The demon is magically compelled to ignore their comings and goings. The only ones who need a password are normal human visitors." Radulescu smiled. "Like us."

Mitspieler sighed, and seemed to discard his misgivings, whatever they had been. "Well and good then. Let's get on."

In a matter of moments everyone had packed up, and the party was moving on, with headlamps lighted against the darkness that Radulescu warned was just ahead. Mark felt uneasy at the thought of his first encounter with a demon, now soon to come, even though he was basically confident of Radulescu's magical protection.

They had only just left the cave of rest, and were passing the place there the tunnel branched, when a faint sound like a distant yell came drifting down the tunnel that led to the level above.

The leaders muttered briefly to each other, then ignored the sound and moved right on.

Ben asked Mark: "What was that? An alarm?"

"If it was, we're past it now. We might as well move on."

"If they're looking for us up there, we'll run into trouble coming back."

Radulescu had heard this, and turned his head long enough to be reassuring. "There will be ways. I know the caves, backward and forward and inside out."

"But maybe someone besides you has discovered that the dragon's missing. And the entrance stone's been enchanted, so it can be lifted from the inside."

The Colonel frowned. He dropped back a little to walk with them. "Of course, I discovered those things. That's why I felt sure I'd find you all down here somewhere. But I was alone. There are no regular patrols on the surface; Hyrcanus is dozing, as usual, in blissful ignorance. And Benambra, if he's been given any report at all on my taking you away, thinks I'm marching you off to interrogation somewhere. He's fairly bright, but he'll be kept busy for a while yet, disciplining the Field Marshall and his merry men, or trying to do so. Trust me, I know the workings of this place."

The party advanced, but more slowly now, the leaders

proceeding with caution. The tunnel they were following soon opened up on the top and one side, to become
a mere ledge that clung to the face of an underground
cliff. The cliff's smooth face rose vertically here for
about ten meters, and grew higher as the path continued its gradual descent.

The outer edge of the winding path was protected
by a knee-high stone wall, and beyond this wall a
slope went steeply down into the dismal darkness of a
dry ravine. A few meters beyond the ravine, another
cliff went up to meet the roof. The slopes were littered
with fallen rocks. Mark expected to see more bones
among them, but discovered something else. When he
turned his light fully on one strange object he realized
that it was either a grotesque doll, or a human body,
clothes and all shrunken to the size of a withered
child. But once it had been bearded like a man.

"One of Dactylartha's victims," said Ariane, walking beside him. Her voice was more dreamy than
afraid.

"Dactylartha?"

"That is the demon's name."

"How do you know?"

She didn't answer. The two warbeasts were uncomfortable now, prowling first ahead of the human party,
then hanging back. Radulescu had to call them frequently to keep them close to his side.

The air in here smelled strange, thought Mark. No,
it was not so much a smell as it was a feeling, as if the
temperature were uncomfortably high. Or perhaps
low. . . .

"He leaves his victims so?"

"Some demons do. Others . . . do other things, perhaps even uglier." Her abstracted voice perturbed him.

"What do you know of demons? Where have you ever met one?" This was from Ben.

Again Ariane did not answer. She walked on, moving steadily and smoothly enough, yet almost as if entranced. Mark and Ben exchanged a momentarily helpless look behind her back.

The . . . wrongness . . . in the air increased. Mark had heard that demons sometimes advertised their proximity so, but he had not felt the effect before. Looking at the others, he thought that now it was bothering them all. Except for Radulescu, who might be used to it, and perhaps Doon, whose pride probably refused to let a feeling of illness show. Even Mitspieler, who presumably could defend himself to some extent, looked paler than before.

Now the officer stopped and turned. With a gesture he stopped the others, who were now all following him at a distance of a few paces. "Wizard, you come forward with me, if you will—just in case, as you suggested, there is some difficulty about the password."

"Why should there be?" demanded Doon.

Radulescu doubtless would have liked to ignore him, but knew better than to try. "I don't know. But just in case. The rest of you wait here. Imp, come with me, lad." This last was addressed to the grayer and larger of the warbeasts, which whined at the command but reluctantly obeyed.

Seven humans and one warbeast waited, while Radulescu, Mitspieler, and Imp went on, following the ledge around the next bulge of the cliff. Mark did not know exactly what he was expecting to happen next, but what did happen surprised him. It began with a show of multicolored lights, playing on the far wall of the cave, thirty meters beyond the ravine.

For a moment there was little to hear. Then some words, indistinguishable, cried out in Radulescu's voice. Then a frightening bass tremor, and screams in animal and human voices.

The animal did not reappear, but the two men came into sight, reeling and staggering back along the path. Mitspieler turned once, gesturing behind him, as if he might be hurling invisible weapons from his fingertips.

Those who had been waiting needed no urgings, no spoken warning, to turn and run. Ben dragged Ariane, who was screaming something and seemed for a moment hesitant, along with him. Mark, taking one final look over his shoulder as he fled, saw Mitspieler with gestures erecting a haze of magic on the path, then turning to run also, with Radulescu. Beyond the two running men Mark saw the figure of the demon, looking itself like a tall man clad in dark armor. And the strangest thing of all about the sight was that the very rock of the path seemed to be stretching and sagging beneath the demon's feet.

Doon, running unabashedly in the lead as ever, had his Sword out, held in front of him. And Mark was sure that he was not willing it to find him treasure now, but refuge.

"The cave!" someone shouted. Mark saw Doon turn hard to his left, and leap into the room in which they had just been resting. The others went pounding after him, in headlong flight. Mark, running right after Ben and Ariane, was the last one in before the wizards. Just before he entered, he was almost knocked off his feet by the remaining warbeast, which was running about insanely, across the path and up and down the slope.

The two wizards, sobbing for breath, made it somehow, and threw themselves down just inside the narrow doorway. They grabbed implements of magic from their sleeves and pockets, and from Mitspieler's pack. Gripping these, their four hands wove across the opening a fine net of magic, whose substance seemed to be drawn into being right out of the air itself. They completed it none too soon. There sounded heavy footfalls, right outside the door, and the feeling of sickness and wrongness that heralded the demon reached in insidiously to grip them all.

But the pressure remained bearable. "We are safe, but only for the moment," Mitspieler gasped.

"The password," Radulescu panted, "must have been changed." And he dug yet one more object from his pocket, and used it as if in afterthought to strengthen the defenses of the doorway. What filled the doorway now had the look of translucent paper, or thin cloth; but it was evidently stronger than it looked. Dactylartha was trying to do something to it from the outside, but so far it gave no sign of yielding.

"Of course it has," said Doon coldly. "So Hyrcanus must be out to kill you after all. That means he's aware of the whole plot, now."

Radulescu stared at him. "Even so, we can still get away, if that ship you promised is truly waiting for us."

"And if we can get out of this room without being devoured. Tell me, you who know the caves forward and backward, how do we do that?"

The Colonel was saved from having to answer, at

least for the moment. For now the demon's voice boomed forth from beyond the door, smothering all other sounds. "Come out, humans, come out. A pair of warbeasts make but a small meal, and I am starved. My hunger cries for human minds and bodies."

Inside the cave all was silence for a few moments. Then Ariane in her little girl's voice offered: "I was taught a charm of old white magic, once, when I was small." No one bothered to reply to her. All eyes were on the wizard, and the priest of the Blue Temple.

Mitspieler let out a small sigh. "We have done all we can to seal the door. It will not be enough, for very long." Then he turned to Doon and spoke deliberately: "I think it is time now."

"Time for what?" Mark wanted to know.

But Doon understood, and he was ready to explain. His manner, as much as his words, served at first to calm the others.

"The failure of the password need not be fatal. Mitspieler and I — and Indosuaros — considered the possibility of something of the kind happening, before we ever came near the cave. We knew we needed some other method of getting past the demon, to fall back on. And Wayfinder found us what we needed."

The Baron's eyes turned now toward Ariane. But it was to Mitspieler that he spoke. "Wizard, are you ready? Can we do it?"

Mitspieler's answer came in a changed voice, tones harder and more powerful. "Yes, I'm reasonably sure we can. Not only is she a virgin, but the daughter of a queen as well. I've now made sure of that. But we must waste no time. Our defenses are not going to hold this doorway for long."

As if to underscore this point, a raging though muffled demonstration by the demon now took place outside. The light filtering in from the passage changed, and rage and hatred and choked noise oozed in as well.

Inside the cave a silent pause stretched on. It was long enough for a multiple exchange of looks, for calculation, for a sudden tightening of muscles, and shifting of weapons.

Then Ariane leaped to her feet with a sudden shriek. "They mean to kill me!" The terror in her voice now, like the wistfulness of a moment ago, was that of a young girl. And, recoiling from the reaching arm of Doon, she scrambled across the cave, and got herself into a position between Ben and Mark.

"What is this?" Ben was on his feet and roaring. And his Sword, like Doon's, was out already.

Doon was smiling at him from across a few paces of sandy floor. Now that blades were drawn in anger, the Baron looked vastly more cheerful, and even at his ease.

But he was in no hurry to attack. "I don't want to kill you, lad," he said to Ben, his voice quite calm and reasonable. "Look you—and you too, Mark, if you stand with him. We all of us now have only two choices. First, we can stay here, and wait for the demon to break in upon us. That'll happen soon, and we'll all perish—nay, perish is too good a word. You saw, out there, what Dactylartha likes to do to those he takes. We'll face what's worse than dying—unless we kill each other first, or kill ourselves.

"But there's a second choice, and that's the one I'm going to take. So are the rest of us. To sacrifice one now—" At these words the shouting of the three across the cave rose up in opposition, but Doon only raised his own voice and went on, "—the daughter of a queen, a virgin girl. Her death properly offered will bind any demon for a time—at least it will bind this one, and for long enough.

"And then the rest of us can go on freely. On to the gold. Have you forgotten?"

Here the Baron paused again, long enough to make sure that the silence from across the cave still represented stubborn refusal, and not a sullen wavering toward assent. "Ben, your own girl on the outside, have you forgotten her? What will you choose, your little shop somewhere with her, or withering for a century in Dactylartha's gut?

"And Mark. Those Swords Sir Andrew needs so badly are down below, waiting for us. How many lives of his people can they save? You've already killed to get them. Now one more small life stands in the way. That of someone you hardly know . . . hey?"

Again Doon halted briefly. When he went on, his voice was still calm. "I'll say one thing more, before we come to kill you. This demon is the last sealing that we'll have to face . . . six is the true number, and the old song lies. Am I right, Radulescu?"

But the Colonel clumsily chose this moment to attempt to assert an officer's authority. "You three, lay down your arms, at once!"

He was ignored, of course. Mark had an arrow already nocked; to draw and loose it would take an eyeblink only. I must get Doon with my first shot, he told himself. Get him, get him certainly, before he can come within a blade's length of any of us. We none of us can match him with a blade, and none of the others over there are likely to be half so dangerous.

Mitspieler, standing with hands half-raised in front of him, made an incoherent sound. He looked almost ready to collapse. A physical fight within this chamber would only weaken the barrier at the doorway, and bring the demon ravening in upon them all; so it seemed he might have pleaded, if he could have found clear speech.

Again the demon stirred outside. Mark could hear and feel it passing the doorway, like a bad wind, like a vicious dog, like the hunter who is coming back.

At last Mitspieler managed to find words. "Mark, lay down your bow. Make your friend see sense!"

Mark had noticed meanwhile that Dmitry, having no regular missile weapon, had picked up a small rock, as if he were getting ready to throw it. Mitspieler's son was looking across the cave at Mark. He was perhaps clever enough to follow Mark's thought on the coming fight, and take the plan one step farther. If the rebellious three were to be pacified without too much damage to the stronger side, then Mark must be prevented from shooting Doon in the first moments of the brawl. Dmitry, while ready to attack with a small rock, was also prudently sheltering most of his own body behind one of the larger ones. . . .

And Willem and Daghur had disappeared altogether; but Mark doubted that they were attempting any kind of a flanking movement, and doubted even more that the configuration of this cave would lend itself to such a try.

Afterwards, Mark was never able to say just whose sudden movement had triggered the outbreak of the fight. One moment, all were statues, limned in the different headlamps' light. Next moment all were blurring in violent motion.

Mark loosed his arrow, aimed at Doon, but missed. Dmitry's rock, flung with unexpected speed and skill, missed Mark but at the last instant just grazed the bow held in Mark's hands. The shaft flew wide, to break against a rock.

Some headlamps went off, others flashed on, beams dancing crazily about the cave, as different people tried different strategies. It was hopeless now to try to use the bow, and Mark dropped it along with his quiver; he had already slipped out of the straps of his backpack. Switching his own headlamp off, he drew his long knife and crouched down waiting.

Darkness was conquering the cave as that strategy became unanimous. Mark thought he could hear Ariane's sling, a short distance to his right, whine softly, one spin, two, and then unload itself at high velocity. Amid the faint staccato of scrambling sounds within the cave the result was impossible to distinguish.

Now the darkness was total, except for the strained glow from the besieged doorway. Outside, the demon still mumbled in his wrath and tried to paw his way in through the spells. Inside the room, rocks continued to click gently, as furtive feet and crawling knees disturbed them. Some people were repositioning themselves, while others waited listening. Those on the other side would be trying to close in on Ariane. She had Ben as one defender to her right, Mark to her left. And she herself, even if her voice did sometimes turn childish, was no timid, helpless . . .

Mark started, as Mitspieler's voice cried out, shouting

at full volume into darkness: "Stop it, you fools, all of you!" There was a momentary pause; then the wizard's voice came back, a notch lower: "Ben, Mark, isn't it better for one to die than—"

He cut off there, abruptly. It was as if he had heard or sensed something that stopped him. Now to Mark all was utter silence in the cave, except for the muted rush of the small stream. Whatever Mitspieler had sensed had probably been perceptible to him alone.

Now there were stumbling footsteps in the darkness, those of one person moving, careless of being heard. And now Mitspieler had turned his headlamp on again, deliberately, as if he had decided or divined that the time for fighting was now over, or else that fighting had become irrelevant. The back-reflection of his light revealed his own face, aged, untidily bearded as were the faces of all the men, and slack-jawed now with fear or awe.

The wizard stood in the middle of the cave. He was looking at the sealed doorway, the translucent barrier that he had himself erected. Again he spoke, and yet again his voice was changed.

"Wait. This is no ruse. The demon is gone. Gone somewhere . . . I don't know how far, but . . . "

Suddenly Mitspieler slumped to his knees, still staring at the fragile-looking barrier of magic.

Now Mark could hear a new kind of movement just outside, different from the demon's. And there was a change in the faint light, a brightening out in the tunnel. And now something appeared in the center of the barrier. It was a hand, not armored, and quite human-looking, except that it was larger than the hand of any normal human being. But it had neither the Whitehands' deformity nor the armor of the giant fist of the demon. The hand, whomever it belonged to, brushed Mitspieler's blocking spells out of its way just as a man might have flicked aside a cobweb.

Now the owner of the hand entered the cave behind it, bringing with him his own kind of alteration. A giant human figure, male, youthful-looking and lightly clad, wearing a Phrygian cap and carrying in one hand a staff. Mark understood that for the first time in his life he was looking at a god. And in the next moment he recognized the god as Hermes.

Most of the cave was now—not lighted so much as revealed, by Hermes' presence. The beam of Mitspieler's headlamp had become irrelevant. Mark's own vision was now able to peer into the far recesses of the cave, and it seemed to him that he could almost see behind the rocks. Hermes had come here seeking something, and in the face of that seeking any kind of human concealment seemed to have become impossible.

None of the humans moved or spoke. All of them remained sitting, crouching, kneeling, just as they had been. Casually Hermes looked around. Then, with the matter-of-fact movements of a strong man who had to interrupt some toddlers' squabble in the course of business of his own, Hermes approached Ben.

Ben was down on his backside, the Sword still in his right hand, quaking as the god approached him. At the last moment he was unable to keep his eyes open, and had to raise one hand to hide his face. When Hermes reached out and took Dragonslicer away from him, Ben's huge frame quaked in a spasm that might have been meant as resistance—but it came too late, and in any case would have been hopeless.

The god dropped something small into the sand in front of Ben—Mark caught the flash of gold. Then Hermes turned away, already seating Dragonslicer in one of the empty scabbards at his belt. Only now did Mark notice that Hermes was wearing perhaps a dozen empty sheaths in all, hanging like a fringe around his waist.

And now Mark found himself getting to his feet, he was not sure why. He was standing straight up, even though his knees were shaking with the fear of it.

Hermes observed this movement. The god paused in mid-stride, on his way back across the cave. He turned his head and looked at Mark. It was a brief look but expressive—even though Mark was not quite sure what it expressed. Recognition—*what*, you *here*? —seemed to be at the start of it, with unreadable complexities trailing off from there.

But the pause and the look were only momentary. Hermes had come here on his own business, in pursuit of which he now approached the Baron.

Doon, finding himself in the path of this advance, made a great effort and struggled to his feet. With both hands he raised Wayfinder to guard position.

Hermes halted in front of him, and spoke for the first time. His voice was huge, remote, aloof. "Give it me. That Sword that you are holding."

"Never. It is mine by right." The words were barely understandable, but Doon managed to get them out. He was shaking almost as badly as Ben had been, as Mark's knees still were. Shaking with what must have been fear, compounded by anger and helplessness.

The deity deigned to speak to him once more. "I suppose you're going to argue that you've been using it properly, unlike some of the others. In accordance with the game. Well, perhaps you have. But that no longer matters."

"I am. I have. It's mine, it's mine."

The god reached out impatiently. Doon struck at him. The stroke would have been a killing blow against a human, but appeared now as no more than some child's petulant protest against authority. Then the Sword was in the hand of Hermes Messenger, who with a flick of his staff, more a gesture than anything else, stretched Doon out on the floor of the cave. The man lay there in agony, crying with pain and frustrated rage.

"Unseemly pride," the god remarked, sliding Wayfinder into a sheath. "In one as mortal as yourself."

The only human being standing now was Mark— and why he should be standing was something that he hardly knew himself, though it was costing him a tremendous effort. He could see that the great wizard Mitspieler was down on his face in the sand. Doon sprawled, groaning. Ariane was somewhere out of sight. Ben was sitting up, but with his face still buried in his hands. And Mark was thinking: This is what my father had to face, some small part of what he endured, when Vulcan took him to help create the Swords. Always until now Mark had felt for his father some faint buried touch of shame, for the implied weakness, for Jord's letting himself be used, letting his right arm be taken. But no more. Now Mark had some idea, some appreciation of what Jord must have felt.

Only a moment had passed since Hermes had last spoken. But something else was happening now, a new presence was announcing itself. Just as light had spread throughout the cave upon Hermes' entrance, so now it was with shade. The wizard Mitspieler, sensing the new presence, raised his head, and the beam from his headlamp was engulfed and blotted out by the intensity of shadow gathering inside the unguarded door.

Mark, still on his feet, could see the dim form of the newcomer, roughly human, standing within the pall of blackness. The voice issuing from the shadowed man-like face was strangely reverberant; it seemed to swell up out of the rocks, out of the earth itself.

"The underworld is my domain. What are you doing here, Hermes Messenger? What is there in my world that you seek to change?"

Hermes Messenger did not appear to be disturbed. "I am collecting Swords—as you ought to realize, Hades. I am going about the business of the gods."

"What gods?"

"Why, all of us. You too. All of us who know what's going on, at least. I only carry out the gods' collective will."

"Hah!" The sound was more like a stony impact than a syllable of speech. "Since when have all of us agreed to that extent on anything? Say rather that you are determined to cheat in the game. That's how I interpret your behavior."

Hermes stood up very tall. It seemed to Mark that the ceiling of the cave must be bending a little to make room for his head. "The game has been—suspended. At least for the time being. There are certain dangers in it that at first were not fully appreciated."

"Oh, has it, indeed? By whose decision?"

Now both gods, as if by common agreement, were

starting to move toward the low cave exit, as if their argument would be better carried out elsewhere. Hades was already stooping his tall figure to go out.

But Hermes paused, arrested by the sight of Doon still moaning at his feet. He prodded the helpless form with the end of his great staff.

"Well, man, what treatment shall I give your pride before I go? Perhaps I'll give you a loadbeast's head to wear from now on. What say you to that idea? Hey? Answer me!"

Hades at the doorway was bored by this distraction, and stood waiting for it to be over.

"No—no, don't. Spare me . . . please." Doon's voice was almost inaudible, and almost unrecognizable, too.

Hades in his impatience grumbled something, in a bass voice pitched too low for Mark to understand. Hermes on hearing it forgot his human toy, and both gods went on out of the cave. Just as they emerged into the corridor outside, Mark heard the sound of the demon out there again. Hades spoke again, and then did something; and Dactylartha fled, yapping and bounding like a kicked cur.

And with that the gods were gone. Inside the cave the humans were stirring, shakily, as if each and all of them were trying to recover from an illness.

Even as others were getting to their feet, Mark sat down, his knees suddenly shakier than before. Why, he realized, I have just looked upon the face of Pluto himself . . . and here I am. Mitspieler, or Indosuaros, one of them, told us once that no man can do that and live. And here I am. . . . Mechanically he picked up his quiver and slung it on his back. He picked up his bow. What was he going to do with it now?

When Doon sat up, the first thing he did was to look around him suspiciously, to see who might have been a witness to his weakness. Mark noticed this vaguely but his own thoughts were elsewhere. Dmitry had emerged from hiding, and was calling out all demons and gods to witness that Daghur was dead.

"Look at that, a rock got him, it looks like. Who uses a sling?" All Mark could see of Daghur was a limp arm as Dmitry raised it.

Ben was calling out too, calling for help, from where he stood bending over Ariane. Mark rushed to them. The girl was sitting up, but blood from a head injury was streaking down one side of her face. Either a stone from the other side had hit her, or she had fallen during the scrambling in the dark.

And now Mitspieler was on his feet. He pointed, with a shaking arm, to where the doorway of the cave yawned unprotected. "The demon!" he choked out the words. " . . . is stunned. Run! Run for it now!"

Ben scooped up Ariane, disdaining any help from Mark. With Mark running as a rear guard, the big man hurried out of the cave. He moved quickly but the others were already gone ahead of him. Outside, they could see headlamps bobbing on the downward path. Doon's Sword might have been taken from him, but his determination was not yet dead. And if he had had any thought of running back instead toward the upper levels of the cave, it had probably been squelched by the sound of human yells that now came drifting down from that direction. The alarms were louder and closer than before.

The demon had retreated or fallen into the chasm of the ravine. Mark could see multicolored lights flash up from those dark depths, and could feel the waves of hatred, as distinct as spoken curses.

Doon was running in the lead, gaining with every stride. After him came Mitspieler, who looked back to find his son, then increased his pace again as both Dmitry and Willem rushed past him at top speed. Radulescu, who supposedly knew better than anyone else the best place to seek safety, was running in the same direction. Ben with Ariane in his arms pounded in the same direction with surprising fleetness, Mark keeping right behind them.

They passed the curve of the path where the demon had first sent them dashing back. Mark had a quick look at the body of the first warbeast to die. It was draped limply over the low wall beside the path, dropped there like a chewed fruit-rind, shrunken, still steaming or smoking.

Just as animals that were natural enemies might flee together from some disaster, so did the humans overtake and pass each other on the path, taking no more notice than did strangers in a crowded city.

Ariane had partially regained consciousness, and was struggling to get Ben to put her down.

And now the demon had recovered, from whatever the gods had done to it in passing. The lights of it again spun and flickered in the air, the noise and sickness of it came trampling, hurtling in pursuit.

Mitspieler, now fallen to last place among the racing humans, unable to run faster, was now unable to run any more at all. He turned and struck with desperate magic against the flying thing. Mark, looking back with some remnant of a wish to help the man, saw bolts of fire shoot from the wizard's fingertips, to splash into

the light that roiled in midair and represented Dactylartha. And then Mark saw the stronger fire strike
back, along the pathway of the first, and he saw what
happened to Mitspieler when it engulfed him.

The demon now flashed throught the air, easily
overtaking and passing Mark and Ben, and Ariane,
who now moved on her own feet supported between
them. It was obviously trying to cut off the leaders of
the human rout, who now fled down the last section of
the path toward a dark doorway. It failed. The last
man of the advanced group vanished into that portal
just before it got there.

Balked, it turned back. Three living victims yet
remained to it.

It spewed its sickness at them. Blue immaterial
flames burst around Ben, and he fell, choking and
gasping. Mark felt the pain. . . .

Ariane pushed herself erect against the wall of rock
beside the path, and faced the thing directly. Her
girlish voice rang out, in what must have been the
charm learned in her childhood:

"In the Emperor's name, forsake this game, and let
us pass!"

There was a burbling and a shrieking in the air.
Dactylartha's substance boiled and spurted. It struck
at the three humans but it could no longer reach them.
A wall as of glass, invulnerable and invisible, was
outlined along the path, imaged in midair by the
demon's fire that splashed against it harmlessly. The
pathway, just to one side, was clear.

The flames had disappeared from Ben's body, leaving no signs of physical damage. Mark with an effort
got the big man back on his feet and shoved him

forward. Then Mark took Ariane by the arm and pulled her along; he realized that he was in better shape than either of the others, but at the same time he knew he was half-dazed himself.

Supporting themselves and each other as best they could, the three of them limped and hobbled forward, passing shielded just under the storm of the demon's wrath. It deafened and blinded but could not touch them. Now the dark doorway was close ahead, and now they were entering it, and now, with a shock of sudden silence, the domain of the demon had been left behind.

They stood in a quiet place, of stone and friendly darkness; a little light was coming from somewhere ahead of them and below.

"This looks like a drainpipe," Ben muttered dazedly. "Or a sewer."

Maybe it did, thought Mark. But it was a passage to where they wanted to go, and even reasonably clean. As they moved forward and the descent steepened, there were steps and grips to use.

Ben was starting to come out of his confusion. "What happened back there?" was the next thing he asked. "I thought it had us for a moment. Did Mitspieler fight it off?"

Ariane had nothing to say. She kept moving along, putting down one foot after another, but she looked bad, her face stark white behind the bruise and the dried blood.

Mark made no answer either. Not now. Later, when he had had time to think, he would have questions of his own.

"Look," said Ben, and stopped momentarily, opening his hand, displaying a gold coin.

"Yes," said Mark.

They moved on. The tunnel was bottoming out. Mark could see that just ahead it widened into a level space, wide and open, extending farther than he could see from here. Some Old World lights there appeared to be turning themselves on in welcome. And the light that shone up into the tunnel was yellow with the reflected burden of the gold.

CHAPTER 16

The ugly dazzle of the demon's influence faded quickly from Ben's mind as he moved on. But his mind did not really clear. Instead the more entrancing glamour of the gold came on to absorb his thoughts.

Down here long hallways were lined with shelves displaying gold. Niches and alcoves and entire rooms were filled with the yellow hoard. As far as Ben could see it was all unguarded, open, free to their touch whenever they wished to reach out and touch it. There were neat piles of bars and ingots, heavy baskets filled with ore and nuggets. Wordlessly the three walked past stack after stack of coin, cases of jewelry, shelves crammed with artifacts of gold. Some of these were simple, some were ugly, some were of intricate workmanship whose origin and purpose Ben could not identify.

In the rooms of the treasure cave nearest to the entrance, many of the stacks of coin were toppled, many of the shelves were disarranged, as if intruders' hands had already played and sported with them greedily. Doon and Radulescu, Dmitry and Willem, must have passed this way only a little earlier.

The rock ceiling here was relatively low, only a meter or two above the wooden walls and partitions and stacked shelves that held the treasure. In the ceiling Old World lights were mounted somehow; lights in individual rooms and halls and alcoves came on individually ahead of Mark and Ben and Ariane as they approached, and lights behind them darkened again as soon as they had passed. Ben, looking very far ahead—this cavern like those above it went on for a great distance—could see that there, too, lights in other rooms were going on and off. He assumed that Doon and the three others were probably there, had probably by now ceased marveling and were busy stuffing their pockets and their packs . . . come to think of it, he doubted that anyone still had a pack, after that last chase. Neither he nor Mark nor Ariane had one now, though Mark had somehow retained his bow and quiver.

And there continued ever more piles of bullion to marvel at, more stacks of coin, more shelves of golden ornaments, all yellowing the light. High shelves of stored gold lined the passages between rooms, and made up the partitions between rooms, and covered the walls of the rooms themselves. There had to be, Ben supposed, some overall plan of organization to the hoard, but so far he could not tell what it was.

They walked on and on, saying nothing to each

other, discovering more and more. Their wonder at the vastness of the treasure grew, until it blurred into a sense of unreality. This was too much. This must be some enchantment, or some joke. . . .

At an intersection of long aisles, or galleries, Ben looked down a long vista—a hundred meters? two hundred?—to a rock wall at the end. About halfway down, he glimpsed an end to gold, if not to treasure. Another light had just come on there, where someone else must be moving through the hoard, and it illumined a kind of borderline where it seemed that yellow metal might give way to silver. And might that starry detail be the twinkle of distant diamonds?

It was all too much. It somehow carried matters beyond the enjoyment or appreciation even of successful robbers that there should be *this* much.

Then, without warning, turning a corner into a room that had just lighted itself ahead of them, the three of them encountered Doon. The little man, who had probably just entered from the other side, recoiled at first, as startled as they were. He said nothing. Dirty and disheveled as were they all, he appeared somehow shrunken without his Sword. There was a dagger still at his belt, but he made no move to draw it. After staring wildly at the three of them for a moment, he mumbled something, but it was evidently addressed only to himself.

Ben had automatically drawn his own remaining weapon, which was a simple dagger also. But in spite of their recent fight, he felt no urge to strike the man in front of him. At the moment the Baron seemed more pitiful than dangerous.

"Where's Radulescu?" Mark demanded sharply of

their former leader. "Where are the Swords—the ones kept here in the treasury?"

At mention of the Swords, a gleam of purpose came into Doon's eyes. He again mumbled indistinguishable words, and stumbling past the three who confronted him, he ran on, searching his own search. They could follow his progress for some little distance, by the lights that went on ahead of him, and winked off again when he had passed. If the irregularity of his path indicated anything, he did not know where he was going.

"Hermes has undone him," Ben said.

Mark asked: "What are the three of us going to do? Separate and search? I assume that the Swords here are kept together in one place."

Ben briefly and silently considered his own plan, the plan that had brought him here, for enriching himself. In the midst of all this it somehow now seemed almost inconsequential, a detail that he could take care of at any time by simply stretching out his arm. But the Swords . . . yes, they were indeed important.

He looked at Ariane, and almost forgot about the Swords. She looked bad, not right yet by a long way, far from being out of the fog from that blow she'd taken on the head. She gave him a weak smile in return for his look, but did not speak.

"No," said Ben. "Let's stick together."

They moved on. Now, just around another corner ahead, lights were on. And now a crash sounded from that direction, and then another, like pieces of pottery being smashed, one at a time. They moved on, Mark with an arrow nocked, Ben with dagger drawn.

Rounding the corner, they beheld a room crammed

with small statuary. Dmitry and Willem had located it already. The two of them were standing there, the pockets of their ragged clothing bulging, spilling gold coins. Each had a sword in hand, and they were playing a game of smash among the statues.

Willem and Dmitry looked up with animal wariness as the three appeared, and paused in their game. They smiled vaguely at the bow and dagger, but said nothing. They swords they played with were only their own ordinary blades.

Mark, with a small motion of his head, signaled his two companions. The three of them moved on, watching with a wariness of their own.

Some distance farther, in a room along one of the main aisles, another light was on. When they peered in cautiously through the doorway, they discovered Radulescu, quite alone. This room was filled with statues too. These were all of fine clear crystal, and the Colonel was holding a small example carefully in his hands. As the three came in, he looked up at them almost indifferently, certainly without enmity, and went on fondling his prize; his mind was clearly somewhere else. It was as if the effort to sacrifice Ariane had happened twenty years ago, or in another lifetime.

He looked down at his little statue again, then held it up for their inspection. "This was my first theft," he explained. "Pretty, isn't she?" Then he gazed at his visitors with more awareness. "You can relax now. We can all take our time, rest a little. Gather what treasure you want, and then I'll show you the way out."

"Show us now," said Mark. "Didn't you hear those yells?"

"There's time," said Radulescu. "Enough time now

ιor everything." He gazed again at his little figure. It was of a woman dancing. " . . . my first theft. I took it out of here once before, you know. Smuggled it back to my quarters, wrapped up in my cloak, enfolded against detection in protective spells that I had devised myself. I took it to my quarters guiltily, as if it had been a real woman, and I some kind of acolyte sworn to celibacy. Of course she is more real, more vital, than any woman I have ever seen in flesh. But . . . there was no way for me to keep it, without discovery. I knew even when I took it that I couldn't keep it, that I'd have to bring it back before the next formal inventory."

"Show us the way out now," said Ben.

Radulescu looked up, startled, as if he had forgotten that they were there. "We'll take it shortly. Rest a little first."

Mark demanded: "Where are the Swords kept?"

"Ah." Radulescu thought a moment, then pointed. "You'll find them down that way . . . if you should be planning to kill me when you have them, remember that I haven't shown you the way out yet."

Ben turned away without answering. His two companions followed him, leaving Radulescu to the contemplation of his treasure.

His solitary communion with the crystal dancer did not last for long. Presently he looked up again, to see the two surviving deserters from the garrison standing in the doorway gazing at him. Their eyes were almost blank, and they had their swords in hand.

They didn't look at Radulescu for long; the surrounding roomful of treasure was obviously more to their liking.

"Come in, gentlemen, come in," said the Colonel, stretching a point in the interests of harmony. "Come in and help yourselves. There's plenty here for us all."

Dmitry's eyes came back to Radulescu, then fell to what Radulescu was holding in his hands. "Give me that one," Dmitry said.

"No." The officer backed up a step. And noted, with hardly more than irritation, that the one called Willem was shifting his position as if to come at him from one side. "And if you're thinking of attacking me, remember—"

But before he could get the next word out, Dmitry's drawn sword was thrusting at his chest.

Ben and Ariane and Mark were already a good distance away from the room of crystal statuary when the bubbling scream reached their ears. They turned their heads at the sound, but no one thought of stopping, still less of going back.

Ariane spoke her first words in some time. "The seventh sealing . . . we've reached it now."

The others looked at her.

"The greed of robbers . . . the old song hints at it." Then she clenched her eyes shut, and walked leaning on Ben for guidance and support. "Gods and demons, but my head hurts. It's bad."

"I don't wonder." And Ben kissed her softly as they kept walking, and wished that they could stop to let her rest. But he knew better.

They passed more chambers filled with crystal, and long rooms occupied by one special rack after another, holding tapestries. When they came to rooms of jewels, Ben detoured for a moment to grab up a handful and stuff a pocket with them. Next was a hall lined with shelves filled with glass jars, containing unknown powders and liquids, all brilliantly lighted to allow for easy inspection by someone simply walking past. There were labels on the jars and on the shelves, but written in a language or a code that was unreadable to Ben.

And now there was another lighted room ahead. It was very near to the wall of living rock that formed one end of the treasure-cave.

They peered into the bright room through the partition that made one of its walls, and was composed of racks of glittering weaponry. Inside the room they gazed upon a mad variety of other weapons still. These were not made, most of them, merely for use; gold again here, silver again, gems in profusion. Ben thought he saw a poinard worked from a single emerald, and arrowheads of diamond.

Toward the far side of the room there stood a great tree-like wooden rack, no thing of art or value in itself, but good to hold display. It had twelve wooden branches, and from each branch there hung a woven belt and sheath, each of the twelve a different color. Nine of the tree's branches — Ben counted quickly — and nine of the sheaths were empty.

And three were weighted down with Swords, heavy fruit with only the black hilts visible.

Baron Doon was standing alone in the middle of the chamber of weapons, and holding one more Sword in his hands. The hilt was concealed in his two-handed grip, but there was no mistaking the perfection of that blade; it could have come from nowhere but Vulcan's forge.

The Baron had his head bent low over the weapon,

and seemed to be mumbling something to it. He stood with feet braced wide apart, legs tensed, as if he wanted to be ready to strike instantly some prodigious blow.

Mark's hand had gripped Ben's arm, enjoining silence. Ben's eyes flicked up again to the three Swords that were still hanging on the tree, seeking the white symbols on the hilts. Mark, he thought, probably knew what they all were—Dame Yoldi had taught him years ago—but Ben himself didn't recognize any of these. One looked like a tiny white wedge, splitting a white block; a second was just a simple circle, a rounded line returning upon itself. And the hilt of the third Sword was turned away, making it impossible for Ben to see its symbol; like the hilt itself, the sheath and belt that held that one were black.

Doon's mumbling voice suddenly rose louder, and for a moment Ben thought that the three of them watching through the rack of arms had been discovered. But if Doon was aware of their presence there he did not care about it. He went on mumbling—not to himself, Ben realized. It was some ritual that he was chanting, the same few words over and over:

" . . . for thy heart, for thy heart, who hast wronged me! For thy heart . . . "

Standing in the middle of the open floor, Doon bowed toward the one dark doorway of the room, a gesture apparently directed toward no one and nothing. Then he turned, and in the same motion crouched, crouched down and in the same motion continued turning, so that in an instant he had become a spinning dancer. And now it was as if the Sword in his hands had somehow been activated, and it was dragging him around. The blade, held out in his extended arms, turning ever more swiftly, became a blur. Quickly the whine of its passage through the air acquired an unnatural timbre. It swelled and hummed, the noise of some great flying insect.

Above this whine, the last words of Doon's grim chant came through: "—thy heart—who hast—wronged me!" And with that Doon released the Sword—or it, perhaps, let go of him.

He staggered and fell down in his tracks. The great whine vanished abruptly from the air, as did the Sword itself. At the speed with which it had leapt from Doon's hands, it must have struck one of the partitions or solid walls that formed the room, or whirred out through the open doorway. But it had done neither. It was simply gone.

For a long moment there was only silence in the cave. Then—

The cry, when it came, even muffled by great distance and by walls of rock, was truly unlike anything that Ben in his whole life had ever heard before. For a moment he could think only that the earth itself must be in torment. Or that the gods were fighting again among themselves, and some landquake was coming to bring the whole headland crumbling down, carrying all the caves and creatures and treasure inside it into the sea. The cry went on and on, beyond the capacity of any human lungs to have sustained it.

Then silence fell again.

Then Doon was laughing.

He sat there in the center of the floor, just as the Sword had dropped him, with his legs crumpled awkwardly underneath his body, and he laughed. His mirth was loud, and hideous, and to Ben it sounded at

least half mad. And yet it was also the most human
sound that he had uttered since he had faced Hermes.

Mark moved at last. He was into the weapons room,
and past Doon, and standing beside the tree of Swords,
before the Baron took notice of the fact that he was no
longer alone.

Doon did not appear to care much. "Not many
men," he began to say—and then his laughter burst
up again, and he had to pause to conquer it before he
could continue. "Not many men—have ever slain a
god. Hey, am I right?" He looked at Mark, and then at
Ben and Ariane, who now stood in the doorway of the
room. "But here was Farslayer—here, waiting for me.
Even the gods must be subject to the tricks of Fate."

"Farslayer," Mark echoed, in a voice that held wonder,
and concern.

The Baron got to his feet, his eyes glittering, and
turned toward Mark. "The Sword of Vengeance," said
Doon. "You who know the Swords will know what has
just happened."

It was at that moment that Ariane collapsed, quite
softly and without fuss. Ben, who was standing right
at her side, was only just in time to catch her. He
lowered her gently to the floor, and bent over her in
anguish.

A girl's fainting or dying was of no consequence to
Doon. "One god is dead," he said. "I'll be my own god
now, with these." He took a determined step toward
the tree of Swords, and stopped just as suddenly
as he had moved. One of the three Swords that hung
there had come sighing out of its black sheath into
the hands of Mark, and Mark now stood confronting
him.

"All three of these are going to Sir Andrew."

"Oh? Ah?"

"Yes . . . if you're willing to come with them, he needs good fighting men, as much or more than he needs any metal."

The Baron squinted at him. Then asked, almost happily: "Which one do you have there in your hands, young man? I took no complete inventory when I came in; not after I had seen the one I needed."

"I have the one that I need now," said Mark. And the Sword in his hands had come to some kind of life, for it was throbbing faintly. Ben could hear it, though it was almost too low to hear: the tap tap tapping as of some distant but determined hammer, working at the hardest metal.

"So?" Doon raised an eyebrow, considering this. "It seems that you do. But we'll see. I've never yet given up on a fight—even against a god—nor lost one, when I had to win."

And with marvelous sudden speed he feinted a movement toward the tree; then, when Mark moved to block him from it, he spun away to reach for another rack of elegant weaponry upon another wall. From this he snatched down a small battle axe and a matching shield, both of beautiful workmanship, embossed with silver and ivory and gold.

"Ben," called Mark, "stay out there. I'm all right. Stay with her."

And in his hands Mark could feel the faint, cold hammering vibration of the Sword he held. This was not Townsaver with its impressive scream, but perhaps equally powerful, perhaps more so . . . in his mind's eye Mark again saw his father dead, his brother too, who had held that other Sword, that had saved nothing. . . .

Doon said to him considerately: "You should first drop your bow and quiver, lad. They'll hinder you. Go ahead, I'll wait."

Mark made a little shrugging motion, meaning: it will make no difference. Doon seeing his shoulders move perhaps thought that Mark had been distracted, that his grip on the hilt was poor, that the ruse had worked. For the Baron brought up his axe and shield, and closed with a rush.

Mark expected the axe to come at him from one direction, and realized too late that it was swinging from another. His arms unaided could never have parried it with any weapon.

But the weapon he was holding was no longer subject to his control. Shieldbreaker only emphasized two notes amid the almost hypnotic streaming rhythm of its sound. Its movement on the two beats drew Mark's arms with it unhurriedly, melding him into its own power and speed. The parry caught the flashing battle axe in midstroke, ripped it from Doon's grasp and hurled it like a missile across the room, where it smashed into a jeweled breastplate and set a whole rack of fancy armor toppling, a crash that seemed to go on endlessly.

The backstroke of the Sword of Force came at Doon himself, but he was able to catch it on his shield. The steel buckler was ripped almost in half, the strips of its precious metal inlays torn loose and sent flying. Doon was knocked down, but he scrambled back to his feet almost at once, ridding his numbed left arm of the useless twisted metal. He darted to another rack of weapons, grabbed up a javelin with a jeweled point, and hurled it with all his strength at Mark. Shield-breaker flashed to shatter the weapon in midair, the pieces flying like slung stones.

Mark, breathing only a little harder than normal, held the Sword easily in his two hands—rather, he stood there letting it hold him. He could not now have let go the hilt if he had wanted to. "Ben. Move her back a little farther. Out of the way."

But, just then, Ben's wordless, helpless cry went up. Mark understood, without taking his eyes from Doon, that Ariane was dead.

Doon had already rearmed himself from the walls of this mad arsenal. This time with a morningstar. He spun the spiked head rapidly on its chain, and probably meant to try to tangle the blade of the Sword of Force and pull it from Mark's grip. But Shieldbreaker's shining blur this time intercepted the weight itself. With the clang of a split anvil, the spiked iron ball, points tipped with bronze and gold, spun free to give up its momentum in the devastation of another shelf or two, from which inlaid helmets and gilded gauntlets cascaded in metallic thunder.

Doon had a broadsword now; in his hands the silvered blade of it made a blur that looked as swift and bright as the arc drawn by the Sword of Force. But when the two met, only one remained.

Staggering amid the wreckage of the room, marked with blood from minor wounds from metal fragments and splintered wood, the Baron grabbed up a spear. Holding this like a lance under one arm, and swinging a scimitar with the other, he let out a scream of defiance and despair, and ran with all his force at Mark.

"Stop! I—"

Whatever argument Mark might have made, there was no time for it. The Baron closed with him—or came as close to him as will and skill could drive. The Sword hammered briskly, blurred impersonally. How many teeth of the gleaming millsaw bit at Doon, Mark could not count. The spear was in three pieces before it hit the floor, and Doon himself was left in more than one. One of his arms was gone, and when the Sword of Force at last came to rest it had transfixed his body.

Mark watched the life depart from Doon's eyes, which were fixed on him. And Shieldbreaker's rhythm, perhaps keeping time with the heart it pierced, went thudding softly down into silence.

Still the body stood almost upright, glaring as if the Baron's will were not yet dead. But in fact the Baron's flesh was supported by a set of tilted shelves that he had crashed into, and by the thrusting Sword itself. Mark raised a foot and pushed. The dead weight slid from the blade, away from the supporting shelves, and fell amid debris with a last crash.

The Sword was suddenly a dead weight as well. Mark let it sag. He turned to the doorway, where Ben still crouched, oblivious to everything but the dead girl he rocked in his arms.

Just then, a strange voice boomed, from somewhere out in the dark cave: "You four in the weapons room, surrender! We have taken your two friends already, and you are trapped!"

Mark forced himself to move methodically. He turned first to the tree of Swords, and got down the belt that had held Shieldbreaker, and put the weapon bloody as it was into the sheath, and strapped it to his waist. He called: "Ben, come on. You must leave her, for now. Come here, quickly."

Ben came lumbering toward him. "Where's Dmitry, Mark? He threw the rock. He hit her." The big man was obviously in shock. "I've got to get him. But—she's gone. She's gone, Mark. She . . . just . . . "

"I know. Come on, Ben, come on. I know where Dmitry went. No, just leave her there. You've got to leave her." He dragged Ben almost unresisting to the tree of Swords, and there loaded him with Doomgiver and its belt. Then Mark took down the last Sword, Stonecutter, for himself, for the moment carrying it belt and all in one hand. For a moment, touching Stonecutter and the Sword of Force at the same time, he was aware of the old feeling that when he was still half a child had terrified him to the point of fainting— a feeling of being taken out of himself, of what he had imagined death itself to be like.

Now to find a way out. Or make one.

He went to the set of huge shelves that stood at the far end of the room, almost against the rock wall of the cave. "Ben, help me tip these back."

The big man followed the order mechanically. The shelves toppled until they caught leaning against the wall of rock, more treasure spilling and crashing from them unheeded. Now they made a high ladder, or crude steps. Mark led the way, climbing up them.

Again the distant voice called: "Your last chance to surrender!"

Ben had mechanically strapped on the first Sword, Doomgiver, that Mark had handed him; and now, while they balanced awkwardly atop the leaning shelves,

Mark gave him Shieldbreaker to hold, saying: "Fight them if they come."

Ben nodded numbly. "What are you doing?"

For answer, Mark turned to press Stonecutter against the wall of stone, feeling the blade come alive in his grip as he did so. Like Shieldbreaker, this Sword generated a hammering vibration, but Stonecutter's was heavier and slower than that of the Sword of Force. When Mark pressed Stonecutter against the wall, the point sank right in, as if the stone it touched had turned to so much butter.

The first piece he cut free, an awkward cone the size of a man's head, came sliding out. It fell heavily between the two men's feet, bounced from the angled, tilted surface of the top shelf, and crashed down to the floor below.

"You're carving steps? To where?"

"It'll have to be more than steps."

The next pieces that Mark cut out were larger. Quickly their crashing fall became an almost continuous sound. Mark was cutting them at an upward angle, so that each block when loosened slid free of its own weight. This meant that the men had to keep their feet out of the way; it also meant that the hole now rapidly deepening in the wall was angled upward. But that was all right, they wanted to go up anyway. Rough-cut pyramids and lopsided cones continued to fall free at an encouraging rate.

Soon Mark had to widen the mouth of his excavation, to be able to step up into it and continue to reach the receding workface, while still keeping his feet and Ben's out of the way of falling blocks.

Ben was coming out of shock a little, belatedly

getting the idea. "We can cut a tunnel, and get out!"

"So I hope. If we have time. Watch your feet!"

There were renewed cries for their surrender, coming from somewhere cautiously out of sight. Ben and Mark were now completely inside their ascending mine, and the Old World lights somehow registered their departure, and turned themselves off. One headlamp, tuned to a dim glow, gave enough light to work with.

There was a rush of invisible feet below.

Ben said: "Let me cut for a while. Take your bow and lob an arrow or two at them."

Now, for just a moment, it was Ben who had two Swords in hand at once. Seeing his expression change, Mark said to him: "It'll be all right. Go on."

With Ben's hand driving the heavy Sword, the work of tunneling went even faster. The tunnel grew, wide enough to let them keep clear of the sliced-out pieces as they fell, its surface rough-hewn to give them footing and handgrips where needed. The blocks, hewn out as easily as so many puffs of smoke, still came falling and crashing down like the heavy stone they were. The constant barrage of their falling had already broken down the tilted wooden shelves, splintering them and pounding their load of treasure into twisted metal and debris, beneath the fast-growing pile of the rock itself.

Now the enemy below was lighting torches, trying to get a better look at what was going on; the presence of Whitehands evidently did not trigger the Old World ceiling lights. Mark fired all his remaining arrows but one at torch-lights, and heard cries of pain. Now he could hear the Whitehands climbing on the talus of rock that grew under the strange new opening in the wall, but more rock continued to fall upon them there, crushing them and beating them back.

Ben had begun to bend the tunnel around a corner. Already the whole opening was some five or six meters deep, and still growing fast. Presently the bend began to afford them the protection that Ben had forseen they'd need; when the first flung stones began to fly up from below, they could make themselves safe around its angle. The Whitehands, like the cave's regular garrison of soldiers, were used to fighting in the dark or by poor light when they fought at all, and bows or slings were not in common use among them.

As the work progressed, each loosened piece of rock slid and fell for a greater distance, building up a greater speed, before it struck anything or anyone. The blocks swept the tunnel clean of climbing Whitehands faster than they could be made to enter it. Before long the attempt was abandoned, and the yells of the wounded were heard no more.

The carving and crashing down of rock, the climbing, went on for a long time. Rock dust began to choke the two men's nostrils. The beams of their headlamps were white now with the fog of it.

Pausing to try to breathe, Ben asked: "What if we're below the level of the sea when we come out?"

"I don't think we can be. Or the cave down there would be already flooded." As he spoke, Mark hoped that he was right.

"How do we know where we'll come out?"

"We don't. Keep going up, and we'll come out somewhere. Unless you've got a better idea."

Mark took another turn at digging. Again touching Stonecutter and Shieldbreaker at the same time, he wondered aloud: "Why didn't Blue Temple ever *use* these Swords?"

"You don't know Blue Temple. If it's valuable it's treasure, and if it's treasure you bury it in a hole in the ground so you don't risk losing it. We'll hear Benambra screaming all the way up to the surface when he sees what's gone."

And at last, without warning, the cutting Sword broke through, broke upward into clear space, and what had to be daylight, though it was dim and indirect. The two men muttered and marveled more than they had for jewels and gold. Some fine dirt trickled down.

Mark quickly widened the hole, then climbed up through it. Ben followed. They were standing in a narrow, cavelike fissure that ran horizontally toward the light, and in the opposite direction from it. Walking, climbing toward the light, they soon got a glimpse of misty sky. Now they could smell the ocean, and hear the steady waves.

At a couple of places Mark had to use Stonecutter to carve a secure step, or widen the fissure so they could squeeze through.

They emerged at last upon a narrow ledge, in living sunshine, halfway between the clifftop and the sea.

CHAPTER 17

Blinking and squinting in the mild sunlight that contended with clouds of blowing mist, they emerged from the crevice into full view of the sea. Mark realized that it must be early morning. The air was warm, and summer had evidently not yet departed. Beyond the first reach of water, slate gray and shaded blue, the opposite headland was half in sunshine, half in shadow.

"What's that?" asked Ben, cocking his head. There had been some kind of distant clash and cry.

"It sounded like a fight. But it didn't come from behind us, in the cave."

"No. Maybe from on top of the cliff?"

The sound was not repeated. "Anyway we're going down. Get to the shore, and then try our charm-words to bring in Indosuaros' ship."

They began to work their way down, carefully.

Rounding a bulge of the cliff, they came upon a broader ledge, and stopped. A marvel lay before them, half-wreathed in mist.

The giant figure had fallen sprawled out, in a prone position. It was crumpled and broken over rock, and as dead as any corpse that Mark had ever seen. The Phrygian cap had fallen off, the great head was turned to one side, the sightless gaze bored at a surface of rock only centimeters from the face.

"It's Hermes." Ben whispered it.

There was a long pause before Mark whispered: "Yes."

"But—he's dead."

"Yes."

The two living men looked at each other as wildly as if it were a dead friend that they had found, and more fearfully.

"Doon boasted that he had slain a god."

"But—if a god is mortal—what does it mean?"

They looked at each other and could see no answer.

Small wreaths of smoke, or steam, were rising from the figure, as if it might be beginning to dissolve into the sea-mist that had come to lave around it. In the middle of the naked back there was a raw, fresh wound. It was just of a size, thought Mark, to have been made by the thrust of a broadbladed Sword.

He said aloud: "It was Farslayer that Doon threw, with a spell from the old Song of Swords. It must have done this. But where is it now?"

"And where are the other two Swords, Dragonslicer and Wayfinder, that Hermes took from us?"

They counted the empty sheaths that were fringed around the fallen giant's waist. Whatever the number had been before, now there were only ten, and all were empty.

Mark made a violent motion with his hand, rejecting the whole situation. "Let's leave this. The death of gods is not . . . let's move on down, there's nothing for us here."

"Except it seems that Hermes will not be coming after us, to take away the Swords that we have now."

They went on down the cliff. It was, as elsewhere on this face, a difficult climb but not impossible.

They had just gotten down to where the slope began to gentle, when a Blue Temple infantry patrol sprang upon them in ambush, leaping out of shadows and caves and fog. Ben had just time to cry a moment's warning; he had felt Shieldbreaker come suddenly to life in his fist. It thudded loudly, and when the warbeast leaped at him, chopped its life out with the first stroke.

The rush of another of the trained animals had knocked Mark down; Stonecutter in his hands only wounded the beast, and he almost despaired of his life before Shieldbreaker's blur passed over him to kill it. He lay there, still half-stunned, knowing that men in blue and gold were crowding in. Shieldbreaker raised its voice, in a sound like the hammering of Vulcan's forge, and their shattered ranks went reeling back.

Then more help was arriving, in the form of fighting men in black and orange; the enemy fled scattering, crying out as if they expected help of their own to be at hand. Mark saw the helmeted head of one of his rescuers bending over him, and then the helmet was lifted to reveal a broad, strong, familiar face. The mustache and beard were of sandy gray. The strong,

slow voice of Sir Andrew himself was asking Mark
how he did.

Helped to sit up, Mark recovered enough to deliver
a quick report. He outlined their raid on the Blue
Temple treasury, and described how they had just
gotten out of it. He concluded: "We've got with us all
the Swords that were there—except one. And there'll
be no use in your trying to get back into the hoard
now—unless you've brought your whole army with
you." He paused there, not understanding how Sir
Andrew had come to be here at all.

"Hmf, hah, yes. Hyrcanus has done that, it seems."
Sir Andrew threw back his head, gazing up the cliff.
"Perhaps the Chairman suspected that his great secret
was out. Well, let us not fall victim to greed. You have
there all that we really hoped to get." The knight
turned to a waiting officer. "Sound the horn, call in
our ships."

Mark, helped to his feet, was able to move without
help, feeling only minor injuries. Another familiar
face, that of Dame Yoldi, loomed into sight. Her sturdy
frame was dressed in man's clothing, prudently ready
for cliff-climbing and combat. Mark began to blurt out
to her the tale of slain Hermes. At the first words the
enchantress hushed him, then drew him and Ben
close to her and Sir Andrew, so that she and the knight
could hear the news privately even as they made their
way down the remainder of the slope.

As Mark related what had happened to Hermes, he
could see the three longships, orange and black at their
mastheads, appearing out of the mist. The oarsmen
were pulling hard in light surf; and the ships' prows had
grated in sand before the shore party reached the water.

Mark was saying: "I knew that Farslayer and the other Swords were powerful, of course. But I never expected . . . " He let it die away.

"Nor would any of us," said Dame Yoldi. She looked shaken, and repeated: "Nor would any of us."

Sir Andrew asked the two men: "And you saw him before? He took Dragonslicer, then it was gone again?"

Ben and Mark both nodded.

There was no time for much discussion now. They waded into light waves with the rest of the patrol that had gone ashore, and reached for gunwales.

Barbara came jumping from a ship into the water to greet them, wrapping her arms round Ben. Quickly she explained how, instead of returning to the carnival, she had taken Mark's goldpiece on to Sir Andrew, together with the story of the treasure-hoard. Ben when saying goodbye to her had told her of its location.

There was sunlight bright upon the opposite headland as the longships pulled out to sea. Ben was gazing in that direction.

"What do you see?" Barbara asked him.

"I . . . nothing."

Mark looked. Someone standing there, perhaps? But the impression faded. It was much too far off to be sure.

Ben was pouring jewels from his pocket, joylessly, into Barbara's outstretched hands, while her eyes questioned him.

Mark stood watching. For the moment he was quite alone.

THE END

All Futura Books are available at your bookshop or newsagent, or can be ordered from the following address:
Futura Books, Cash Sales Department,
P.O. Box 11, Falmouth, Cornwall

Please send cheque or postal order (no currency), and allow 55p for postage and packing for the first book plus 22p for the second book and 14p for each additional book ordered up to a maximum charge of £1.75 in U.K.

Customers in Eire and B.F.P.O. please allow 55p for the first book, 22p for the second book plus 14p per copy for the next 7 books, thereafter 8p per book.

Overseas customers please allow £1.00 for postage and packing for the first book and 25p per copy for each additional book.